Praise for *What We Did in the Storm*

'A clever, complex, layered story that plays with your head. Baker is the mistress of the jaw-dropping reveal. *What We Did in the Storm* is one of those books that leaves you gripped in its pages long after the story is over. Absolutely brilliant'
Helen Fields, author of *Perfect Remains*

'A big recommendation from me... Love the subtle and dry, dark humour laced into the thrills'
Emma Curtis, author of *One Little Mistake*

'A brilliantly atmospheric book, where a community is tight but the secrets run deep... Unwavering in its intrigue, loved it'
L.V. Matthews, author of *The Twins*

'Claustrophobic and compelling, haunting and suspenseful. I was utterly gripped'
Lisa Hall, author of *Between You and Me*

'Fizzing with electricity, evocative and unputdownable. Tina Baker has done it again'
Alice Clark-Platts, author of *The Flower Girls*

'Another impeccable, intriguing and infectiously irresistible tale from the brilliant Tina Baker... A wild and windy holiday read'
C.E. Rose, author of *The House on the Water's Edge*

'A stunningly executed portrait of an island community seething with secrets that are ready to burst free... Baker's writing is by turns amusing and achingly sad, but always beautiful. Batten down the hatches and clear your schedule because this is an absolute gem and it will ravage you'
Heather Critchlow, author of *Unsolved*

Also available from Tina Baker and Viper

Call Me Mummy

Nasty Little Cuts

Make Me Clean

what
we did
in the
storm

TINA BAKER

First published in Great Britain in 2024 by Viper,
an imprint of Profile Books Ltd
29 Cloth Fair
London
EC1A 7JQ

www.profilebooks.com

Copyright © Tina Baker, 2024

1 3 5 7 9 10 8 6 4 2

Typeset by Crow Books

Printed and bound in Great Britain by
Clays Ltd, Elcograf S.p.A.

The moral right of the author has been asserted.

A CIP catalogue record for this book is available from the British Library.

Hardback ISBN 978 1 80081 184 3
Trade Paperback ISBN 978 1 80081 185 0
eISBN 978 1 80081 187 4

FSC
www.fsc.org
MIX
Paper from
responsible sources
FSC® C018072

I love the Isles of Scilly, a cluster of unique unspoilt gems off the coast of Cornwall. I met my lovely husband Geoff on the beautiful isle of Tresco (not in the aisle of Tesco as most of my friends assumed), and we had our wedding blessing there. I have only ever experienced kindness from the people who live and work in this magical part of the world.

And this is how I repay them!

The North End

May, Before the Storm

He notices the figure high on the cliff above him, buffeted by the gale, leaning forwards, trudging on, long dark hair whipping wildly in the wind. This part of the island is never welcoming, let alone in savage weather, although a few horny teens might chance it. Take me up the North End, the old joke.

Stupid maid. Stupid bleddy tourists! He can't fathom them. If you don't have to work in it, why the hell would you be out battling these elements? A big storm is brewing – soon be bucketing it down, a gale threatening.

Ted the boatman likes rough seas. Brings back that time as a kid on the rollercoaster, one of the few bright memories in a grey childhood. Can't think about that. Needs to get cracking. He urges on the boat, forging through outraged waves.

End-of-the-world skies today. Clouds glowering green as an old bruise overhead, evil black tumbling in fast from the west – a whole lot of nothing between this tiny island and America; nothing but the vast vicious ocean.

Slices of sunlight pierce the gloom to light up the cliff. Two of them up there now. Another maid by the looks of it, a bright pink coat rather than a rubber-duck-yellow waterproof. He turns to cock his head at a new engine noise he does not like one bit.

The next time he looks up it seems like the women are dancing up there, daft beggars.

He's distracted by one ramshackle seagull heading in low over the water, its flight jerky, straining for land. Unusual for them to get caught out. The rest are already roosted down to wait out the storm. Perhaps this one is brain damaged, or bladdered. He smiles to himself. A pint with his name on it at the Old Ship just as soon as he settles this deal over on St Mary's – a dirty business as his missus would put it, wrinkling her nose at anything he's involved in. Still, needs must. This gig championship weekend is the busiest time on the islands and he has to capitalise on it.

His mind drifts, comforted by images of cold beer served by a hot barmaid. When he glances back, there is only one woman up on the cliff.

I

The Previous June

1

Hannah and Beatrice

The animal is desperate, eyes insane with fear, spittle flying. Its lips are pulled back, fangs bared as it throws itself against the bars with all its weight. It would rip out her throat if it had half a chance to escape the cage. A killer. As far as she can make out, some sort of chihuahua crossed with a gremlin and possibly a feather duster.

Hannah might also be yapping with terror, but she clenches her jaw shut tight, her hands squeezing into fists beside her.

The noise is extraordinary. An assault.

This is her first time in a helicopter. Someone like her wouldn't usually travel this way, unless she was being airlifted to hospital, her life hanging by a thread. This journey is also 'a matter of life and death' according to Jane, but not really. Of course the girl's wedding day is vitally important to her, and she's the one paying for the flight, or rather her father is.

In the seat across the aisle from Hannah, Beatrice Wallace makes *there-there* noises to soothe her fur-baby.

'Primrose, darling. Hush now. It's okay, sweetheart. Mummy's here.'

Poor thing! How she adores the dog. She always wanted a daughter.

Sitting next to Beatrice is her actual goddaughter, Charlotte. The girl has not looked up from her phone once, checking photos of her own face by the looks of it; as bad as a teenager, although Charlotte is now in her early twenties. She is missing the exceptional views. Blue for days!

Beatrice is very much looking forward to this holiday – the wedding of one of her best friend's daughters, and a week away from the grind of London. Marvellous!

Hannah, however, is not thrilled to be returning to the island so soon. She has been summoned back from her first proper break in a year, to 'save the day' and put a stop to the bride-to-be's theatrical tears which garbled her words in the frantic phone call the previous evening. She begged Hannah to be a last-minute replacement for her first choice of hairdresser (from a London salon, naturally), who has reportedly been poleaxed with food poisoning and will not be making the long journey over to Tresco.

Hannah told the girl she'd get back to her as she was just disembarking from the ferry at Penzance, but there immediately came a call from the island estate manager Bobby, who pointed out that Hannah's job is to serve the likes of Jane and her family, whatever the request. The plans of worker bees like Hannah are never in the same league as those of the valued guests.

Hannah needs to keep in Bobby's good books, and this, as

much as the assurance of the fee and a paid flight back to the Isles of Scilly from the mainland, persuaded her to return.

By morning, it was as if the churning waves which had assaulted the evening ferry crossing from Tresco to Penzance had never happened and all was calm and bright. It likes to play tricks on you, the weather here – three seasons in an hour is not uncommon. Hannah caught the first flight back.

Today there are nine passengers on the Penzance to Tresco helicopter (aviation fans will know it's a Sikorsky S-76) and while Charlotte seems a tad jaded by the transport (not a patch on the helicopter from Nice over to Monaco), most are excited by this leg of the journey and the prospect of their well-deserved holidays.

Passengers have been assured by a briefing video that it is only a fifteen-minute flight. Hannah wonders if her heart will hold out so long. It batters frantically, every instinct fighting against her current incarceration. Humans are not supposed to fly in deafening tin cans. She stares hard at the sea far below, trying to concentrate on something other than her fragile mortality. There is hardly any sense of scale from up here, just an unfathomable expanse – a terrifying watery void peppered by a sprinkling of miniature vessels which could be tiny fishing boats or mighty ocean liners.

A toddler squeals with glee, Primrose yelps in terror, Charlotte yawns theatrically, and Hannah squeezes her eyes shut and screams internally.

An eternity later – finally – a glimpse of land ahead!

Seeing the island from above as they approach is like the beginning of a film. Hannah almost forgets her sense of imminent death as they approach the intense turquoise blues of the shallow waters surrounding the small land masses. It is like the Caribbean – or at least what she's seen of those tropical shores on television. There are even palm trees, despite this being, technically, England.

Return visitors know this view from the postcards sold at Tresco's innovatively named Island Shop, purveyor of goods including caviar and baked beans, although not in the same tin. The photos on those cards do not do the scene justice.

The helicopter swoops over the crazy castle where The Family live – the island's ultimate bosses, although they are off holidaying on some other paradise island at the moment – and comes to hover over the giant penis of the heliport.

'Oh! Really!' Beatrice nudges her companion and points. 'Look!'

'Wow!' replies Charlotte, hastily chronicling the *artwork* for her Insta feed.

This is a new attraction. Someone has recently drawn said appendage on the grass, using weedkiller or bleach. Hannah has walked past this *installation*, but she hasn't experienced the full glorious effect of the prank from the air. It amuses her to see the startled reactions of the elderly couple in the seats in front of her, and she can afford to smile now they are finally descending to hover over solid land.

As they touch down, she offers a sincere prayer of thanks.

Beatrice waits for a moment after Charlotte has alighted, so she can descend the steps alone like Joan Collins, although the hair is always an issue thanks to the downdraft. *How on earth did Joanie's wigs survive*, she wonders?

Hannah's legs are wobbly as she exits the helicopter, the last one to disembark because she allows the holidaymakers to go ahead, although they'll get their bags at the same time as she does.

When she nears the waiting room she perks up and gives a wave, wink and a wiggle for the benefit of the heliport workers – Vlad and the two new lads, all of them in the pub every night living their best lives. She gets an appreciative whistle in return.

The travellers congregate in the bijou waiting room, gabbling and checking their phones. Beatrice scoops Primrose into her arms and the small dog, delighted to be released from her travelling cage prison, wiggles delightedly, licking her mother's neck. Charlotte pulls a face at this display.

Bobby arrives ready to execute his estate manager meet-and-greet, giving Hannah a thumbs up, acknowledging her swift return to rescue the bridal party. Beatrice notices the interaction and smiles at Hannah, now recognising her from the Old Ship where the girl works primarily as a barmaid.

Meanwhile, arrival bags are offloaded while another batch is transported across to be stored in the hold. Passengers who are departing then walk across the green to board, bracing themselves for the return trip to the mainland. By the time everyone in arrivals has their bearings, the helicopter has already taken off again and a small group of seagulls has settled on the ball area of the graffiti cock, watching the proceedings with reptilian eyes.

There are no cars on the island, part of its USP, so heliport passengers are transported to the Old Ship Inn and their various timeshare cottages via the *Wacky Races* style tractor-bus. Workers and visitors generally use pushbikes or walk, and there are golf buggies to help those less mobile get around.

There is a short wait as a beefy heliport worker brings round a wheelchair for one of the larger passengers. Beatrice turns to Charlotte and whispers, 'If she lies on the beach, do you think marine biologists will throw water over her?'

Charlotte giggles then snaps a selfie of her arrival. She will need to take precautions here – sea air is brutal on the complexion.

2

Beatrice

As soon as they arrive at Falcon, the family's spacious timeshare property with one of the best views over to the neighbouring island of Bryher, Beatrice settles Primrose on her blanky at the foot of the bed. She knows she's lucky to be able to bring her – visitors' dogs aren't usually allowed to stay on the island in June, only in winter, but special dispensation has been given due to the wedding.

She unzips her bag to air out the wedding outfit – the silk crepe palazzo pants and flowing blouse in soft blues with a faint shimmer of gold, one of her favourites ever since Charlotte helped pick them out on their latest girls' shopping expedition. She lays out her toiletries and checks herself in the dressing-table mirror. All shipshape.

The grocery supplies have already been delivered, so she pops downstairs to make herself a restorative Bloody Mary before tackling the rest of the unpacking. She is very much looking forward to trying the complimentary bottle of Westward Farm Gin later.

Beatrice Wallace owns six weeks here at Falcon, one of the larger holiday homes on the island, sleeping twelve at a push. She might have booked a smaller cottage for these extra nine days as it's only herself, Charlotte and her son Kit staying this time, but it's nicer to be somewhere that feels like home.

All of the guests are relieved they weren't fogged in on the mainland, but Beatrice especially so, as she didn't want to cut it fine for the wedding ceremony this lunchtime.

She told her infuriating husband that they should have booked a flight for yesterday in case of bad weather, but he was adamant that he was far too busy to think of taking another day off work. And after all the extra stress that caused, Henry still had to stay behind – a 'crisis in the markets'.

'There's always a bloody crisis in the markets!' snapped Beatrice, before disconnecting the call. She seethed on the train all the way from St Pancras to Cornwall, which took some seething.

'Helloooo!' comes a call from outside.

'Kit! Darling!' shouts Beatrice in reply, hurrying to open the door. Charlotte dashes down from her own bedroom to greet the rather gorgeous young man in running shorts stretching his calves on the doorstep, but Primrose beats her to it. Hugs, kisses and delighted woofs commence.

'Char! Looking good!' beams Kit, who decided to come to the island a day early.

'Oh, please don't!' blushes Charlotte. 'I'm a state!'

'You are not! What are you going to do while the *mothership* and I are at the wedding of the year?' he enquires.

'I'll go for a walk, look in on the pub, the usual,' she smiles. 'But perhaps we can meet up later if you like? Have a few drinks?'

Kit seems oblivious to the note of hope (some would say yearning) in the young woman's voice.

Beatrice addresses Charlotte. 'I'm sorry you weren't invited to the wedding, darling, but you hardly know Janey, and it is only a small do. Oh, damn!'

'What is it, Mum?' asks Kit.

'Please don't call me *Mum*, darling, I hate it! There seems to be no celery for my Bloody Mary,' she informs him. 'I shall have to be very brave.'

Kit is about to sit in the kitchen chair, but Beatrice says, 'Oh no. Chop-chop! Time to get ready, darling!'

'You make a start. I've only got to shower and put on my suit,' he replies. He turns to Charlotte and says, 'I hate weddings. Sooo boring.'

Beatrice is aware that Charlotte not only loves weddings, but that she would have loved to attend one with Kit.

'I wish I'd come over yesterday with you, darling,' sighs Beatrice. 'I do not like to be rushed.'

She hurries upstairs and commences preparations, worrying about her son as she applies a well-practised subtle smoky eye.

Kit has seemed rather down in the dumps lately. He has recently moved back home after splitting up with his latest girlfriend, and Beatrice thinks he now seems a little . . . lost. He has no job lined up, and he spends most of his time skulking round his bedroom all day, gallivanting to parties all night – so nothing much has changed since he was home from uni in the holidays.

Many of Beatrice's friends wail about their empty nests, but she tells them, 'Darling, I yearn for the day!' although she is joking.

Kit's father accuses his son of lacking a work ethic, but Beatrice defends him, saying that *it's just that poor Kit's had a few false starts; he's not yet found his true path; he's a sensitive soul.*

He gave up on the business course, as well as the foray into public relations. He was never keen on the idea suggested by his cousin to join him with the landscape gardening enterprise, and he only worked on one TV production as a runner. Sticking at things does not seem to be Kit's forte.

Yet despite his mother's unwavering support, he frequently mocks her.

'Why do you need a PA?' he challenged Beatrice only the other week. 'You don't even have a job!'

'I do so, as you well know!' she responded.

'And what might that be exactly?'

'I plan things for your father. Events. Charity functions.'

'You don't even clean your own shoes!'

Exasperated, Beatrice snapped, 'Darling, you're almost twenty-seven and you're jobless and living with your parents, so I rather think you should sort yourself out before you start offering me career advice, don't you?'

But then he looked so hurt, she felt awful.

Beatrice takes another sip of her drink, wishing she knew what would make her son happy, or at least happier.

She rolls out her shoulders and looks around the tastefully decorated bedroom. The whole place is spotless, but there are splatters of seagull shit on the window. She doesn't know why they can't cull the bloody things. If they gave her a gun she'd do it herself.

It is easier to stoke her anger about that than admit her disappointment that, yet again, her husband has let her down.

3

Hannah

Due to the wedding emergency, Hannah is one of the first passengers to be dropped off at Hawk, the largest holiday property on the island. She knocks, walks in, and is met by one of the bridesmaids, a girl with sparkly braces on her teeth who she's never seen before, and she's swiftly ushered upstairs. The master bedroom is already a hive of activity awash with decreasingly fizzy champagne and escalating fizzy anxiety.

'Hurrah! The cavalry!' squeals Jane, the blushing bride, rising from her chair where *dewy* make-up is being professionally applied, rushing towards Hannah in a haze of perfume. The girl's fluffy dressing gown is gaping, and Hannah's own impressive chest is squished against an ample, corseted bosom.

'Yesss!' shouts one of the younger bridesmaids, already in acres of tulle, running around in non-specific giddiness.

'What a lifesaver!' adds Jane's mother, one of several Right Honourable Tresco regulars, lightly holding Hannah's shoulders and air kissing her cheeks, careful not to make contact and smudge her own recently applied lipstick. Hannah has served this woman's family in the bar for five seasons, and this is the first time the mother of the bride has ever acknowledged, let alone touched her.

'Can I just get a coffee before I make a start?' asks Hannah.

'Of course, of course,' says Jane.

While she's in the kitchen making her drink, Hannah calls Alison, her boss at the pub, and is put back on shift to work early doors tonight. No point not earning now that her holiday's been cancelled. Just as she's adding milk to her coffee, she hears a scream upstairs and rushes back up.

'What happened? Are you okay?'

'A bird just crashed into the window,' says Jane. 'It nearly gave me a heart attack!'

'Is it alright?' asks Hannah. A small ghostly impression of the poor creature remains on the pane.

'I don't know. Will you have a look?' says Jane.

Hannah goes back down to collect her coffee and checks outside. There's no sign of the bird on the grass beneath the bedroom window, so it might have simply stunned itself and flown away, thank God. She applies a smile as she returns to the bride's boudoir. There's no need for her to share her thoughts on the omen with the wedding party.

Hannah's hairdressing kit has already been brought up to this impressive holiday home from the much smaller worker's cottage she shares with two other girls. She assumes Bobby did the honours, but anyone might have collected the bag because no one bothers locking their doors here.

'It's like Britain used to be in the fifties,' enthused Bobby when he first introduced Hannah to the accommodation which has been her home for the last six years. 'Honesty boxes for flowers and farm produce, and you can leave your bike anywhere and no one will vandalise it like they would on the mainland. No crime here. No pollution. It's a proper paradise!'

At that time, Hannah hadn't been on a bike since she was a small child, back when they visited her *babcia* in Poland. (Hannah's actual name is Zuzannah, but nobody here has ever bothered with that, so she dropped it.) When she first met Bobby and his bright, rainbow-painted bicycle she had no idea that it was the principal mode of transport on the island and wondered why he might wax so lyrical about his place of work.

Now she understands people's enthusiasm. The island is heart-achingly gorgeous. Wildflowers festoon gardens and fields, red squirrels cavort in trees, the air is pure. Walkers embrace the immaculate views and wave and smile at each other – the people who come here generally drop no litter to spoil the pristine beaches and the water is crystal clear, although bloody freezing.

Isolated from the mainland, Tresco engenders the sense of a true getaway. It is remote, as in it once took Hannah twenty-three hours to return to Croydon to see her mother – the journey entailing tractor, boat, ferry, train, tube, taxi, plus the obligatory delays. It is also exclusive, as in shockingly expensive.

And life here is from a time gone by – a time of fresh air and strolls along perfect sandy coves, of cheery bunting and fine paintings of vast horizons and cheeky sailors. A time of board games and sing-alongs and cream teas and old-school racism and servants and masters, where even today girls like Hannah work like dogs, while a few of the privileged guests treat them like shit on their deck shoes.

'You are so lucky to live here!' people exclaim.

Hannah knows she's lucky.

But sometimes she can't bear the everyone-knowing-every-one-else's-business-in-and-out-of-each-other's-houses-*tight-knittedness* of this community and she marches up to the cliffs to get away, where to the accompaniment of screeching sea-birds and crashing waves, she can scream out loud.

4

Bobby and Hannah

'Oh, she do look pretty, don't she!'

'I'm no expert on the fairer sex, as you well know, Miss Elisabeth,' says Bobby.

'Ooh, she do! A very pretty maid. Well, the dress and the hair. Shame about the face!' cackles Miss Elisabeth – former teacher, former councillor, part-time postmistress, tour guide, community centre assistant, playgroup assistant and church volunteer. The oldest worker on the island. The woman is nothing if not adaptable. Everyone calls her Old Betty, but never to her face.

'Do not let them hear you!' warns Bobby.

'And a lovely service. Proper lovely,' she witters on.

Bobby nods. The church side of things has gone down well. Plenty of photo opportunities, which will hopefully flood social media and drum up business. Standing outside the church for the official poses, the bride indeed looks . . . bride-like. The hair is a triumph, adorned with tiny pearls to complement the gown, a beautifully draped off-the-shoulder number with shades of Vera Wang if he's not mistaken. Bobby loves a little *Vogue* glamour on the island – a welcome change from Barbours and wellies. Everyone here smells like wet dog. Even those who don't have dogs.

'They done her up a treat,' says Betty. 'The bride with the beautiful blue eyes.'

The bride's eyes are obviously brown.

Bobby is confused. 'Blue eyes?'

'Oh yes,' nods Betty. 'One blew east, the other blew west.'

'Will you behave,' he hisses.

Bobby makes his way across the path to praise Hannah. A good manager should give positive feedback whenever it is warranted. So many bosses only admonish, which saps morale.

'An excellent job with the hair there, Hannah. Well done. I love the little pearls. A very nice touch.'

'Thank you.'

'Good tip?'

'Fair enough.' She looks away as she says it, so he guesses it wasn't impressive.

'It stands you in good stead going the extra mile like this – cancelling your own break, rushing to the rescue. The guests appreciate it. The Family will appreciate it.'

The bride's people are friends with the island's ultimate bosses, *The Family*. Bobby reports directly to The Family, who report to the royal owners, or rather the minions in their employ, and the royals, of course, report only to God. Many of the regular visitors, like Jane's family, have been coming here to holiday for decades. Most tourists only manage a day trip over to see the Abbey Garden – it's all normal folk can afford – but those who stay, those who come back year after year at peak season, like Jane's clan, timeshare owners who visit several times each year, they are usually dripping with assets.

The bride has appreciated Hannah's effort to the tune of an extra fifty pounds on top of her fee – and while Hannah is grateful for the cash, it is more a Blue Peter badge level of thanks rather than a full commendation. Jane's family spend more than fifty quid on a round of drinks in the Old Ship most lunchtimes. And Hannah hasn't gone the extra mile for them – as the crow flies from Land's End, she's gone twenty-eight extra miles.

Still, her effort has pleased Bobby, which means word will get back to her immediate boss, the redoubtable Alison, who governs the pub with an iron will and a slick of Estée Lauder lippy. A good word from Bobby might help grease the wheel the next time Hannah wants to swap her shifts.

The wedding party no longer notices Hannah. As soon as she'd fulfilled her purpose she was dismissed and subsequently ignored. Jane, her relatives, and Glorious Greg the groom – thus named due to his habit of declaring everything on the island 'glorious!', from the shooting and fishing to the *evocative* Malbecs he downs like water – are back with their own kind now. Even Primrose is on her best behaviour and part of the inner circle, sporting a pink cape affair with a giant bow attached to her collar.

The guest holding the dog catches Hannah's eye and makes a funny face, followed by a wry smile, as if to say, 'It's ridiculous, isn't it?' He mimes shooting himself, which makes her laugh. She recognises this good-looking young man from a past visit, but she's forgotten his name.

Hannah was invited to the church as an afterthought. It's an open invitation, although regular visitors know that most islanders will be far too busy working to come to mid-week midday nuptials. A few, like Miss Elisabeth, have stopped by for a few minutes to see the couple outside St Nicholas's Church – built in 1878 by the rather innovatively named Thomas Algernon Smith-Dorrien-Smith, although presumably not single-handedly, aptly dedicated to the patron saint of sailors. None of the workers have been invited to the reception.

Hannah needs a lie down. She's tired after yesterday's bad crossing, a disturbed night's sleep in the B&B, and today's early start. Her body clock is more used to late nights behind the bar than early mornings, although when she'd first come over as a chambermaid she'd worked totally different hours. Now, along with her bar work, she's added 'unofficial hairdresser' to her skill set, not that there's an official hairdresser on the island. She's been doing cuts and colours for friends, workers, and a few guests for the last couple of years. She also gives house-keeping a hand when they need, and she recently started help-ing the interior design team.

'You'll soon be managing this place at the rate you're going,' said Bobby, teasing her. But everyone has to pitch in here.

Hannah watches Bobby walk over to shake Glorious Greg's hand, beaming at the bride and doing his best professional fawning. Bobby has a low centre of gravity and a suggestion of bowlegs, possibly from spending so much time tootling around on his bike, overseeing the smooth running of the island busi-ness. A peal of laughter trills out at something he says. Hannah is about to head back to her room and get some rest when Old Betty grabs her arm.

She comes up close, the old girl's teeth always a shocker, and says, 'Lovely job on that hair! Silk purse out a cow's ear!'

Old Betty has an unusual turn of phrase.

'Miss Elisabeth!'

'Pity she didn't get the genes, hey? That bleddy dog had more luck than her!'

'You did a lovely job with the church flowers,' says Hannah.

Betty ignores the compliment, as women tend to, and says, 'He has an eye for you, that youth. Proper 'ansome, him. Proper tall.'

The tall young man holding the dog's lead seems to divine they're talking about him and gives them a small apologetic wave and another grin. His mouth is beautiful.

'He is a bit lush,' smiles Hannah, who has a vague recollection of kissing him under a bunch of mistletoe at the pub last Christmas. But then, who didn't she kiss under that mistletoe.

Betty leans in and whispers, 'You take care! Hear me? You take care!'

'Why?' asks Hannah.

'He'll be gone soon enough. One of you'll end up broken-hearted. Or worse.'

'Are you the island soothsayer now,' laughs Hannah, shrugging Betty's fingers off and trying to make her escape.

The old woman sweeps her into a farewell embrace. Hugging Old Betty is like hugging a sack of sticks.

Just then the wedding golf buggy, decorated with pink and white ribbons to match the flowers in the opulent bridal bouquet, sets off to a cheer, the newly hyphenated Bamford-Lloyds waving regally from the back. All the workers wave in reply – if they didn't it would be noted by Bobby – and Hannah sets off in the opposite direction.

She wonders how anyone could bear to marry someone like Glorious Greg. The man's a buffoon. But Hannah will be thirty-two next year, and her mother has been nagging her that it's time to settle down, time to start thinking about giving her a grandchild. It's not that Hannah's against the idea, but it's not so easy when tourists are only here for a couple of weeks at a time, plus there are very few eligible workers on the islands, and most of them usually only stay for a season or two before disappearing. Anyway, she tells herself, she's having a fun time as she is.

And she's been stung in the past. Before she came to the island she was engaged to be married for an entire five weeks – well, her boyfriend at the time asked her, but never supplied a ring, and never mentioned it again. They broke up the following month when he suddenly left the country, claiming it was for a new job, although it turned out to be a new woman. Hannah blames herself for not seeing how flaky he was. She doesn't have the best track record in her love life.

She sighs and walks on.

Buttercups and daisies, honeysuckle and wildflowers in pinks and blues that she can't name, adorn the path as she makes her way down to New Grimsby. She'll have time for a nap before getting changed for her shift at the pub. She meets Angie from the shop walking Sadie Dog the other way up the path and greets them both, to the dog's delight. She waves to Isak from the cottage gardening team who looks to be in mortal combat with a giant dead Echium over in Tern's front yard. She texts her mother again – *Sorry! I'll try to get over to see you soon.*

A soft silence suddenly engulfs her, and she's hit by a wave of nausea like she's still at sea. She's overtaken by a strange sensation where the world seems to tilt and darken. She has to steady herself on a garden wall.

Exhaustion, probably.

This strange episode is observed by one plump baby gull which sits on the nearest cottage roof, bleating heart-rending cries in the perpetual hope of food. A single magpie remains on the chimney opposite watching her impassively. It calls out three sharp, scornful cries, and swoops away.

Hannah salutes it and hurries on.

The Graveyard

The screeching is insane, the fight bloody. High above the church roof, attacks and retreats, feathers and fury. The larger gull dive bombs its rival aiming to impale it with an evil beak, intent on murder. The flock shrieks encouragement. Brutal.

The gulls are too intent on violence to notice the silent ones below.

Beneath the lush green grasses and whispering leaves of the watchful trees a favoured few are buried here. There will be no new grave. Miss Elisabeth feels it in her bones – there will be no body to bury. They will never find the missing girl.

She lays her posy next to Florence's headstone – her friend and former teacher; one of the few select islanders allowed to sleep beneath this hallowed earth. The graveyard is full. People who live and work on this tiny island now have to be buried elsewhere.

Elisabeth herself has a nice plot already sorted in Helston, where her people were from. Her mother and father and baby brother already lie side by side over there. She can't remember her brother as she was only little when he was taken by the angels. She wonders if she'll recognise him. She hopes they all get on when they're reunited in the great hereafter. Elisabeth is looking forward to seeing her mum and dad again. She'll be able to say 'I told you so' now they realise it was not her who left the gate open, allowing the horse to escape, even though she got a smacked bottom for it.

Funny, she remembers that time as if it were yesterday, but she can't quite place what she had for breakfast.

How Elisabeth loves this church. But her faith is of the little England 'All Things Bright and Beautiful' variety, not the snake-wrangling hysteria and speaking in tongues favoured by Americans like John What's-His-Face, the expert up at the Abbey Gardens. Seemingly ecstatic in the pews, booming out hymns, dispensing hearty handshakes afterwards. So embarrassing. He was from the Bible Belt. Elisabeth is sure she wouldn't like it there. A real Holy Joe. Didn't do him much good though – a terrible business, that.

Miss Elisabeth is at her happiest arranging flowers for the altar, cocooned by the profound peacefulness of the church. The moment she steps outside, she is untroubled by thoughts of sin. She does not approve of Catholics with their guilt and handwringing and over-the-top ceremonies. She does not trust any form of passion in religious practice.

As she walks away from Florence's grave she says a silent prayer for the poor lost girl. They've just started searching for her – police from the mainland, volunteers – but the waves have already taken her, Elisabeth feels sure of that. Still, she will join them this afternoon – it is only right, a community effort.

Eventually, though, the search will be abandoned.

*There might be a plaque of some sort at some point in the future –
a few words on a bench near the church. Nothing that might really
commemorate a woman's life.*

Men get the statues.

5

Bobby

'Yep, yep. It all went well. I passed on your good wishes to the bride and groom . . .

'Delighted. They're all delighted! . . .

'Only thing to report is there's been some . . . um, a small amount of, er, vandalism at the heliport. A prank. No real harm done . . .

'You don't want to know. Really. Being sorted now . . .

'Yep. Yep. The Robinsons will be down next week . . .

'Change of plans . . .

'Will do. Lots of interest in taking over the Easter weeks. We'll accept the best offer of . . .

'Aha. Aha. Builders' accommodation all sorted . . .

'Yep. Very unfortunate. The new constable came over from St Mary's to have a word. Read them the riot act. The uniform had a sobering effect, ha ha . . .

'No, no, of course it's no joke. Agree entirely. It only takes one drinking game to get out of hand like that and . . .

'No, no, no. I'm sure there won't be a complaint, no. We've offered the parents a week next year free of charge . . .

'Yep. The lad was discharged after he'd sobered up. Gig-championship levels of stupidity . . .

'Pretty much the entire bottle of vodka. The blue stuff. Stomach pumped. All ship shape now . . .

'There's the . . .

'Oh, okay. Okay. Yep, yep, yep. Catch you later.'

Bobby puts the phone in his pocket and starts walking up to the farm – if he cuts across from here it will be as quick as going home to get his bike and cycling round. Sam should be up there sorting out the tractor engine for Farmer Michael and Bobby needs a stern word with Sam about the golf buggy repairs – four out of action today! Unheard of! All the rest will be needed for Alice's birthday bash at the community centre, which means there'll be none available for guests. Totally unacceptable.

Complaints are the last thing he needs right now. He has more than enough on his plate.

Sam is an excellent engineer and handyman, or at least he was when he first came to the island. But he's too fond of the sauce. So much so it's being remarked upon, and that's saying something here. Fine for a single man like Bobby himself – although he has cut right back after that unfortunate business last year (it involved nudity; don't ask) – but a damn shame when you've a young family to care for. Bobby feels sorry for Sam's wife, poor Christie – the last thing she needs is a drunk to look after along with the four young boys she already has to cope with.

He walks on. It's a warm day and he's already sweating, but the exercise will help soothe his anxiety.

After sorting Sam, he plans to check in on the wedding reception, then head down to the community centre to take a birthday card over for Alice. Lovely to see the old girl again. Retired to Penzance – not a place he'd have chosen, but she said she wanted to feel as near to the island as she could.

'But that would be Land's End,' he'd replied.

'I don't want to be crawling with bloody emmets,' she'd snorted, trying to stop her tears. 'And I want to be able to get my shopping without a song and a dance, thank you very much.'

How long ago was that – when Alice was asked to leave? Eight or more years back now. It doesn't seem that long.

That final scene – leaving the island – will come for him too, one day in the not-too-distant future. Years ago, there was some leeway in how long a worker might keep going. Now it's encouraged that you retire when you're still at the top of your game. There's no room for passengers here; no excess fat. Bobby glances down at his belly, swiftly glances up again.

Miss Elisabeth is the last of the old guard, the only islander working long past retirement age, and even The Family wouldn't dare to mess with her. Old Betty knows where the bodies are buried.

No one is allowed to live on Tresco after they retire. As soon as you stop working, you have to leave; accommodation is linked to your job on the island. In theory you might go to St Mary's, but, thanks to second homes and timeshares, the prices are well beyond the means of mere workers. *The same for most of Cornwall now, with or without a sea view*, thinks Bobby bleakly.

He does not like thinking of leaving his home and his friends, so he doesn't.

He makes his way through the field of Farmer Michael's

happy cows, greeting those who amble over to sniff him. He strokes one on its tufty head then trails his hands along the tops of grasses on the edge of the field, admiring the splashes of poppies. It's a rare moment of calm in his hectic day.

He strides on. So much to sort out. Squeaky-bottom time with the accounts. Even with a fair number of bookings this summer, they've still not recovered from what is locally known as *The Quiet Times*, globally known as the pandemic. And there are always mixed reviews on TripAdvisor from the hoi polloi who pop over for a day. Of course it's bloody expensive here! This island is unique! What do they expect, Butlins? And now some ridiculous endangered newt might put paid to the building work up on the site of the former hotel. Always something unforeseen to deal with.

Thinking of endangered, at least the Egyptian vulture is back. Well, it is according to Vlad. No one would take much notice of Vlad in normal circumstances – he's one of the more committed drinkers, like Sam – but Bobby has enthusiastically stoked the lad's recollection of what he *might* have seen up near Pentle Bay, because a rumour like that will bring over the birdwatchers in their droves. Sure, most of them will stay on St Mary's or brave Bryher's campsite, only visiting for the day, but every little helps. Weird-looking thing, that creature – but birds have never been Bobby's bag, so to speak.

A plan forms itself as he crosses the next field. He considers asking one of the girls who post on social media if they could perhaps whip up a rumour into a story; fluff up the vulture gossip. A blurry picture from the year the bird really did alight on the island might set things off nicely. It's only a white lie, just a bit of fun like the Loch Ness Monster.

The screech of a sickly tractor greets his arrival at the farm. Bobby calls out, 'Hello!' and Sam's head appears from within the engine. Bobby smiles and waves as he approaches, belying the fact that Sam is in for a reprimand. The engineer stands and wipes his greasy hands on a rag. There are dark shadows beneath his eyes and a nasty bruise on his cheek.

Bobby isn't surprised the young man looks so exhausted – three young lads and a baby in one tiny cottage. He can understand why he might choose to stay drinking in the Old Ship rather than going home, but that's no excuse for letting his work slide. Much as he dislikes this part of his job, Bobby has to give him a verbal warning.

The tractor engine makes a horrible clattering sound as it dies. Bobby's no expert, but it sounds totally knackered. And it's not just Michael's tractor having issues – there are some pretty large cracks in the smooth running of the island *machine*, truth be told. It's a worrying time all round, plus some of the natives are restless – wage demands as usual. When they sign their contracts employees have no idea how expensive it is to live here: the Island Shop is extortionate, and if the weather's rough and they can't get over to the Co-op on St Mary's and deliveries from the mainland are held up, it's the only place to buy anything. Bobby himself has a cupboard neatly stacked with dried goods and tinned foods, but youngsters these days rarely plan ahead.

Despite the challenges, Bobby adores his job, and he would do anything for The Family and the island. He's given his entire adult life to this place. Yes, there was one very brief period when he'd thought he might start again, somewhere warm like South America but—

He shakes his head to rid himself of those silly dreams and strides towards Sam, as much as he can stride with his rather stumpy legs.

Sam needs to up his game. Everyone does. They all need to dig deep to make this season work. This island is a special place, a fragile ecosystem. This is the quintessential English idyll. Some say it is the resting place of King Arthur. Others disparage it as a bunch of alcoholics clinging to a rock.

Bobby would defend it with his life.

6

Kit

It is a glorious afternoon. A pearly sky and a benign sea, the surface a silky skein reflecting the whole colour chart of blues, from the clearest turquoise to the deepest inky indigo. The Scilly Isles are at their most alluring.

Kit might be enjoying this out on the skiff – delicious solitude! Or he could be walking and musing, nodding to hikers, 'A nice day for it, yes!' all that is required of him. Or sitting in the pub garden enjoying a few cold ones, the odd comment about cricket drifting over him. As it is, he's enduring a forced bonhomie akin to that displayed by the band on the *Titanic*, sitting alongside his mother with not one, but two of the bride's dowager aunts in attendance. A very particular circle of hell. No wonder his father bailed.

If the weather holds, he might go out on the boat tomorrow, although he needs to collect his supply box from the office first. These treasure troves are where the family store items they only use on the island: wetsuits and hardcore wet-weather clothes; sunhats, deck shoes, walking boots; his father's fishing equipment; his own painting gear; his mother's IOS rugby shirt in pale violet and the bright fuchsia waterproof she acquired earlier this year – *In a sale, darling. Couldn't resist!* – which, thankfully, he's never seen her wearing. How old does the woman think she is? Twelve?

Kit's daydream of escape is cut short because Bobby is now ambling over to their table, enquiring, 'Everything going well here? All good food-wise?'

'Oh yes, Bobby *darrrling*,' slurs Aunt One. 'Organ Morgan has whipped it out!' She titters.

Morgan, the new head chef, has catered the event. He is very Welsh and very red in the face. His nickname has nothing to do with his musical skills, rather a long story involving a pair of obscenely short shorts.

Kit cringes. His mother rolls her eyes. Aunt One is veering towards the acutely embarrassing stage, and they've not got to the speeches yet. He averts his eyes from her performance, staring hard at the remains of his duck confit as if it might contain the secrets of the universe.

He tunes out. They have been blessed with the weather. It is balmy rather than scorching, but Kit is already a little sunburnt on his nose and forehead, while his mother is perfectly florid. Dowager Aunt Two, sitting next to him, is daintily perspiring into her pale grey linen. She is a drab sparrow against Aunt One's showy purple plumage.

There is an arrangement of strange spiky pink flowers on the table. He pokes his finger to the darkness inside and is surprised to find it soft as a bird's feathers.

'*Protea neriifolia*,' announces Aunt One, as if addressing a rally. 'Beautiful isn't it. Twenty thousand varieties of plant in the Abbey Garden, from eighty thousand different countries!'

Kit wasn't aware that there *were* that many countries, but he says nothing to disillusion the woman, who is already tilting at least fifteen degrees to the perpendicular.

His mother sighs.

A loud hoot from the visiting vicar is accompanied by a tinkling of laughter from the top table in the garden. The clergyman, who usually oversees a parish in Barbados (where the bride met her groom during one rather splendid Christmas getaway), is the only black person at the occasion. 'Oh, what a pity for the photos,' whispered Aunt Two as they sat squashed together in the island's small but perfectly formed church. 'Contrast,' she'd added hastily, noting the outrage in Kit's expression.

Now Aunt One suddenly leans over her plate to grab Bobby's arm and announces, in a booming stage whisper, 'Give the chef *all* my compliments. Tell him . . .' She straightens, smiling and fluttering what must be assumed to be a saucy twinkle, 'Tell him I am very particular about what I put in my mouth, but he will be granted entry any time.' She stifles a small burp. 'Any time at all!'

A smear of *jus* remains on the brocade covering her left nipple. *Kill me now*, thinks Kit.

His mother unfolds her long legs from beneath the table and re-crosses them as she turns away from the aunts. Kit gets his height from her, rather than his father – one of those compact, bolshy trader types who delights in his elegant wife; one who towers over him in both height and class. Or rather he used to delight in her.

'Pure gold, your mother,' was one of his father's sayings when

Kit was a child. This view has since tarnished somewhat. His parents have been leading separate lives for years.

Kit has reached a level of mandatory drunkenness required to survive any wedding reception, but his mother has become tight-lipped. This is one of the tiny outward signs that she may be heading towards her own version of alcoholic Armageddon. At this rate she may not last the night and he'll not only have to haul the aunts back to their own holiday home, them squawking protests all the way, but he may also have to deal with one of Beatrice's moods – doleful eyes, heavy exhalations and barbed comments – behaviour which he finds draining.

Bobby is attempting to prise Aunt One's talons off his arm just as Jane the bride slinks by, gracing Kit with a radiant smile as she heads inside to the toilet. She can afford this generous display of *no hard feelings* now she has Glorious Greg in the bag. Their break-up, instigated by Kit some years ago, was not taken in the same spirit.

Bobby somehow manages to deftly disentangle himself without breaking the aunt's knuckles and moves on to glad-hand a couple from Chesterfield at the next table. Kit has heard the rumour that these friends of the mother of the bride are thinking of buying a timeshare in Barn Owl for the Easter holidays – a whopping thirty-year commitment. This is a particularly lucrative period, rarely available, which has only recently come up for grabs due to the tragic yet rather convenient death of a former QC, his widow retiring to the Mijas mountains of Spain with a dapper antiques dealer from Brighton, with what some have judged as indecent haste.

These potential buyers are not to know that Bobby has flirted with three other interested parties in as many weeks, according to those in the know, talking up the rarity of the opportunity. He seems rather desperate to bring in a good offer.

Aunt One suddenly makes a lunge towards the wine bottle, startling Beatrice, who tuts threateningly. Kit resolves to leave the women to their imminent downfall and head to the pub as soon as is socially acceptable.

Aunt Two starts questioning Kit on his *future plans*. Not having any, his will to live seeps further away as he tries to answer in polite generalisations, and when that fails, he trails off, falling into a silent funk.

He is wondering whether he might get a chance to do a little painting while he's here this time, when Jane swoops by again just as his mother knocks her wine glass flying. It is already empty, so there is that, but Kit is forced to grab Aunt Two's arm to stop her hurtling onto the grass after it.

'I'll do it!' trills the bride, curtseying prettily in her gown to scoop up the glass, knees demurely together, which is a first, thinks Kit unkindly. 'Intact!' she crows, which is more than can be said for Kit's temper.

'Oh, Janey!' sighs his mother. 'You are incandescent, my darling. This silly oik must rue the day he let you slip through his fingers!' She lays a perfectly manicured hand on her son's chest, murmuring, 'Silly, silly boy!'

As Jane faux toasts his mother, Kit has an overwhelming urge to snatch the glass from the bride's hand and smash it into her smug face, then grab the stupid fascinator from his mother's stupid head and ram it into her stupid mouth.

The best man chinks a glass to announce something or other, shattering the image, and Kit grits his teeth so hard the neighbouring guests might hear them splinter.

7
Alison

The Old Ship pub is quiet enough right now in the lull between lunchtime and evening sessions. Most punters are in the garden, including two young families shoving vegan pizza and sweet potato chips down their kids' gullets. The little ones drink organic pop (same sugar content, higher smugness quotient than the normal stuff) while the parents unwind with very large G&Ts, because (hurrah!) the sun has long passed the yardarm. They are probably regretting their choice to come here rather than holidaying at an all-inclusive with a children's club somewhere in the Algarve, which would have worked out far cheaper, even if they'd bathed in asses' milk.

Bar manager Alison Smith is bracing for a deluge of customers later. Along with the regulars, there'll be a few birthday-party oldies and their handlers from the community centre bash, plus a slew of wedding guests. Some will stay back at Hawk post wedding reception – not that they'll help clear up, they have people for that – and of course there are drinks at Hawk, but the truly dedicated will troop down to the bar to achieve a more professional state of inebriation.

Alison checks her optics and calculates if she'll need more spirits. All in order. Good.

The single new thing that catches her eye is Bill Thatcher's urn up on the shelf alongside the tankards. Bill's wife, Phyllis, only plucked up the courage to bring it over to the pub last week. It was a highly emotional and somewhat disturbing moment for punters, friends and family alike, not least Bill Thatcher himself, who was sitting in the snug nursing a pint of Betty Stogs (queen of Cornish ales), minding his own business at the time.

This grand gesture was accompanied by Phyllis yawping for all the pub to hear, 'You touch that bloody cleaner over at the Mermaid one more time, mister, and you'll be in that, you dirty bugger. Think on!'

Phyllis is northern.

Hannah brings a tray of cups through from the garden. A large group of happy hikers are sitting out there, still ordering cappuccinos, which Alison considers very bad form. This is the cocktail hour, happy hour – the magical, pivotal moment when it is socially acceptable to commence the process towards messy.

Alison doesn't mind the ice-cream and coffee mob – good profit margins – but that clientele is not her forte. The whiskers and furry-knee brigade, as she thinks of the hikers (and that's just the women), are too health conscious to spend an entire week's wages in a single night, which is a regular occurrence on the island. Alison thrives on those epic events of profligate inebriation; nights when she's required to break up fights between rival gig crews, flinging out irascible builders, knowing when to say yes and when to refuse a lock-in, and forging her fearsome reputation as a successful woman in a man's game by sheer bolshiness and brute strength honed by a lifetime of humping barrels up and down cellar steps.

Given that one of the barmen is currently down with 'flu' – a summer cold, but youngsters these days have no stamina – Alison's delighted that Hannah's holiday has been cancelled and her best barmaid has since volunteered to work for a couple of hours early doors.

'Do you want to take a break now before it all hits the fan?' she asks Hannah.

'I'm fine. Got a couple of hours' kip earlier,' replies the barmaid, coming round to the business side of the bar.

'Good,' says Alison, stacking the clean pint glasses she's polished.

They are now both a little antsy, bracing for the wash of human plankton that will soon fill the place with laughter, sweat and midweek marauding. People always behave foolishly in large groups – behaviour they would never consider when alone becomes the accepted norm whenever they're in a gang, whenever they're on holiday, and whenever alcohol is involved.

The great leveller, alcohol. *Booze! Helping ugly people have sex since 3000 BC!* as one of Hannah's off-duty T-shirts proclaims. What a gift to the gene pool.

Alison admires the barmaid. Hannah's a hard grafter. But she does not approve of her florid love life, which can cause complications and resentments. The flirting might make her popular with punters and nets her fabulous tips – on top of the fifteen percent service charge, shared equally by the team – but it isn't great for business when things go further. Alison herself used to get away with stuff like that back in the day – too long in the tooth now. She wonders if she might be a little jealous.

People like to gossip about Hannah – and not only about her relationships. Weird rumours swirled around the darker recesses of the pub last year, spread initially by one of the housekeepers:

'Saw her dancing up there at Cromwell's Castle, buck naked under the full moon. . .'

'You reckon she's a witch?'

'Devil worship, probably. . .'

She's not usually one to spread gossip, but Alison couldn't help but pass that extraordinary nugget along. Hannah had read the tarot at last year's Summer Fayre, so the tittle-tattle got plenty of traction.

Three of the housekeeping team are cackling together on Table 3 right now, sitting in descending order of size as you look from the bar, like a nest of tables, trashing someone else's reputation by the looks of it.

Hannah goes to gather the last of the afternoon glasses as Alison sets about sorting the till. Thor from the shop comes up to the bar and Alison gives him her professional smile. Super polite, nice enough bloke, moderate drinker. The bad skin is a pity. He wears a T-shirt with the sleeves rolled up to show off the new godawful tattoo he recently acquired in Penzance – the face of some bald bloke who looks like a pincushion. Ted the boatman calls him Hammer Boy, although Thor has to be mid-twenties. This is not on account of his chosen name of Thor, but because, 'He's a right tool, that one.'

For want of something better to comment upon, Alison says, 'Those biceps are coming along nicely.'

'Thank you,' he mumbles.

'You'll be breaking a few hearts this summer.'

'Chance would be a fine thing,' he replies, without making eye contact. He blushes, thanks her again, pays for his pint and scuttles away to stand alongside a group of gardeners, at a slight distance yet near enough to be included in the conversation if they so wish. They do not wish.

Poor bugger, thinks Alison.

The couple from Razorbill turn up with a group of teenagers in tow. One of the pretty girls is only wearing a bikini top and her jeans are more hole than material. It's hard not to stare. Alison notices Thor looking with an expression of pure longing. *Not even if you won the lottery, mate*, she thinks.

She's finishing Razorbill's order when Maisie Willis and her mother arrive from Sanderling, which takes some doing. Maisie huffs and puffs as she attempts to manoeuvre her mother's wheelchair inside, so Hannah goes round to give her a hand.

'Thank you, thank you,' flutters Maisie. 'You okay, Mum?'

Maisie's mother, Edith Willis, has been coming to Tresco for donkey's years, initially along with the dearly departed Mr Willis. He didn't die or anything, just shacked up with a dental hygienist and moved to Launceston, which some might think amounts to pretty much the same thing.

'Arrived this afternoon?' asks Alison when Maisie comes up to the bar, flustered and sweating.

'This morning,' says Maisie, pushing damp hair out of her eyes. 'But we've not even unpacked everything yet, have we, Mum?'

Her mother is already studying the menu. Alison guesses it'll be cheesy chips for Edith and is proved right.

The women have matching pink waterproofs, Edith's hung across the back of the chair – Alison assumes for draping purposes because it'd not do up across the expanse of Edith Willis's chest – and matching pink headbands. Maisie fusses over her mother, continually asking if she's comfortable, if she needs anything. That would scare the hell out of Alison, constantly having to *care* for someone. She doesn't even own a pot plant.

A flurry of activity follows. Islanders finishing work pop in before heading home for tea, while the blow-ins from the time-shares and rentals commence their holiday evenings early.

There's a brief moment of respite while Alison slices more lemon, then the first of the wedding guests arrives. The son from Falcon as memory serves her . . . Kit. She's good with names is Alison – part of the job. The bride and groom must have just departed for the Hell Bay Hotel over on Bryher. Alison's worked here three seasons, but she's only visited it once as she's been so busy. The hotel is hailed for its *dramatic views*, although pretty much everywhere you look round here there's a dramatic view.

As Kit approaches Alison chirps, 'What can I get for you, my lover?' (She's not Cornish, but she occasionally gives it her best *Doc Martin* for the punters.) The young man sports a strained look on his face which is easily and accurately interpreted as *get me drunker right now!*

'A large vodka and a new life,' says Kit, leaning on the bar and gracing her with a lovely smile as he adds a heartfelt, 'please.'

A handsome young man with nice manners. Alison catches Hannah giving him the eye, and thinks, *here we go again.*

8

Charlotte

Her high heels clickety-clack down the road towards the pub and Charlotte opens her exceptionally tiny handbag to reapply her lip gloss. It's a nervous habit – she already has ample coverage. Ditto the perfume, which she spritzes on her neck and her cleavage just in case he kisses her there. The light's too low for a good selfie but she pouts and flashes the peace sign anyway – she can brighten it up later with a filter.

In preparation to see Kit, Charlotte has had her eyebrows threaded, her regular facial, a gel manicure, plus a lymphatic drainage massage as she was still feeling bloated after giving in to that pasta dish at Golly's birthday bash – always irresistible. Damn Golly, who seems to be immune to carbs, which is really bloody unfair. Charlotte's *downstairs* is regularly tended, but she booked a waxing session the week before the trip, just to be on the safe side. Plus a blow-dry before setting off, but thanks to the sea air, flyaway strands of hair are already making a bid for freedom.

She's forgotten her brolly and imagines Beatrice saying, 'You know it can turn in the blink of an eye here, Charlotte!' but Kit might let her shelter under his golf umbrella, pulling her close to him. And he knows she's not one of those welly-and-horses types he grew up alongside in the Gloucestershire countryside. She's always been a city girl at heart, Charlotte. Yes, she might have given him the impression that she liked sailing, but that was when she'd assumed they meant proper yachts, not the sad little boats and dinghies Beatrice's friends and family use here, bobbing around like pathetic corks.

Anyway, she doubts a brolly would do much good because it's not raining, it's just super-moist. Out of nowhere too. It was gorgeous on the mainland and really hot earlier this afternoon, but now the temperature is plummeting and Charlotte is shivering.

She'd called for a golf buggy but was told they were all busy with some pensioners' jolly at the community centre, which was very inconvenient, so she's had to walk.

Charlotte has been to Tresco with her godmother several times before, but this will be her first time on the island without her parents (who are in the middle of a messy divorce), and the first time while Kit is here too. There will be so many gorgeous backgrounds for her Insta. Kit and sunsets! She can't wait!

If she gets her numbers up, one day she might get on *Made in Chelsea*!

She imagines Kit standing on the terrace at Falcon, framed against the sea. He might step forwards to kiss her then and her legs would turn to cooked spaghetti.

As she rounds the corner to the pub she tosses her hair upside down in preparation.

'You having a fit, maid?' shouts one of the oiks sitting on the sea wall. She'd failed to spot them in the gloaming. Locals. Nothing for them to do here but drink. Lovely as it is on the island, Charlotte knows she'd go insane in about a fortnight here – so cut off from all her pals in London.

She offers the smile as expected and then takes a pic of herself posing with the pub sign above her head, although as signs go, it's pretty basic.

The light is now falling fast. It's a pity about the coastal fog because dusk is usually the sweetest time for atmospheric shots. It would be so romantic if she and Kit could sit stoned and happy in the garden back at Falcon, watching the sun sink into the sea. The light would be just right. A post with her squishing her head next to Kit's with the setting sun glowing behind them would get so many likes.

Charlotte sucks in her stomach and pulls back her shoulders to give her breasts a boost as she walks into the crowded bar. The heat hits her hard and she realises she shouldn't have started on the gin back at the house.

She spots him immediately – Kit is a head above most of the scrum. She wriggles her way through the throng towards him, and as she gets nearer she notices his arm is slung around the shoulders of a tiny girl in an even tinier skirt; one of the barmaids, wearing the uniform T-shirt featuring the Old Ship logo which is straining against her breasts.

Charlotte calls, 'Kit! Kit!' but her voice is drowned out in a huge roar from a group of gig rowers. She tries to push her way through, calling again, but before she can reach him, she sees him bend and take the barmaid's face in his hands, cradling it, before giving her a long, deep kiss.

9

Christie

'Sam. Sam! Put him down, you'll make him heave!'

Sam is spinning Tommy round the kitchen like a chair-o-plane. The lad is screaming at a level beyond seagulls, ecstatic with giddiness, and the twins, Ben and Dan, are hooting encourage-ment.

'Can you take the baby? Sam! Can you take—' No one ever listens to Christie.

'YAGGHHH!' Tommy shrieks at his final rotation before Sam gently plonks him on the kitchen floor and he takes a wailing baby Finn from his wife's arms, thank Christ.

Tommy stands and weeble-wobbles around, knocking into furniture, spilling the small vase of wildflowers on the table, until he collapses flat on his bum on the floor.

'What's wrong, little man?' says Sam, peering at his youngest son's enraged face. 'Want me to take this one outside for a bit? See if he quietens?'

'Yeah. Thanks.'

Sam jiggles the baby, and as he walks him to the bottom of the garden, Finn's furious shrieks fade like a siren.

The relief is physical.

He has the knack, her husband. The kids adore him. The neighbours, his gig crew, his colleagues all love him. The Family rate him . . . or used to. That's her Sam. When he's good he's very, very good. When he's bad, he's total rubbish.

Christie takes a deep breath to rid herself of those thoughts.

'Right, Tommy, get your coat on.' The boat which takes the lad to school on St Mary's is on its way. Last night's mist has already cleared, and she can see it approaching Bryher across the channel before it heads over to Tresco. 'Now, please.'

'My head's still woozy,' he complains.

If he's sick down his school clothes on the way across she'll bloody kill Sam.

As soon as she gets Tommy off, Christie has the twins to see to, then she'll tackle the devastation of the breakfast ruins and if she's really, really lucky, at some point this morning, with the twins in front of the telly and the baby in his bouncer, she might have time for an uninterrupted wee.

What did she do in a former lifetime to deserve a house full of lads? Even the cat turned out to be a tom. Outnumbered. She does her best in this sea of testosterone, but it's a constant battle. Just once she'd like to go into the bathroom and not have to wade through—

'Mum!'

A flurry of activity follows as her eldest son departs for school. His first year over there, but he acts so grown up already and he's only eleven. Where did the last decade go? She had Tommy when she was just eighteen, only a kid herself then.

Sam shoves the baby at her as he comes in from the garden, pecks her on the cheek, and leaves for work. She envies his escape.

She hoovers, mops, takes the mince out the freezer, puts the kettle on. She's loading the dishwasher when a memory from last night hits her like a truck. She has to straighten, reaching for a glass still covered in greasy fingerprints, filling it from the tap. She takes three long gulps of water. The cat, lying on the kitchen counter like a loaf of bread, regards her impassively.

She was a bit tipsy herself last night. It was good craic at the bar – a party atmosphere after yesterday's wedding and Sam was drinking to celebrate a great gig training session. But there's always something to drink to on the island: if the rowers do well, if they lose a race, if there's a Y in the month . . . or the day. Sam's idea of a balanced diet is a beer in each hand.

Of course, Christie felt she couldn't say anything. The least hint of her disapproval and it's another excuse for him to stay out playing euchre or poker with the lads until the small hours. And it was one of their few nights out together since the baby was born – a rare night off when her friend Emma, the playgroup manager, had volunteered to babysit. Aunty Emma to the rescue! A night of freedom! Christie was determined not to let her concerns about the level of Sam's drinking sour things.

But the effort required to stop her exasperation showing is grating.

She'd had a couple of pints herself, and as she came back from the toilets she noticed John and Mary-Jane kissing in the corner, snuggling together like lovebirds, the new garden expert and the café worker; *The Happily Marrieds*, as some call the Americans, the edge of sarcasm belittling the couple's displays of affection. Christie always feels a pang of envy when she sees them. They're older than her and they're still all over each other. She takes the mick like everyone else, although she'd love for Sam to kiss her like that, to hold her hand, sit with her, just acknowledge her in public. But as soon as he's out the house, he's off with his mates – rowing with them, drinking with them, standing at the bar talking with them, spending all his bloody time with them, ignoring his own wife. She wishes she didn't, but she still loves her husband, still craves his attention.

When had Christie last managed a proper conversation with Sam? The demands of the kids prevent any heart-to-heart when they're awake, and she doesn't chance pushing things when he's drunk or hungover, which leaves a very small window of opportunity.

At least the set-to in the pub last night had nothing to do with Sam this time, although skanky Hannah was involved yet again. One of the timeshare guests was caught snogging her as far as she could make out, although she only caught the aftermath because she was getting a round in from the smaller bar down the pavilion end of the pub at the time. She heard the shouts, and saw a sobbing blonde girl storming out of the pub.

Christie started grumbling about Sam to Alison. The bar manager tutted and nodded until Christie felt guilty and added, 'He needs to blow off a bit of steam, I know that. I do.' And she plastered on a happy face, took a slug of her cider, and said, 'At least he's keeping it in his pants now.'

It was meant as a joke, but the look of pity on Alison's face told her something different.

Christie made her way back to the table with her pint just as

Hannah gave the tall tourist's bum a squeeze. And even though she wasn't coming onto Sam, Christie itched to wipe the big grin off the barmaid's face.

St Mary's Quay

May, After the Storm

Nurse Kelly sits waiting for the boat to take her over to Tresco, glad of a few minutes to herself.

Sitting alongside her are two little ones eating ice creams, excited by the activity in the harbour, the mother and father enjoying the innocent pleasures of holidaying in this delightful destination.

'We're going to see the whales!' announces the taller of the children.

'The whales!' echoes the other.

'Well, we might not see them,' says the mother, managing expectations. 'They might be somewhere else. Or asleep. Or . . .'

Kelly wishes she too could go out on a pleasure trip to see the whales, but all she can see is her patient's face – not just the injuries, but the expression of terror. The poor thing flinches at any sudden movement. When Kelly accidentally knocked her phone off the hospital bed onto the floor, the girl actually yelped.

The mother turns to Kelly and says, 'We love coming here. It's so . . . you know, wholesome.'

Kelly forces a smile in return.

The sun today is relentlessly jolly, the birds and the harbour master delightfully chirpy, but two women have been attacked and another is still missing. Hardly wholesome.

10

Kit

He wakes to the world pitching and yawing.

Incrementally, tentatively, he turns onto his side, trying to focus on the light switch to stop the spinning, and as he slowly stretches his limbs, he tries to knit the shreds of himself into a whole, wincing at the state of his head, attempting to piece together the story of the night. He senses it was epic.

He is not in his own bed. He seems to be covered in . . . *curtains*. No pillow. His neck is incensed. And he's cold.

The sense of loss. She's gone already.

Ah, yes! The barmaid. *Hannah.* A pleasant throb reminds him of the night.

He remembers he's in Puffin, so at some point he will have to make his way back to his mother's.

He recalls abandoning the wedding reception, although he did stick it out through the appalling speeches. Why does everyone think they're stand-up comedians when it comes to weddings? He'd left Aunt One dancing with Glorious Greg the groom, or rather the man was gamely attempting to prop her up as she swayed, fascinator at half-tilt, laughing her loud braying laugh, '*HEE-HEE-HEE!*', while his mother sat aloof, quietly judging for Britain with that smug superior expression on her face that made him itch to stave in her skull with a jeroboam.

The thought of his mother makes his early-morning semi shrivel.

He thinks hard to retrace his steps. He'd made it to the Old Ship, sobering a little on the walk down, then he'd had a vodka at Table 1, chatting to Big Bob (thus named to distinguish him from Bobby), got his buzz back, flirted with the barmaid, drunk more, upped the flirting. Big Bob painted seascapes on bits of driftwood in the naïve style, which meant a child of five could do them, but he was fun to talk to – encyclopaedic knowledge of early Motown and the more picaresque aspects of island life.

Kit was informed that Big Bob and Vlad sourced cheap booze and a few basic drugs for the locals, and they could also sort a couple of chosen guests like Kit, who, Big Bob informed him, was deemed a top bloke, despite the accent.

It was the first time Kit had ever talked to Big Bob, but they were now apparently *best buds* because he'd just bought a little weed from him, the exchange happening in the toilets, Big Bob acting like a cross between Tony Montana and El Chapo.

When the gig crews invaded, Kit had a drink with Sam, who he'd chatted to on a previous visit, and a drink with someone else.

Whenever Hannah passed on her way to collect glasses, she joked with him, ruffling his hair, touching his arm.

'Maid's got the hots for you,' winked Big Bob.

It became loud and blurry, or perhaps that was just him. One of the old boys joined their table and spouted a slew of garbled words which Kit took for Cornish, but apparently he was just arseholed.

When Hannah came by to deliver bowls of chips, he'd got up and followed her back towards the kitchen, grabbed her hand, and led her around to the corridor near the back stairs. In the corner there they'd had their first kiss – well the first since their brief fumble under the mistletoe last Christmas, which was red hot as he recalls.

Later, Hannah had finished early for the night, and when she came round to the punters' side of the bar he'd stood, hugged her to him, bent to kiss her again, and while he explored her mouth, the noise and bustle was still there all around him but no longer inside him.

Then a push in his back and Charlotte was there – appearing out of thin air, confusing him, because as he stood there gormless and swaying, there'd been shouting which he couldn't quite make out and Charlotte suddenly hit him hard across the mouth, making his lip bleed. A torrent of tears out of nowhere, making no sense.

When Charlotte disappeared, he immediately forgot her.

He sat back down at Sam's table and Hannah came round with ice cubes in a cloth to put on his lip, but all he wanted on his mouth was her.

Another drink, avoiding the split, dribbling some of it down his shirt. More laughter.

The barmaid from this season, who was leaving in a couple of weeks, not even staying for the August rush (couldn't hack it), joined them, and Alison went upstairs and left them to it.

Hannah and her friend had put on their own music, but not loud, so's not to disturb the guests upstairs, and the girls danced together, putting on a bit of a show. Hannah had a throaty, filthy laugh.

Then he was the only one left with Sam and a couple other workers.

And *her*. Sexy as all hell. A total knockout. Really long dark hair, like a mermaid. Dark eyes. A wicked smile and amazing breasts.

Desire licks up from his groin as he remembers.

Eventually she sat next to him and asked him about Charlotte.

'Was that your girlfriend?'

'Never saw her before in my life!' he joked.

'Really.'

'Honestly, I don't know what's got into her. She's my mum's goddaughter. She's usually a sweet girl. I've no idea why she kicked off.' (And he genuinely doesn't have the faintest idea.)

At some point there was *the look*.

He didn't want to go back to his mother's, and they couldn't go back to Hannah's – no room – but she had the keys for Puffin, one of the cottages up by the lake. In the middle of being redecorated.

Properties on the island are generally only locked during refurbs, because there might be ladders, drills, sanders and saws left around, and Tresco's free-range kids, used to running in and out of the workers' cottages, are fascinated by the timeshare homes, mainly because they're not allowed in them. During building work these holiday lets are locked to stop the youngsters sneaking in, poking around and hurting themselves.

'Sea savvy, land stupid.' One of Old Betty's sayings.

Kit left the pub first, then he waited in the shadows outside. Moonless. No streetlights. A couple of steps away from the pub, it was pitch black apart from the stars – so many stars! Hannah wheeled her bike round and joined him a few minutes later. She'd acquired a bottle of vodka.

He wrapped his arms around her, pressed himself into her, enjoyed the sting on his lip when she kissed him, and then he tripped, knocking over the bike.

She picked it up and they snuck away, giggling.

It was cold inside Puffin, the furniture enveloped with dust sheets, ghostly in the dark, the smell of fresh paint. They soon warmed up.

And she swept him away.

The thought of that and Kit is instantly hard again. And he feels a shift deep inside; something irresistible – the point where the moon's pull turns the tide. It is light already, and somehow he knows his life has changed.

Like a teenage girl he checks his phone and smiles to see a message from her. She asks him to lock up, leave discreetly, bring the keys back to the bar this afternoon when Alison's not there. His lip hurts as he grins at the thought of seeing her again.

But first he will have to return to Falcon and the thought of his mother, no doubt nursing her own hangover, makes him feel slightly queasy. He wonders if she'll have remembered to let the dog out for a wee. And he'll have to face Charlotte, who must have been off her head on something . . .

He swings his legs off the bed. Another memory – one so

sweet, far more intimate than the sex, it makes him blush. As they finally lay down together in the small hours of this morning, exhausted, sated, he reached for Hannah's hand.

And that's how they went to sleep, the same as sea otters do, holding paws so as not to drift apart.

11

Hannah

She showers back at hers, aching and swollen and full of him. She's probably still a little drunk, but despite the lack of sleep, she feels wide awake, renewed.

She'll have to manage the situation, so Alison doesn't go ballistic. There's no rule about dating guests, but it is very much frowned on if things turn nasty, and even though Alison didn't see it because she was down the pavilion end of the pub at the time, everyone will tell her boss about that little scene between Kit and the drunk blonde – the girl screeching about him 'leading her on' and slapping him about the head, calling Hannah a whore and ugly crying.

But it was worth it. Hannah shivers in delight as she towels herself dry.

In bed, after that first frantic fuck, even before the second and third time, she'd realised Kit was something special. He told her he was young, free and single; he swore there had never been anything romantic between him and the blonde girl. But she's been caught out like this before. Holidaymakers forget mainland life as soon as they get here. Different rules apply. What happens on the island stays on the island and all that, although Tresco is hardly Vegas.

Hannah never expects much from these holiday flings. She takes them at face value, enjoying the fact that they burn so much brighter than ordinary relationships.

And she'd really enjoyed last night. *Kit* – a buffed-up Timothée Chalamet face, all chiselled cheekbones and sexy lips. Tall, good body, wavy reddish-sandy hair. Not really her type. Young. *Keen.*

She'd guessed he was a fire sign, an Aries as it turned out. She's a Scorpio. Aries and Scorpio matches are often passionate. *Incan*-bloody-*descent*!

She manages a couple of hours' sleep, jerks awake at the alarm, dresses in her vintage silver leggings and her favourite leopard-print hoody, and swings by the shop.

John, the numpty from the garden team, waves at her as he's coming out and Hannah's going in. He's by himself, which is unusual because he and his wife are normally joined at the hip, walking to and from work together most days. 'Bless-ed day!' he trills. He says 'bless-ed' like they do in *The Handmaid's Tale*. He was a former pastor or something back in the swamplands of America. He gives Hannah a smile, and the creeps.

She ignores him, but no matter how rude she is to him he continues grinning. Something about him makes her want to hit him in his beaming beardy face.

Inside the shop, Hannah grabs a bottled Frappuccino. It always makes her think of the time two daft timeshare lads put up an announcement on the notice board by the mini post office (on estate headed notepaper, which was a clever touch), announcing Starbucks was opening a branch on the island, and all hell broke loose.

At the till, Thor is already in full investigative mode, obviously having heard about the altercation in the pub from earlier customers.

'All kicked off then last night?' he mumbles. Very little eye contact as usual, which puts Hannah on edge.

She makes a non-committal grunt.

'The guest from Falcon?'

'Mm.'

'What happened?' He rings up her purchases.

'The usual,' Hannah shrugs, putting the coffee and a bar of chocolate into her bag as swiftly as she can, keen to be off. When she offers nothing more, Thor gives her the death stare.

His attitude annoys the hell out of Hannah. They'd had one kiss at a party last year. That was it. But he's not let it go since. Hannah tried to let him down gently, saying she wasn't in the market for a relationship, not adding that even if she was, Thor would never be in with a chance. But ever since, he's acted like a bloody stalker.

'I want details,' he demands, a fake smile plastered over poorly hidden jealousy.

'Nothing to tell really,' says Hannah.

Thor refuses to hand over Hannah's change. He crosses his arms, to show off his muscles, and says, 'But I want to know.'

'None of your business,' snaps Hannah.

'Don't be a tease, Hannah.'

'Don't be a prick, *Alec*.' That's his real name. Thor is an affectation.

64

He looks furious.

Hannah might have said more, but Emma from the playgroup comes in and she makes her escape.

Outside, her phone buzzes. A text from Bobby asking her to meet him in Puffin. Bugger.

She drinks her coffee and eats her chocolate, collects her bike, fires up a quick breakfast cigarette, then cycles over, a fresh sea breeze behind her back. It's only ten minutes to Puffin, although pretty much everywhere by road here is only ten minutes to cycle. Her skin's tingling by the time she arrives at the cottage.

Luck is on her side. She doesn't have to explain why she hasn't got her key because the door's already open and she finds Bobby in the kitchen. If he's aware of what went on here last night, he doesn't mention it.

'Will you give me a hand with the curtains?' he asks. 'We have a new rental coming in next Tuesday.'

'That's good news,' she says. 'Shall we air the place out now most of the painting's finished? Put the heating on for a bit?' The advantage of that suggestion is that she's hoping for a replay with Kit tonight.

'Yep, yep, yep,' says Bobby. He seems preoccupied.

She switches on the boiler, goes upstairs to bring down the curtains – checking the mattress for any of her incriminating long dark hairs – and then she and Bobby remove dust sheets and wrangle pieces of furniture back into place downstairs. They re-hang the curtains together, Bobby straining as he holds up his end.

'You okay?' she asks.

He mumbles a non-committal reply.

Hannah knows Bobby well and something's bothering him. She wonders if someone saw Kit sneaking into the cottage with her last night.

'What's eating you?' she pushes.

'Just . . . bloody guests!'

'What have they done now?'

'We had one dopey cow come into the office first thing this morning to ask us to turn *the big light off* because it was keeping her awake – the bloody *lighthouse* light! You couldn't make it up! And the complaints about being fogged in the other day! "I'm expected in Munich. I can't possibly stay another night." Spoilt brats! I just . . .' He trails off.

It's unusual to hear Bobby talk like this. The guests annoy everyone, but they're a necessary evil. Usually it would be Hannah bitching about their insane demands: 'Do you make your ice with tap or filtered water?' Moaning that the foghorn's too loud!

Bobby falls silent.

Hannah doesn't mind his mood. He doesn't require conversation, which makes a change from her always having to be *on*, being chatty and flirty behind the bar however she really feels. And in this companionable peace, she relives the restorative images of the previous night.

12

Thor

Thor scrubs violently at a sticky spillage in the fridge. Hannah knows exactly how to wind him up. Only his cousin Kelly insists on calling him Alec, rather than his chosen name. Life here is shit at the best of times without the barmaid making it worse.

Underneath the dark and dangerous persona he carefully crafts online, Thor still feels like a boring little kid from Dudley. Well, Wombourne, which isn't even the mean streets of Dudley proper. He's twenty-four but Hannah doesn't take him seriously; treats him like a kid.

When he finishes his boring work at the boring shop this afternoon, he will get the boat over to St Mary's to visit Kelly, who's a nurse over at the hospital there. Thor doesn't really get on with his cousin, as Kelly's much older, far too nosey, and far too bossy. He doesn't see a lot of her because she often has other plans – she's either working or out drinking with her mates.

For all the time he spends in the pub on Tresco, Thor doesn't really have mates he drinks with. He has his online friends – but those blokes are not the type you can have a laugh with exactly. *BDE666* is almost as bossy as Kelly, but at least he can unload stuff online. He could never tell anyone face to face what goes through his mind.

But sometimes loneliness forces him over to St Mary's to spend time with the only relative he keeps in contact with. When dark feelings threaten to overwhelm him, his cousin is the lesser of two evils.

But Kelly is a *medical professional*, and she never lets him forget that. She's always trying to *diagnose* him. She reckons his social anxiety is down to growing up with a mother who herself had various *issues*, problems denoted by acronyms: BPD, ADHD, OCD, GAD – all of which made her a total CUNT. No wonder his father fucked off.

If Thor thinks too much about any of that he spirals, and he has to list things he can see and hear, to stop those thoughts getting out of hand.

He is not obsessing about Hannah either, definitely not, but he can't stop thinking about her. For months now, Thor has lived on scraps – reading into what Hannah says and how she says it. A simple, 'Nice day for it,' could suggest the barmaid is in a good mood and therefore there might be a possibility of a replay of the kiss they shared last year. 'I'm hanging this morning' might signify Hannah's in a bad mood or, perhaps, scared of getting involved.

Thor considers all angles, apart from the obvious – Hannah is simply not interested.

And now by all accounts she's hooked up with that long streak of piss, Kit, the son of the snooty Beatrice woman from Falcon. A ginger! Thor has not been as gobsmacked by Hannah's choice of partner since that time she had a fling with that Aussie sous chef from the Star Castle Hotel on St Mary's. After all her boyfriends, Hannah had suddenly gone lesbo!

He'd asked her if she'd had other girlfriends, but she just laughed and said, 'Babe, the difference between gay, straight and bi is about four vodkas or half a spliff.' Like it didn't matter! Like she didn't care what people thought or said about her!

As he prices up the *local beef* in the freezer (far more expensive than normal meat), Thor entertains himself by imagining how he might get his own back on Hannah. Teach her a lesson. Who does she think she is, calling him Alec?

He'd get her drunk and bring her back to his room, although his housemates would have to be out. Then he'd strip her and tie her naked to a chair, cut off all her hair, and whip her with barbed wire (he'd have to order that, or they might have some up at the farm) until she screamed and begged for mercy.

Such daydreams pass the time.

13

John

This is the best season to appreciate the Abbey Garden, when God rewards his creation with blooms unfurling like slow-motion fireworks. Late spring on the island! A cornucopia of beauty!

Iris Murdoch once said that people from a planet without flowers might think humans would be mad with joy to be surrounded by them. And he is!

What hurts John, no, enrages him, is that the next logical thought does not follow – what Supreme Being created such miracles? The minds of most humans are so dulled and atrophied, ruined with temptations and false idols, they do not seem to be able to hold the concept of the Almighty. It has become a Godless land.

Except here. Except this Paradise. Yes, there is war and famine in some corners of the earth, but here there is an embarrassment of riches; here is a sanctuary.

Who could fail to believe in the benign power of Our Lord surrounded by nature's bounty? Take this *Echium pininana*, the tower of jewels – he trails his fingers up the blue foliage on the tree-like erection. Technically a weed, some think, including the garden curator, who exhibits an unsettling snobbery regarding certain plants. John has no time for such a concept. Every single thing here is one of God's creations. Originally from the Canary Islands, this stunner. He and Mary-Jane are also foreign implants, hailing from Georgia, USA. Will they too be able to settle on this rich soil, in this temperate micro-climate, this divine archipelago? Will the sweet breezes and gentle showers allow them to take root? He prays it will be so.

They are blessed to be here. He is doubly blessed to work here – his hands in the soil all day, working the land like his forefathers, going home to the woman he loves at night. His heart might burst with joy.

Yes, his lumbar region sometimes nags him, after all, he's in his late thirties now, but that is a small price to pay. He smiles watching a ladybug amble across a soft green leaf. He knows he's in fine physical fettle apart from his back, although he must focus on gratitude that it is so, rather than indulge in prideful thoughts.

One of the giant flower heads nearby has been flattened, either by a clumsy visitor, a squirrel, or a blundering pea-brained pheasant. He breaks it off. He will take it home for Mary-Jane, place it in a tall vase for her to appreciate as they eat their evening meal together, although her beauty far surpasses any bloom.

An instant surge of jealousy. He sees the way other men look at her. He— He prays to quiet his rage and churning emotions.

To clear these base thoughts he breathes in the heady scents surrounding him and takes a moment to gaze out to the horizon, appreciating the consonance of sky and water, flora and fauna.

His attention returns to the flower. Some call this soaring perennial the viper's bugloss, but if John were to find an actual serpent here in this garden, he would dash its brains against the rocks and cast it out. Nothing can be allowed to threaten this Eden.

14

Kit

They fall on each other as soon as they shut the door to the cottage. He pulls her hair a little. She bites his neck. They scramble upstairs, a jumble of buttons and zips and desire.

He laughs with pure joy as he comes.

After they disentangle, Hannah leans out of the window for a cigarette, then closes the newly hung curtains, and Kit lights the candles he's brought with him. They wrap themselves in the duvet Hannah has cycled up from the laundry, hidden in a garden sack, and take turns sipping the flask of chilled Cosmopolitan he prepared earlier in a moment of genius. He's also brought Mini Magnum ice creams in a freezer box, which has impressed and delighted Hannah.

This is like a really excellent first date.

He's giddy. He acts the clown to entertain her, juggling the plastic glasses, badly, before pouring her cocktail. He loves how her eyes go crinkly when she laughs. He loves how she enfolds him, as he lies on the warmth of her breasts.

Wisely, Kit didn't make an appearance at the pub this evening. He had avoided both his mother and Charlotte by staying out on the water all day and drinking at the Flying Boat Club until Hannah had finished work. Hannah said they'd been so busy in the pub that Alison hadn't even had time to read her the full riot act for the preceding night's scene with Charlotte. Thankfully there had been no sign of Charlotte in the bar either.

However, surprisingly, Kit's mother had made a point of popping into the Old Ship to apologise to Hannah on Charlotte's behalf.

'She told me that Charlotte has a crush on you and she'd somehow got it into her head that you were going to get together during this trip,' Hannah informed him. 'She'd had too much to drink and then—'

'You don't say!' He laughed at the thought and informed Hannah there was no way he'd be getting together with Charlotte.

'Not my type and way too immature. Mum only invited her here to cheer her up. I think there's been some sort of falling-out with her folks.'

Hannah and Kit are currently very cheered. They're now at the relaxed and riffing stage of the evening, sated for the time being, getting to know each other in ways apart from the carnal, where they appear to be extremely well suited. She tells him she likes his eyes, 'greeny-blue, like the sea'. She laughs and informs him, 'You're a very, *very* good-looking date.'

He glows with the compliments.

'Why have we wasted so much time getting together?' he muses. 'I remember the very first time I saw you – it was a couple of years ago at New Year. You were dressed as a crab. The claws were hilarious! They were so bad.'

'I made those claws!' she protests. 'Cornflake boxes. But you can't have been at that party. I would have remembered you.'

'You weren't really noticing much by the time I got there,' he laughs, although he's hurt that he'd made no impression. 'And then there was the Christmas kiss last year in the pub.'

'I do remember that.'

'So why didn't we do something about it then?'

'We inmates are not encouraged to fraternise with the guests.'

'Inmates?' he laughs.

'Those of us trapped here.'

'I adore it here,' sighs Kit. He starts waxing lyrical about the island. He's been visiting since he was a baby, although he hasn't been over very often recently.

Hannah says she used to love it, but she now wants to move on. 'I'm over it. Been there, done it, bought the T-shirt.'

'But it's gorgeous,' he says. 'Where else would you go that's so lovely? I managed to do a little painting up at the Old Blockhouse yesterday but I can't do the views justice.'

'It's great to visit,' she explains. 'But it's not a place to stay too long. Not enough to do. Too many temptations.'

He grins. 'A beautiful temptation.' His breath catches as he traces the line of her breasts.

Hannah continues, 'You stop really *seeing* it after a while, you know. You stop noticing what's right in front of you. It's like you can only truly appreciate it in short bursts, otherwise you become immune to it.'

'I'd like to stay here forever,' he sighs, wistful.

'No, you wouldn't. It's too small. If you stay here too long you get. . .'

'Bored?'

'More . . . *ossified*,' she tries. 'That's okay for some, like Bobby. This place has shaped him, and it's a shape that suits him. But if I stay much longer I'll get crushed.'

He asks, 'What about Miss Elisabeth? She's happy enough and she's been here donkey's years.'

'Old Betty? I think it was different in her day,' says Hannah. 'They were used to accepting their lot. Servitude, you know. They didn't resent it or question it. But I see the cracks in the others – Alison, Thor, Mary-Jane.'

'Mary-Jane from the garden café? She's only been here a few months hasn't she?'

Hannah nods. 'But there's a different time frame for some people. I suppose more sensitive people.'

'You think Alison's sensitive?' he laughs. 'She's terrifying!'

'She'd hate anyone to say that about her. She drinks hard to cover it up. But don't say anything! If she found out I'd told you that, she'd kill me!'

He strokes her hair. 'I could drown in this hair,' he smiles, spreading it over the pillow he's brought over from Falcon. 'What do you want to do if you leave?'

'Hairdressing? Bar work? The only thing I'm sure about is that I want to be my own boss, whatever I do. And I want to travel. I'd love to visit all the big cities. I'd love to work somewhere like New York . . .' She nuzzles into his chest. 'What about you?' she asks.

He admits that he has no clear ambitions. 'I could go into banking, I suppose. Dad has contacts. A couple of pals from uni are starting a whiskey export business for the Japanese market. Or journalism, perhaps . . .'

'Poor little rich boy,' she teases. 'So many opportunities!'

'Yeah, it might look like that but . . .' He props himself up on his elbow so he can see her better. He plays with her hair, winding it around his hand. He finds it so easy to talk to her – totally unlike talking to his parents and their cronies, where there's always the leaden sense that he has to defend himself; that he should have a life plan all worked out by now. 'I don't think I have the drive for journalism, I'm not all that keen on whiskey, and I'd hate that banking tosh. All that selling your soul for business. It's not me.'

'Then don't do it,' she says.

Such a brilliant, freeing idea! It delights him.

'I'll read your tarot for you,' she suggests. 'The cards will help point you in the right direction.'

'I'm afraid I don't believe in anything like that.'

'Doesn't matter,' she replies. 'The cards don't mind.'

He traces the line of her neck and kisses her shoulder. 'Your hair is like a horse's mane,' he smiles.

'Thank you, I think,' she laughs. She knows her hair is coarse. It's not her best feature.

Helping herself to a second ice cream, she says, 'My mum said to do what you love, and you'll never work a day in your life.' There's a pause for effect. 'She did meth.' When she sees the shock on his face she laughs. 'Joking!'

He sips his drink, and sighs. 'My mother is always on at me to push myself, not that she's ever had a proper job.'

'My mother's a teacher,' says Hannah. 'She likes it.'

Kit flings himself down beside her. 'I don't think I'd be any good at teaching.'

Hannah says, 'I'll teach you something,' and she takes another bite of her ice cream before going down on him. He flinches in surprise, then groans.

He is still inside her when his phone buzzes. He ignores it the first time. But it continues, an angry hornet, persistent, again, again, half a dozen times.

'Take it,' she says, the mood ruined.

He sighs and reaches for the phone. 'Yes?' he snaps.

A muted woman's voice.

His body tenses, like someone's punched him. 'I'll be there,' is all he says. He rolls off Hannah.

'What?' she asks.

'My father,' he says. He tries to arrange his face, fails, gulps. 'My dad's *dead*.' His voice cracks.

'Oh God!' says Hannah.

He lies still and she reaches for his hand.

He does not get out of bed and run to console his mother. He cannot make himself move. Instead, he drops the phone and wraps his arms around Hannah, clinging to her, squeezing his eyes shut, appalled with what will be required of him now. And she shushes him and strokes his hair.

She says, 'This is huge. But it will be okay. It will take time, but you will survive it.'

She tells him that when she learned her own father had died – someone she'd never even known – the grief blindsided her.

But she reassures him that he will be able to get through this wave of shock and the difficult, churning emotions which will follow, and as he listens, his shoulders start to relax. She tells him he will not go under. 'We are given nothing we can't survive,' she says. And she rocks him against her and kisses his face, his eyelids, his temple, until parts of him harden once more.

Then he's inside her again, and she's inside his skin, his head and his heart, and he knows there's no going back.

II

The Previous September

15

The Walk

At the time of the exceptional low tides in May and September, there's the unique opportunity to walk between the neighbouring islands of Tresco and Bryher – the Moses Walk, as Old Betty calls it. The tractor can transport the less able, but most people cross the seabed on foot, an eerie experience that some say indeed feels biblical.

Hannah has never done the walk before, but this year, persuaded by Kit, she's planned ahead for a change, arranging time off so she can join him, like she's a tourist.

Kit has been back to the island twice since they got together in June. 'I can't stay away,' he tells her. 'You're irresistible!' Obviously everyone now knows, and everyone has an opinion on their budding relationship.

As the couple make their way down the cool leafiness of Abbey Drive, sunlight filters through the trees, dappling the path. Hannah stops to stroke the velvet muzzles of the horses in the paddock. Above them wood pigeons coo soothingly, thinking themselves a class above the squawking gulls, and a couple of butterflies flutter by, presumably booked by Central Casting.

Hundreds of pink flowers jewel the hedgerows. Kit stoops to pick one and presents it to her with a flourish. '*Amaryllis belladonna*,' he announces in an appalling Italian accent.

'I had that once,' quips Hannah. 'There's a cream for it.'

'There is so much *nature* here. Everywhere!' He spins round, arms wide. 'I don't understand why people want it rounded up in the Abbey Gardens. I like it wild – like you.' He gives her bottom a friendly squeeze.

Hannah breaks off a blade of fat grass, puts it between her thumbs and trumpets a loud hoot which makes a young couple walking ahead of them turn and stare. 'What's the wildest thing you've done?' she asks.

'I once woke up in a skip,' he laughs. 'My chums chucked me in after a rather feral night at the uni bar. You?'

She twirls her flower and considers. 'One night I danced naked up near Cromwell's Castle. Drugs may have been involved.' She laughs. 'I forgot to take out my contact lenses and woke up the next morning and I couldn't open my eyes. My gunky mascara had glued my eyelashes together and I thought I'd gone blind.' She threads her fingers through his.

His smile doesn't waver. He doesn't judge her behaviour. That's one of the reasons she loves him.

The emotion has come as a surprise to her.

They walk on, holding hands, swinging their arms like children, ambling around the island before eventually joining others heading towards Farm Beach in time to make their way across to the sandbar and on to Church Quay on Bryher.

At the crossing point, Old Betty stands proudly directing the walkers in a high-vis tabard several sizes too large, her clip-on sunglasses a little skew-whiff on top of her spectacles. Hannah gives her the flower. Vlad and two other heliport workers who have had basic first-aid training are also in attendance with Ted the boatman.

'What are you lot expecting,' laughs Hannah, 'a shark attack?'

The pace is relaxed. A couple of younger children dawdle behind, poking into pools of seawater, while up ahead, Christie is trying to herd her three boys, the baby strapped to her chest. No sign of Sam.

Emma walks alongside Christie, wearing one of the pink waterproofs Hannah wanted, but by the time she got over to the shop on St Mary's, they'd sold out of her size. She's kicking herself for not being quicker off the mark.

Hannah doesn't notice Christie glaring at her as she and Kit overtake. And she doesn't hear what Emma whispers into Christie's ear.

'Wendy from housekeeping told me,' says Emma. 'She heard Thor telling Big Bob that he saw Hannah at the *clap clinic* over in Penzance.'

Christie pales.

If she stopped to think for a second she might realise this begs the question *What was Thor doing there?* when he's never been seen with either a girlfriend or boyfriend, but never let the facts get in the way of a good story. The rumour is totally made up, but Christie's jealousy makes it sickeningly real.

She tunes out of the walk, worrying at Emma's words like

a dog with a bone. She doesn't notice the sparkling pools of water, the sunshine, the laughter and happy chatter all around her; she doesn't reply when people say hello as they walk past. Instead, her mind niggles away at darker questions: *What if Sam's slept with Hannah again? What if he's not been careful? Will she need to get herself checked out? What if someone sees her at the clinic?*

The barmaid might look all loved up with her latest squeeze right now, but that means nothing. He's not always on the island. Christie will bloody kill Sam if he's been near that little mare again.

It's the perfect day for the walk – a little cloud cover and playful breezes. Kit and Hannah plan to eat at Fraggle Rock, the tiny café on Bryher, before they return by boat. Hannah smiles as Kit, *her boyfriend* as her mates now refer to him, talks about booking himself onto the next island Art Break, a popular painting course, which means he'll be back again soon, which pleases her very much.

Along with the constant flow of compliments, Kit tells her he loves the way she listens to his plans, not judging, not telling him he should be doing something *more productive* with his time, which is his mother's favourite reprise apparently. He says he loves the way she looks at him, as if she really sees him, rather than a version of him – who he might become; someone better. It makes Hannah feel wise.

He tells her that being with her is such a rush. That makes her feel sexy.

They fall in step with two of the lads from housekeeping,

seasonal workers. There's much giggling about Bobby's recent plunge off the wagon.

'He started up the cycling club again last night!' Hannah is informed. The lads stop abruptly, bent double with laughter at the thought.

'The cycling club?' asks Kit.

'The Naked Synchronised Cycling Club,' clarifies Hannah. 'They do it at midnight.'

This was once a popular moonlit pursuit, until Richard Penhaligon came off his bike at Racket Town, doing himself an injury (thus earning himself the nickname Scabby Rick with the Spotted Dick), and news got back to The Family. Obviously the activity has since been banned.

Kit looks surprised. While the island is marketed as sub-tropical, hypothermia is a risk most nights, not to mention how uncomfortable nude cycling would be. 'Who on earth would want to do that?' he asks.

'Old Betty!' quips Hannah. 'She's the founder member.' They stride on, leaving the two housekeepers laughing.

There's a walker ahead wearing the same pink waterproof worn by Emma, bought from the big closing down sale at The Herring on St Mary's – one of several shops that have recently gone out of business, because even the visitors who can afford to come here on holiday are tightening their metaphorical if not literal belts.

No rain is forecast today, but no one's taken in by that predication.

When Hannah and Kit reach the shoreline of the neighbouring island, Kit says, 'We should walk round to Hell Bay for the views. I'd love to do some painting there. And I've heard the hotel is excellent. Perhaps we'll stay at some point?'

'Perhaps.' Hannah likes to pay her own way and her wages wouldn't stretch to that. She's also done enough walking for one day.

'I've heard you can get married there,' he adds.

She doesn't reply, but as she looks back at Tresco displaying itself in all its golden glory, when he kisses the top of her head and whispers that he loves her, she hugs the words close.

Piper's Hole

May, After the Storm

Vlad was up early to catch the tide. He's taken his dinghy and made it round the northeast tip of the island, up to Piper's Hole. There are plenty of legends about this hidden sea cave, most involving ghostly tin miners and smugglers. Vlad's favourite is the one suggesting any dog which ventures inside will emerge minus its fur.

But he is not here leading an excursion of tourists – he's here to search. She has been missing forty-eight hours now.

At high tide the waters smash against the jagged granite rocks and he wouldn't be able to get anywhere close. Now, with the tide out, he manages to clamber over the slippery boulders at the mouth of the cave to make his way inside.

No sun penetrates here and he has to rely on his head torch. Even though he's told the search team where he'll be, he is suddenly gripped by the primitive dreads: fear of the dark; fear of being trapped; fear of the unknown. There's an oppressive stench of brine and decay, like he's within the guts of the earth, the belly of a whale.

Last night in the pub, Ted the boatman told him that if the maid went into the sea this side, she'd be long gone – swept out with the currents over to the nearby island of Samson to rot alongside the ancient burial grounds there.

But Vlad feels the need to check, just in case.

Towards the back of the cave there's a small freshwater pool and a tiny gravel beach. The rocks above glow silver, not from precious metals as he'd first thought, but from microbes. The thought makes him shiver.

And in the corner—

His heart lurches. He tastes acid.

The light from his torch wobbles as he forces himself forwards.

The body lies twisted on its side, the hair tangled and spread out like a mermaid's. There is no face.

His legs rebel but he takes one more step towards it. The shape is all wrong.

He slips, rights himself, creeps nearer and crouches. He makes himself reach out to the deathly chill of the thing before him, perhaps one of the bravest things he has ever done, touches horror, then slowly rolls the slimy torso towards him . . . and he sees it is not human after all.

A bin bag full of plastic bottles has entangled in a fishing net. Pollution, even here. The hair is seaweed.

There was a sighting from a couple sailing around the Eastern Isles yesterday. That body turned out to be a bloody seal! Vlad thought, how stupid would you have to be . . . so he doesn't tell anyone about his own discovery – not until much later that night, after he's had a fair few pints, after he's stopped trembling.

16

John

The bloom before him is *Fascicularia bicolor*, crimson and blue. The specimen boasts a giant eyeball, comprised of other tinier alien eyeballs, all seemingly observing him, although the plant is from the pineapple family rather than outer space.

It irritates John to think that the cult of unbelievers would rather hold a narrative that advanced extra-terrestrials visited to seed Planet Earth rather than accept the Divine Creator. He wants to shout, no, to roar, 'Then who created the aliens?' Idiots!

Not that he believes in aliens, of course.

The tiny eyes of the flower are mesmerising. They seem to bore into him. It disturbs him. They seem to see right into his soul—

His train of thought is interrupted when just then a party of visitors arrive, led through the gardens by one of the horticultural students, and they stand to gawp at the South African

Proteas. Common now. They sell smaller versions in M&S, that most British of stores. John listens as the usual factoids are dispensed chronicling the garden's history – nineteenth century, subtropical, Augustus Smith, blah blah. These are day-trippers, so the basics will do for them. There are more exclusive tours led by Alistair Darley, the garden curator, for the more discerning guests willing to pay for it.

This group will *ooh* and *aah* at the specimens, the views and the seashell art, before treating themselves to cream teas and coffees in the garden café, where his beloved Mary-Jane will serve them, then they will go on to *ooh* some more at the figureheads displayed in the island's tiny museum. There have been many shipwrecks around these parts. Rumours that the islanders used to lure merchant vessels onto the rocks with misleading lights during storms could never be proved as all the witnesses drowned.

John stands smiling, making himself available in case of questions. He and Mary-Jane are both working today so will not be able to join the others on the walk from Tresco to Bryher. Perhaps next year. He is allowing himself to daydream about meeting Mary-Jane for a late lunch, thinking ahead to her birthday next week (she'll be The Big Three-O), when, from within the group, he hears the gut-churning twang of an American voice; worse, a southern accent. A woman in an orange and black checked pantsuit asks if there are 'any plants from the US in the gardens' – and there is a moment of absolute horror, a moment when he loses sight of what is before him, and only manages not to cry out, not to flee, by taking a long slow breath and offering a desperate, silent prayer.

The odds are impossible. This woman could not be from

Georgia, let alone the small city of Madison from which he and Mary-Jane hail. But southern folk are chatty, inquisitive, *gossipy*, and he cannot risk it. He might give himself away.

The smile wavers on his lips. He turns, and forces himself to walk at a steady pace, dreading a call, an accusing finger, and only when he is finally hidden by foliage does he hurry away, his heart battering.

17

The Art House

The Art House gallery is flooded with early evening sunlight. The extraordinary blues of the paintings stand out against a white so bright it hurts your eyes. Prices are similarly eyewatering.

It feels wrong to have a jolly arty party with current world affairs being so unmitigatedly shite – wars and famine and natural disasters – but the gallery drinks and mingle is a regular event, where timeshare owners are plied with half-decent wines as Bobby and gallery manager Fiona introduce them to the work of new artists in the ever-changing exhibition. Tonight there's a chap who specialises in rather brutal landscapes from the smaller off-islands like St Martin's (anger issues, suspects Fiona), and a female poet-painter whose pastels are more soothing to the eye.

Bobby and Fiona have put on this evening to take advantage of the extra visitors who have come over to do the walk across from Tresco to Bryher.

It is rare to make a sale to a day-tripper, unless it is a smaller item such as an artisan flower vase, or a limited edition signed print. Timeshare owners are the guests usually invited, as they're far more likely to invest in an original piece of art to remind them of their holidays. How visitors pine for the place when they're not here. How those shackled to this rock pine for the respite of mainland life.

Local artists Maggie O'Brien, who runs some of the painting breaks, and Richard Pearce from Bryher, chat to the guests, answering questions, agreeing that, yes indeed, there is much inspiration here, a mercurial light, a true artist's idyll, while Angry Man and the Poetess stand like sentries alongside their own work.

Fiona is dressed exquisitely, as usual, a floaty pale pink asymmetric dress which signals her expertise in the art world yet does not compete with the items on the wall. A classy act, Fiona.

Hannah, on the other hand, is no such thing. She has flung the kitchen sink at her own outfit. Bobby's eyes widen as she turns up hanging onto the arm of her latest beau, young Kit from Falcon. She is wearing a jaunty fisherman's cap to which she's attached a huge fake sunflower. That wouldn't be so bad, but there's a patch on the back pocket of her tiny denim hotpants proclaiming *Eat The Rich*.

They make an odd couple, the timeshare son and the barmaid. He's so tall and lean – a swimmer's physique, athletic, well-defined pecs, quads and glutes as far as Bobby can make out, although he isn't staring. Kit is a strawberry-blond god, while Hannah is short, dark, voluptuous; wicked, feline eyes. Some would say attractive, but even if Bobby were that way inclined, Hannah would not be his type.

She is laughing loudly at something Kit has said to her. She does not put her hand in front of her mouth.

The exuberance of this display grates against the more refined wine-sipping atmosphere of the soirée. It is almost as bad as if Bill and Phyllis Thatcher had invaded the exhibition, dragging it down to their level of pints of ale and a knees-up.

Hannah waves and heads Bobby's way. 'We're just back from Bryher,' she enthuses. 'We did the Moses walk, didn't we, Kit. It was brilliant!'

'Glad you enjoyed it,' says Bobby. 'But this get-up? It's hardly . . . appropriate.'

'It's my night off!' she protests.

Fiona comes over to greet Kit and asks, 'How is your mother getting along? I've invited her tonight. I hope it's not too soon . . . after your father?'

'She'll be okay,' says Kit.

Fiona notes that he hasn't said Beatrice *is* okay.

'And you? How are you doing, Kit?'

'Thanks to this one,' he hugs Hannah to his side, 'I'm doing very, very well, thank you.'

'Are you on your way to the pub?' asks Bobby. It is more a suggestion than an enquiry.

Hannah bats her eyelashes at him and smiles. 'Keen to be rid of us?'

Kit smooths over the needling, saying, 'Yes. A proper drink! I'm keen to try the new ale – what is it, Water-Ma-Trout?'

'Lord of the Ringz,' sighs Bobby, who is exhausted trying to keep up with the proliferation of local microbreweries and their ridiculous monikers. He is not a real-ale man.

Kit sees his mother looming at the gallery door. She spots

him, waves, and homes in like a heat-seeking missile.

'Darling!' trills Beatrice, kissing his cheeks.

'Mother.'

'Bobby!'

'It is so lovely to see you here again,' says Bobby, swooped up into an embrace.

'So lovely to be back!' beams Beatrice.

'Hello, Beatrice,' chirps Hannah.

The tone could be construed as cheeky. Workers like Hannah would usually address guests like Beatrice as Mrs Wallace. Kit notes his mother bristle a little, but she offers, 'Hello, darling!' and Hannah is gifted a small smile.

'What a fabulous new hairstyle,' enthuses Bobby. Beneath a wide black velvet hairband, Beatrice has gone a shade lighter and is wearing her freshly-blonded hair blow dried and bouffed. 'Very Catherine Deneuve!'

Beatrice almost shimmies with joy. 'Oh, stop it!' she giggles.

'She was my first female crush,' he confides.

'*Before* she chunked up, I assume!' hoots Beatrice. 'That's probably what turned you!'

Kit winces. His mother speaks almost entirely in exclamations, no matter how non-PC her comments might be.

Beatrice addresses her son. 'How are you, darling? Enjoying your break?'

'Yes, we are,' he replies.

His mother disregards the 'we', although Kit has told her that he and Hannah are dating. She sees it as a fling, not *dating* as such. And a dalliance is exactly what he needs right now. It will be a distraction from losing his father.

'Beatrice!' says Fiona, who, as a manager, is on first-name

basis with the guests. 'So lovely to see you. We've missed you.' Good at reading the room, Fiona proffers a glass of wine. 'How are you?' she asks.

Beatrice replies, 'Fine. Absolutely fine!' If she says it with enough gusto, she may start to believe it. Naturally she is struggling after the death of her husband given the *rather difficult circumstances*.

'We're off to the pub. Want to join us later?' Hannah asks Beatrice.

Kit pinches Hannah hard on the bum. He does not want to spend the night with his mother, thank you. He knows he should – ever since his father's funeral, she's accused him of abandoning her – but he finds he can't cope with her grief as well as his own.

'No, thank you. I think I'll stay here,' says Beatrice. 'Go! Enjoy yourselves!'

Bobby, sensing Beatrice is working hard to put on a brave face, takes her arm and leads her away, saying, 'Come and see the new work. I'll introduce you to the artists.'

Kit grabs Hannah's hand, herding her to the door, and they leave Bobby to his work.

There is an hour or more of chit-chat, but apart from half a dozen postcards, there is no sale.

18

Alison

It's not late, but Ted the boatman is already singing melancholy sea shanties. Alison smiles indulgently. Tourists lap up this kind of thing. They watch the sunset glow golden over the sea, congratulate themselves on their good fortune, treat themselves to another double, then retire to their lovely holiday homes well lubricated and moist-eyed.

Alison sends over a free pint and blows Ted a kiss. He is one of her best customers. Everyone knows Ted, one of several boatmen who spend their days tootling between Tresco, Bryher and St Mary's. He's pretty much a fixture in the pub. He does a little crab fishing on the side and the occasional private-hire puffin spotting, not that many get to see the little sods because they're barely bigger than the Scilly bees.

He looks the part of the salty sailor does Ted – nut-brown weather-beaten face, bushy beard flecked with silver, a classic fisherman's cap which now sits on the table in front of him, and a big navy jumper which has seen better days. As soon as he arrives he hangs his battered waterproof on the peg near the door, considerate of the Old Ship's floor. He might be the Ancient Mariner, although visitors are often surprised to learn he's barely fifty. His son, Teddy, shares his father's name, a practice still common in these parts. The lad was born on St Mary's and Ted had hoped he'd follow him onto the boats, as he'd followed his own father into the profession, but that was not to be. It was a huge disappointment.

Alison employs a brand of professional flirting with Ted, the same as she does with most of her regulars and pretty much all the visitors. The boatman's wife is rarely seen – a sour-faced wisp of a woman who moans about the weather and the cost of living. When she does grace the pub with a rare visit, she bleats about how much she misses her son, who left the island as soon as he could, the same as most of the other young people. She's a total wet weekend. No wonder her bloke spends most evenings over here.

Kit and Hannah arrive looking sun-kissed and happy and Alison wonders what he does for a living that allows him the freedom to come over every few weeks. How the other half live.

Leaving the assistant barman serving, Alison starts collecting glasses. She likes to keep an eye on things, checking visitors and workers alike for any signs of potential trouble. Tonight, all seems calm.

Nestled into a corner, John and Mary-Jane look totally loved up as usual. They always seem besotted with each other, yet they've been together since their teens apparently. Alison can't understand why they're not bored as all buggery by now. Her two marriages floundered around the three-year itch.

On her way back to the bar, Alison stops at Table 3 to chat to Hannah and Kit. They discuss the gallery party and who might be in the pub later, then Kit looks at his phone. He shows them the picture Beatrice Wallace's goddaughter, Charlotte, has just sent him – her posing in a tiny bikini on a beach the other side of the world. You do not need to be a psychologist to identify the look of jealousy that crosses the barmaid's face. *Trouble in paradise*, thinks Alison.

She's glad she doesn't have to deal with all that relationship nonsense any longer. But she wonders what it might be like to have someone close, someone to confide in; someone to warm your feet on through the cold nights. It's not that Alison is lonely – not at all, she's always surrounded by customers – but no one else is responsible for running the place and sometimes that weighs upon her. The only people she can talk to as equals are the other managers: Bobby, Angie from the shop, Fiona from the gallery. The Family are a different kettle of fish. Everyone's a little on edge when they pop down to the pub to do a walkabout with the serfs. Alison could never admit her worries to them – it's a cheery smile and the forced-jolly reply of 'smashing' if they ever ask her (or anyone else) how things are going. The Family aren't really asking about the financial state of affairs anyway; they have accountants to keep tabs on that.

By the time she swings back to the bar, Kit has his hand on Sam's arm, saying, 'Cool it, mate. It's fine. He didn't mean anything by it,' and Sam is glaring at Vlad, who's backing away with both hands up, like he's surrendering.

Sam is already well on the way to belligerent. Alison recently had to bar him for a week after he started a pushing-and-shoving row with one of the builders sorting out the roof on the community centre, and the way he's been at the ale for the last few days, she guesses she'll have to do it again soon enough. He's obviously been fighting again – there's a gash on his cheekbone and bruises on his hands. Thankfully Kit manages to sit him down, and the altercation fizzles out. Hannah has enough sense to keep well out of it.

Alison serves Kit, wondering if *Dame* Beatrice Wallace, as she thinks of her, will grace them with her presence this evening. While Kit is now a regular, the mother didn't return for her usual August break. Alison assumes her absence was due to the husband dropping dead back in June – Henry Wallace, good tipper – thankfully not while he was on the island. Always a logistical pain, that.

Mother and son are not staying together this time. Beatrice is currently rattling round Falcon alone by all accounts, while Kit is renting one of the smaller cottages, Guillemot, and after she finishes her shifts, Hannah spends her nights over there with him.

The good news is that Beatrice is keeping the timeshare weeks on Falcon, much to Bobby's relief – hard to let something that size on a regular basis.

Alison has never seen Bobby so anxious as he's been over the last couple of months. He got legless last week and confessed as much. But that's what a few months on the wagon can do for you – it's bloody dangerous when you start up again, and yes, Alison does have experience of that. Best to keep drinking, as far as she's concerned.

As Alison is unloading the glasswasher, Thor from the shop pops in asking for Hannah. Stupid bloody name. Why he wants to be called that rather than his given name of Alec, she's no idea.

Alison looks round to check, but Hannah must be in the loo or outside having a cigarette. 'It's her night off,' she says. That's the truth in fact, if not in spirit. But Thor is a pest. Sometimes he'll spend an entire lunchtime sitting watching Hannah like a hawk, drinking a single beer and picking at a bowl of chips. He's a total buzzkill. She wonders if the lad ever gets outside in daylight hours, he's so pale. Hannah is also coming to the end of her tether with Thor's moping, which has intensified since Kit appeared on the scene. The lad never seems to sit with anybody, just broods by himself, sending puppy-dog glances towards the bar. Alison feels sorry for him.

'I'll tell her you were asking after her,' she smiles. 'And take my advice, yeah? Forget Hannah. You get yourself a nice girlfriend.'

She gets on with serving a group of timeshare guests who arrive from the pavilion end – the clever ones who come after the school holidays when the beaches are less *screechy* and the prices marginally less shocking – and Thor traipses out with the weight of the world on his shoulders.

'Alison! Alison, my good woman!' Colonel Blimp from Gannet comes up from Table 5 and orders a round of drinks for his chums and a mineral water for himself. Sobriety is one of the Colonel's several affectations which some mistake for a personality. His real name, obviously, isn't Blimp.

The Colonel leans against the bar, eyeing Hannah who's just come in from having a cigarette in the garden. 'Who wears short shorts!' he laughs. 'The full gravy, that girl!' He winks. 'The full gravy!'

Talking like he's living in the twenties is another of his foibles.

So polite, so privileged, so handsy with Hannah and the other barmaids who have to wiggle out of his grasp after last orders. Wisely he never tries it on with Alison.

'The quiz on tomorrow?' he enquires.

'Yes,' says Alison. You entering?'

'Of course!' he booms. 'In with a good chance, I reckon.'

Alison smiles. His team won't win. The kitchen workers in Quiz Team Aguilera always take it.

As she serves the drinks, she notices that the housekeeping harpies are whispering together on Table 2 – the two newish lads and their supervisor, Molly, who is old enough to know better. They seem to be pulling Thor apart, and while the lad almost asks for it, Alison intervenes.

'Hubble bubble, ladies and gentlemen,' she calls over to them. 'What will it be – eye of newt?'

All three scowl at her. Let them. This is her establishment, and she can say what she likes – well, to the workers, if not the guests.

An hour or so later and Alison is knackered; she's tempted when Hannah comes up to order another round and says, 'If you want to knock off early I can give you a hand.' It's a kind offer.

'No, you're fine,' replies Alison. 'You have your young man here. Enjoy him!'

What would she do with a night off anyway? You have to occupy yourself on the islands, which takes a degree of energy, and Alison is depleted on that front. Late nights and too many doubles. She hasn't even got a good book to look forward to.

She promises herself she'll go for a walk tomorrow, get back on the fitness kick, but she's also self-aware enough to guess that might not happen. Plus, tomorrow night is her actual night off and her friend Kelly is busy, so, for want of something better to do, no doubt Alison will end up back here, sitting where Sam sits now – a busman's holiday. It's either that or Cinema Night at the community centre, another Tom Cruise *Mission: Impossible* if she recalls correctly, and she isn't a fan of anyone who smiles that much.

Alison reaches for another vodka on the rocks, adding a slice of lemon for the vitamin C.

There seems to be a slump when Ted stops singing. People's thoughts turn inwards.

After Alison has rung the bell for last orders, the boatman will return to Bryher, but he will not go straight to bed. He cannot stand the miasma of disappointment radiating from the back of his wife's brushed cotton nightdress. Instead, he will pour himself a large whiskey and turn on his computer in the back room. Even though he will be up again at dawn to check the weather reports, he will spend an hour or more staring at the screen, hungry to find some solace within the dark recesses of the internet, or watch one of the old films with his favourite actor, Jean-Claude Van Damme.

You have to make your own entertainment here.

19

Hannah

It's a treat to take a slow amble back to Guillemot with Kit, especially after a night in the pub when she's not had to work. They hold hands and dawdle, looking up at the clouds scudding across the moon. He serenades her, singing snatches of pop songs, then brings his arms around her waist to spin her round and kiss her, his lips soft as a dream. Almost four months together and Hannah is still being wooed. And she loves it.

They walk down to the water's edge, where the sea glows unearthly with phosphorescence. They lie back on the sand together and watch a satellite, a shooting star. She feels herself falling away into space, but before she loses herself completely, Kit says, 'Come on, I'm getting cold,' and helps her to her feet. 'Fancy a hot chocolate?' he adds.

'Of course I do. But no whipped cream for me.'

'But you love whipped cream.'

'Need to watch this,' she laughs, patting the roundness of her belly beneath her denim jacket.

'No, no, no!' he protests. 'You're my pocket Venus!'

'What?'

'Small, but . . .' He makes the in-out shape of her figure with his hands and pulls a kissy face. 'My Marilyn—'

'She's dead,' protests Hannah.

He slings an arm around her shoulders and she hugs him round his waist as they hurry back to the cottage to warm up.

Across the sea, the moon makes sequins of the water.

It is a new experience for Hannah, this romance. She hasn't had many long-term relationships, and this has evolved into much more than a holiday thing. Kit is adorable. They laugh, they play. She tries not to think about what might happen next.

But he's different. He suggests they might have a future together and he truly seems to believe that's possible. He offers up vague idyllic plans and looks to her for affirmation. She hasn't the heart to dissuade him from these rather lovely fantasies.

Right now Hannah is perhaps the happiest she has ever been. She's always pleased to see Kit when he arrives, keen to meet him off the helicopter whenever her work allows. Her body delights in his. She doesn't feel stifled by him either. He isn't possessive. He smiles when she flirts with other customers. He allows her to be herself, claims he loves her dancing and her unique sense of style, both deemed 'outrageous' by Bobby; by most people, probably.

Tonight, Alison had said, 'Er, how short are those shorts?

You'll feel a chill wind around the Trossachs in them!' Not that it's any of her business what Hannah wears when she's off duty.

Before she snapped back at Alison, Kit retorted, 'If you've got it, flaunt it,' and he bowed to her, like she was a queen, like he was proud of her, and the barb was deflected.

He is a sweet boy. He even dances with her, and she loves that. How many straight boys has she known who like to dance?

And in some ways he's more adventurous than she is. He persuaded her to swim with him in the sea – as shockingly cold as she predicted. She never understood the wild swimmers here: hardy types who fling themselves into the unforgiving Atlantic water all year round; the women known as the Blue Tits. Even with a wetsuit, it didn't appeal to Hannah, but she did it, for him. The noise she made on entry sent the seabirds flapping away in terror.

She nearly drowned.

She threw herself in and flailed and inhaled water and her head went under, and he had to drag her out. 'Why the bloody hell didn't you tell me you couldn't swim?' he asked, and she said, 'I can. Well, I did it at school. I just haven't done it since.'

Regular swimmers swear by both the health benefits and the exhilaration promoted by their immersion in sea water, but the only joy Hannah experienced was the bacon butties and Irish coffee Kit provided afterwards.

As she dried herself on one of the big towels he'd brought down to the beach from the timeshare, still coughing, still gasping for breath, she watched him frolic in the waves like a giant Labrador. He bounded up to her when he'd finished, and her lips tingled with his icy kisses. The taste of salt on her lips, the salt in her hair making it rougher still.

The afternoon after the swim they walked and found a quiet spot near the bird hide by the lake. He lay down his waterproof across the gorse.

Then he lay her down beneath him.

That night he cooked her cod with samphire, and they spent their time drinking good white wine and laughing at nothing. It was, as Saint John from the gardens might say, a *bless-ed day*.

But there have also been nights when Kit has sobbed in her arms, crying for his father, emotionally unmoored. Hannah wasn't sure what she felt about this tsunami of emotion at first, but she found herself responding with kindness. She'd not thought of herself as a patient person before, but something about Kit makes it easy.

Another surprise is that she finds it easy to talk to him about her own father – the big absence in her life. She'd always resented him on her mother's behalf, but when he died, her mother cried, and Hannah felt the pain stab deep into her own chest.

Back at Guillemot, Kit sets about making the hot chocolate. He adds cream on the top of both mugs and Hannah doesn't complain.

She sips the drink, tucks her feet underneath her on the sofa, and says, 'Your mother looked well tonight. She put on a good show at the art gallery. How's she really doing?'

He wrinkles his nose, shakes his head.

'Shouldn't you go over there to check?'

'You want me there, rather than here with you?'

'No, not now, of course not, but . . . I feel bad for her being

109

on her own. She'd probably like a bit of support from you.'
Hannah's mother had been quite clingy after her father died.

'I can't bear to be around her,' he confesses. 'She's pushed
the self-destruct button.'

'How?'

'She and my father always liked a drink. But now . . .' He sighs.
'She's drowning in it. I feel like, if I'm around her, she'll drag me
under.'

'When my father died, my mum threw herself into work. But
he'd never been around, so I guess it wasn't the same.'

They finish their drinks and go to bed. And long after they've
worn themselves out with sex, their bodies curve around each
other as they try and untangle the messy nets of emotion surrounding dead parents.

He tells her how he found it easier to love his dad than his
mother, even though he felt his father was disappointed in him
for not having a clear career path. He talks for almost half an
hour and then asks, 'What about you?'

Hannah has never talked about her feelings like this before
– not with another lover, nor her friends, not even with her
mother.

'I hated my dad,' she confesses. 'Is that terrible?'

'I hate my bloody mother right now,' he replies.

'I thought his cancer was karmic, you know. It started in his
eye – his *roving eye*, as my mother called it. The grass was always
greener for Szymon. I thought it served him right.' She buries
her head under his arm. 'God, I'm sorry. I don't know why I'm
telling you this. I'm a terrible person.'

'Of course you're not.' Kit kisses her forehead.

'If you'd asked me the day before he died, I'd have said I

wouldn't care a toss. But when my mother called with the news
... I was physically sick. I couldn't function properly for weeks.'

It's been, what ... three-and-a-bit years now, and she might
forget for months on end, but then, around mid-October she
will find herself feeling exhausted, as if she's coming down with
a bug, her limbs leaden, and she realises the anniversary of his
death is approaching. On the twenty-seventh of that month,
she aims to take the day off, not to remember, but to lie very
still until the wave of anger, sadness and regret passes once
more, grieving both for the father she never knew, and the perfect imaginary figure of a dad she'd constructed in his place.

She tries to explain this to Kit. He listens without inter-
rupting, smoothing her hair across the pillow. The unburdening makes her feel lighter. They snuggle closer, arms and legs
entwined, and both sleep well.

20

Beatrice

She wakes sweating, disgusted with her own body. For a second she doesn't know where she is. She reaches out, but the bed is empty. Her husband isn't . . .

Her husband—

She flings off the damp duvet and gets up, stumbling as she hurries to the window. It is still pitch-black outside – a terrible void.

Her stomach lurches at the absence.

Yet she cannot understand why it disturbs her so much to wake to an empty bed. Henry often *worked away*, but then, no matter where he was, no matter whose bed he might be in, there was always the possibility of his return.

Not now. Never again . . .

She is parched.

There is no sound from Kit's room as she creeps downstairs. Her darling boy— then she remembers, he isn't here either. He is off with the barmaid.

She is totally alone.

Beatrice's hands are uncertain as she pours herself a brandy to settle her nerves. She drinks it too quickly, then pours herself another to stop the feeling of something clawing deep inside. She doesn't even like brandy that much.

She thinks she should have begged to bring Primrose. Even though guests aren't allowed to bring dogs to stay in the peak season, surely one as well-behaved as Primmy wouldn't threaten the island's accommodation, flora or fauna. She decides to call the dog minder later and FaceTime her baby girl.

She slips on her coat and shoes and walks to the bottom of the garden. The clouds have shifted, and the sea is now sliced by shafts of moonlight. It is a mild night. The quiet beauty does nothing to calm her. She still has an overwhelming urge to lash out at something.

The thing is . . .

She takes a deep breath. The thing is, Beatrice's darling husband Henry wasn't just *with* someone when he dropped dead of a heart attack, rather, he was *in* them. Some awful secretary-assistant, half his age, naturally, which showed such a bloody lack of imagination! She was from Billericay for God's sake.

Beatrice noticed the way people looked at her during the funeral. Her husband had turned her into the butt of a joke.

'You bastard!' she shouts into the night, hurling her glass at the rocks below. Fuck the wildlife!

That was a terrible night, after the funeral. After the guests had left Kit went out, because he couldn't bear to be in the same house as his own grieving mother, and Beatrice was left utterly alone. She sat in the kitchen feeling sorry for herself.

She can't remember exactly what Kit said when he came home the next morning, but there was something about the way he looked at her. Just like his father. Judging her.

She can admit now that she probably lost control, although she only has the vaguest memory of it.

But she does recall Kit snarling at her, literally baring his teeth, as he said, very quietly, 'If you ever do that again, I will hit you back.' She had no reason to doubt him. She'd never seen that side of her boy before. He got that hidden fury from his father.

She supposes she drove him to it. His eye was a little bruised.

Beatrice marches back indoors, deciding to make herself an Irish Coffee Royale with the brandy – a small treat.

In a few months it will be Christmas. Despite all the rest, her husband had always managed to be with her on the island then. She wonders if she should invite a few chums over to make the best of it this year. Celebrate . . . surviving. Perhaps invite Charlotte again.

The kitchen feels empty without Primrose. She misses the dog so much. Always wanted a daughter.

She puts on the radio and sets about assembling her drink.

By the time the sun has made a heroic effort to drag itself up from the dark sea, Beatrice is, once again, a merry widow.

21

Christie

She only popped to the shop for milk. Sam had used most of it making himself a bowl of cornflakes when he got back last night, whatever time that was, the selfish git. No thought of what they'd need in the morning.

When Christie gets home, she sees Sam at the bottom of the back garden having his first roll-up of the day. She doesn't greet him but goes straight into the kitchen to start breakfast. She's hoping baby Finn is still asleep in his crib upstairs. He should be – the little sod kept her awake most of the night. Another cold. The kid can be a delight, almost angelic, but also a total snotty nightmare.

She's only just put the kettle on when she feels the draft around her ankles. She sticks her head into the hall to find the front door wide open. They rarely use the front door.

She legs it up the stairs two at a time. Tommy's in the bathroom, but while Dan is messing about on his bed next door, the other bed is empty.

'Where's your brother? Dan. DAN!'

No reply.

'Ben. Ben!' she shouts.

No answer.

'Tommy,' she bangs on the bathroom door.

'What? I'm not late,' he protests, emerging pink from the shower, his tufty hair all over the place.

'Have you seen Ben?'

'Which one's that?' This is Tommy's usual joke, pretending he can't tell the twins apart.

'Keep an eye on your brothers, yeah. I think Ben's gone walk-about. I'm off out to look for him.' She tries to keep her voice light, but inside she feels sick to her stomach.

She runs down the stairs, shouting for Sam.

'Sam! Sam, where's Ben? Have you seen him?'

Sam looks bleary-eyed and stupid as he comes in from the garden. There's a bruise and a lump on his forehead.

'Search the house. Ben's missing. The door was open. I'll look out front.'

'What—?'

She shouts in his face, 'Look for your bloody son! You were supposed to be watching them! For fuck's sake!'

She rushes outside. No sign of the lad in the tiny front garden or on the path immediately ahead. She jogs towards the quay. Ben is obsessed with tractors and boats and the ferry is his favourite thing ever.

A group of visitors are walking up to the pub from that direction. In between breaths she asks, 'Have you seen a little boy in his pyjamas? Dark hair? He's only just four!'

They haven't. They volunteer to help look and she sends them back the way they've come as she runs over to Emma's and bangs on the door.

As soon as her friend opens up, she asks, 'Is Ben here? He's gone missing.' Her voice catches.

'No, I've not seen him. I'll call Bobby and he'll put the word out,' says Emma.

'Thanks.' Christie suddenly thinks she should head back and grab her phone.

'Wait,' calls Emma as Christie's already at the gate, 'Try by the *Scilly Maid*. He was playing with Tommy, Dan and my lot down there yesterday.'

Christie takes off.

All her boys have had swimming lessons. The twins are taught in the spa pool with the preschool group. She and Sam have taken them out paddling in the sea on warm, calm days often enough. The baby will start Aqua Tots in a few months. But that means nothing. You can't be too careful. There are thousands of ways the sea can lure a child into jolly wavelets, then turn ugly and evil and sweep them away.

She's read the kids the old book her mother gave her, ever since they were small: *The Book of Sea Stories and Songs* – full of warnings. The verse to keep them away from the blowhole up the North End:

> *We sea dragons gush and roar*
> *Then sweep you through our deathly door*
> *To silt your lungs with brine-slimed fears*
> *While mothers keen their salty tears*

She read them the verse to keep them away from the slippery rocks, even though she worried it wasn't appropriate, with the drawings of the witches too sexy and scary:

> *We sea witches will entice*
> *With gash-red smiles and hearts of ice*
> *To grasp and jag with wiry weed*
> *And split the heads that have no heed*

But warnings to stay away from the sea can never be scary enough.

Christie's gasping now, as much from fear as the run.

The *Scilly Maid* has been pulled up onto the shingle for repairs in the little hidden bay just along from the Flying Boat Club. As Christie sprints down the sand, she sees her son is out beyond the boat poking at a clump of seaweed at the water's edge. How the hell did he get this far? Anyone who saw a child this age out on his own would have stopped him. Perhaps he hid. The twins can be cunning.

'Ben!' she screams. His *Transformers* pyjama bottoms are soaked.

He startles and freezes. By the time she's reached him and snatches his hand, he's in tears. As she hauls him back to the cottage, they're both crying.

'Never, NEVER go near the water when a grown up isn't with you! DO YOU HEAR ME! You must NEVER leave the house without me or your dad! I swear I'll bloody kill you if you run off again!'

Her son sobs.

Christie sobs too, not just from relief – hers are raw, angry tears. When they get back home she swears she'll bloody kill her husband.

22

Kit

The morning after the Moses Walk she takes him up to the high cliffs at the North End, carefully clambering over the rocks at the side, across the steep narrow ledge and down the slope to show him the blowhole. It is nothing but a wide crevice, but at regular intervals it breathes sprays of seawater high into the air.

'Wow! I can't believe I've never seen this before. It's like one of those geysers in Iceland,' says Kit.

'You should see it when the tide's up,' says Hannah.

'This is why I love this place,' he says, hugging her to him as they brace their backs against the granite cliff face, which isn't exactly comfortable, but the wet rocks around the blowhole are lethal. 'This view is . . . everything. I need to grab Richard Pearce for some tips on brush technique. My paintings don't do any of this justice.'

She replies, 'I see why people love it.'

'It's beautiful. How can you not fall in love with it?'

'It makes me angry.'

'Angry?' He's surprised.

'How many people can afford to see this? My mum has only been over once. She said she could have a whole summer back in Poland for what it cost her for two weeks here.'

'But if too many people came it might spoil it,' he reasons.

'And when I look at this, I hate us as a species, pumping our shit and chemicals and rubbish into the sea. We should be taking care of it.' She scrapes her hair out of her eyes. 'Ignore me. I don't want to ruin the day.' She smiles up at him and kisses him. 'Sometimes I don't know what I think until I open my mouth.' She laughs at herself. 'Sometimes it surprises me, what I think, what I say.'

They hold hands as they start to walk back down. Bees and flowers and a gentle breeze. Bliss.

He pauses on the way back to look out at the waves flinging themselves against the land. The day is mild, but the water is not.

'*Thanatos*,' he pronounces.

'Who?'

'That desire to throw yourself over – to take that step into oblivion. The death wish, you know?'

'No, I don't know,' she laughs.

'You've never felt that?'

'Never! No! You want your head looking at!'

More quietly he says, 'I think about it sometimes.'

'Don't,' she snaps. 'It's a waste of energy. If it came to it, you'd fight.'

'I might not.'

'You would. I once found an injured gull down by Ruin Beach.

One wing completely smashed up. It would probably have been kinder to finish it off, but I couldn't do it. The look in its eyes – it demanded to live. I brought it back to the house and we kept it in the yard and fed it. I felt sorry for it watching the others fly, but it was life of a kind. It died in its own time.' She turns away quickly, as if she's revealed too much.

They make their way down to the Old Ship for a drink.

'Do you know who's over on St Mary's?' she asks. 'The actress from that TV show about chess that you liked.'

'Anya Taylor-Joy? Is she? Wow!'

'You should get over there and have a go.'

'Don't be silly.' He assumes she's joking.

'I would. It's a once-in-a-lifetime opportunity. I'd go for it.'

'You wouldn't—'

'Of course I would! Channing Tatum! If he was over there I'd be on the next boat across. I'd have a bash at all the Hemsworths! At the same time!' She laughs that filthy laugh and Kit feels a chill, as if a cloud has covered the sun, but when he looks round, it's still there, all smiley-faced and bright.

23

Maisie

She managed a swim today! Finally. The last three mornings Maisie put on her swimming costume but then her mother needed something or other and before she knew it, it was time for lunch, and Maisie's mum always prefers to go down to the Old Ship, even though Maisie offers to make her something at the cottage.

'Your chips aren't a patch on theirs,' she says. She knows she's not supposed to have chips, but what can Maisie say – they're on holiday.

Mother and daughter had a week on Tresco back in June, so Maisie feels lucky that they've had the opportunity to come for another break now, although her mum never lets her forget that she's the one paying.

The shower pressure is never up to much in the cottage, but Maisie still prefers it to a bath. She angles the shower head, so the warm water massages the tightness in her lower back. Lovely! Lavender-scented handmade soap from the local farm too. She runs the shower tepid and slowly increase the temperature, little by little, until it's so hot it's borderline stinging. She loves it.

She decides to leave her mum another half hour. She's amazed she's not already awake. Edith Willis rarely sleeps in, but then she did get through the best part of a bottle of wine last night. Maisie tried to get her to slow down but it's never easy to persuade Edith because, you've guessed it, *she's on holiday*. Well, her mother is. Maisie limited herself to one small glass of white wine spritzer because she has to keep her wits about her in case Edith needs a hand in the middle of the night, which she often does: if she wants a wee; if she wants a drink; if she has trouble with her CPAP machine – the Continuous Positive Airway Pressure mask that makes the soft Darth Vader noises to stop the sleep apnoea killing her. Maisie is always on duty. But her mother is in a better mood if she has a good sleep and—

God—

She can't scream—

A man stands in the bathroom doorway watching her shower. He's wearing a balaclava.

Maisie can't move. She can't even cover herself—

He stares through the slit in the black material over his face, leaning against the door frame. His silence is worse than anything he might say.

And suddenly she hears herself gabble, 'I'll be with you in just a minute. Kevin and David are upstairs, but they'll be right down and then I'll put the kettle on and—'

The man disappears.

Maisie slides down the shower wall, the water battering the top of her head.

She's not sure how long she sits there, hugging her knees to her chest. Her muscles are shaking. She tells herself to get up, tries to force herself to go and check, to make sure he's not upstairs with her mother. But she doesn't move.

How did words come out of her mouth? What did they mean? David and Kevin are their lovely neighbours back in Wiltshire. They used to come here on holiday, and they were the ones who told Edith about the timeshares, but they're not here now. Perhaps suggesting there were two men upstairs frightened off the intruder.

A weird sound escapes her lips. A bizarre thought – the figure in black is the only man to ever see her naked. Forty-three and she's never been kissed . . . not since the games they played as children.

She starts giggling like a mad person. It must be the shock.

Eventually she manages to turn off the shower and reach for a towel.

She checks the kitchen and lounge then slowly climbs the stairs. She quietly opens the door to the master bedroom, the one with the ensuite. Her mother lies on her back, the machine making its sibilant hisses, which are as annoying in their own way as the violent snores which preceded its arrival.

In her own room, Maisie checks under the bed and in the wardrobe to be sure, then she slumps onto the duvet, suddenly exhausted.

The man has disappeared.

After a few minutes she starts to towel dry her hair as she doesn't want to wake Edith with the hairdryer. By the time she's sipping her morning tea at the kitchen table, she's calmer, and she is clearer about what she wants to do.

She takes the largest knife from the holder next to the coffee pot and puts it in the downstairs bathroom, sandwiched between two towels in the cupboard. The second largest she takes upstairs, sliding it in the drawer of her bedside cabinet.

She has decided she is not going to report the incident. She might not even lock the door. If the man comes here again, she will defend herself. The thought is thrilling.

She sees herself stabbing the intruder – again and again and again, feeling the blade slicing into his flesh, his hands, his face beneath the balaclava . . . and . . . no one will be able to blame her for it!

Her mouth smiles of its own accord and she shivers imagining how it might feel.

'Maisie!' the call comes.

She's awake.

'Maisie!'

Her smile dies.

'Coming, Mum.'

III

The Previous Christmas and New Year

24

Hannah

She is wiping herself when she hears them come into the toilet. There's a blast of music from the live band in the bar – a duo currently singing Oasis covers, customers joining in on soaring choruses – fading as the door shuts behind them. There is bustle and two women's voices.

'. . . and that dancing! It looked like she was possessed!' snorts one.

'*Twerking* isn't it?' laughs the other. Kit's mother. There's no mistaking those haughty nasal tones.

Hannah realises they're talking about her.

'At her age!' says the other voice. This one sounds younger, similarly snooty. Both women seem seriously drunk. 'And she's supposed to be a hairdresser? With *that* hair!'

Hannah freezes.

'Yes. It's ghastly. But I suppose she did a good enough job of Jane's wedding.'

'Yah, I saw the pics on Hil's feed. Her hair actually did look amazing with those pearls!'

'Mind you, anyone can do construction given enough hair-spray, darling, but best leave the cuts and colouring to the real professionals.' There's the sound of the toilet door next to Hannah's being opened. 'No subtlety.' Another laugh and then Beatrice pisses like a donkey.

A bang makes Hannah jump. The woman outside has kicked or stumbled into the bin.

'But he's still with her, Beatrice! He prefers . . . *that* to me!'

Ah! Hannah ascertains Kit's mother must be talking to the goddaughter. *Charlotte*. The one with the eyes of a milk cow.

Hannah has no reason to be jealous. When she and Kit first got together she wasn't. Charlotte went for him in the pub that time, but things like that always happen in the pub. Can't take them too seriously. But now the girl has taken to throwing herself at Kit. She turns up to various parties in London nightspots apparently, has too much to drink, and at some point Kit has to put her in a taxi.

'She just launched herself at me!' said Kit when he reported back on one of these incidents. 'She won't take no for an answer.'

The fact that he tells Hannah this, the fact that he thinks it's a huge joke and seems to feel nothing but pity for Charlotte, should reassure Hannah. She trusts him. She knows Kit's feelings for her are genuine.

But Charlotte is beautiful and she's so much younger. Plus, she has lovely hair. Glossy.

Hannah feels a swift flare of shame. She dyes her own hair and, yes, right now it is a shade too dark, a little too crispy. In two washes' time it will be better, and by next week, at the New Year party, it will be at its best.

Like her mother, Hannah went grey when she was young, only twenty-four. Now she ekes out the dregs from bottles of Olaplex she uses on guests and a few of the highly educated workers who do a season here as something interesting to put on their CVs. But there is never enough conditioner left over. Her own hair remains resolutely coarse.

'He's not serious about her, darling. It's only a fling. Nothing to worry about.' The toilet flushes, the door opens, then the unpredictable tap in the left-hand basin gushes in psychotic spurts.

'I know, he can't be, right? It's insane.'

'He's just been a little destabilized lately, what with his father . . .' Beatrice's voice trails off but does not crack.

'But what can he possibly see in her?' bleats the girl. 'It's been *months* now!'

'It will run its course. Not long now I should think. I bet my bottom dollar he's already bored, darling. He'll move on soon enough, mark my words.'

'She is such a skank! I just want to smash a glass in her face or something.'

'It might be an improvement!' hoots Beatrice.

Enough!

Hannah bursts out of the cubicle without flushing. Both women look aghast as she strides up to Charlotte, who backs away until she's pinned near the wall. Hannah smiles sweetly and hisses into the lovely blonde hair, 'Were you always such a bitch, Charlotte, or did you have to take lessons?'

Charlotte recoils, activating the hand-dryer, which whooshes like a punchline.

Hannah stalks out of the toilets like a queen, seething.

131

25

Christie

The night started well enough. It was rammed in the Old Ship – a fair few guests already over for the holidays, gearing up for Christmas, and workers enjoying their last Friday before the big party-season rush. Everyone smiling and singing, even Thor from the shop – some of the youngsters call him Pizza Face, because of his bad skin, and when they do Tommy has a go at them, saying that's not nice, and Christie sees the way the other kids look at her son then. Too sensitive, too intense, her oldest boy. Tommy worries about everything: global warming, the death of the sea. And Christie has nothing to tell him to quell his fears.

Christie and Sam were having a night off from all that, enjoying the atmosphere. Mary-Jane and John were sitting opposite them at the same table because there was nowhere else for them to sit. They were hugging each other as usual, but their displays of affection didn't sting at all right then because Sam sat alongside Christie, his arm heavy across her shoulders, and they sang 'Wonderwall' together, getting some of the words in the verses wrong and laughing and not caring. She bloody loved Sam when he was like this.

Old Betty sat squashed alongside them, nursing her half a Guinness and a glass of sweet sherry. She does well on busy pub nights, does Betty, rarely having to buy her own drinks.

Christie had already had quite a bit to drink, because the kids were supposed to be at a sleepover with Emma's lot, but then Tommy had called announcing he wanted to come back (a fall out with Emma's eldest over who was better, Ronaldo or Messi), which meant Christie would have to go and collect him as soon as the singers finished up. No chance of Sam seeing to his son, of course, but still, they were having a great time and an early night wouldn't go amiss as she had to help sort the kids' early Christmas party at the community centre tomorrow morning. Big Bob was due to make an appearance as Santa in the afternoon with presents for all, and then it'd be the Christmas Makers Market with lots of homemade goodies on sale to tempt the tourists.

But then, in the middle of 'Stand By Me' Hannah started a row with the son from Falcon – high-season timeshare owners although he's been here loads recently, what was his name? – and Sam had got up, actually climbed over her to go to bloody Hannah's aid. As if *she* needed rescuing, as if she was ever a damsel in distress. Hannah was doing most of the shouting, although Christie couldn't hear the words because the music and singing were so loud.

Christie felt her body go hot. She was instantly furious with Sam after his history with that little mare. The emotional intelligence of a bloody whelk, her husband. Stupid, stupid man. No thought to how tongues would wag about him acting the knight in shining armour for the barmaid everyone knew he'd had a thing with last year. Not just a one-night thing either according to Emma, who broke her bloody neck to inform her of what was going on behind her back. As if she hadn't guessed! But Christie had said nothing, let it slide. Sometimes he made mistakes, but her Sam was a good man, a good father. Usually.

She gripped her pint so hard her knuckles went white as she watched her husband take hold of Hannah's hand, his arm around her waist, trying to lead her away from the tall youth – Kit, that was it, Beatrice Wallace's son.

That was bad enough, but Christie only had herself to blame for the next part. She can't remember having the thought, but when Sam made his way back to his seat, as soon as he came into range, she reared back and flung the remains of her cider in his face.

She went cold. The shock of what she'd done sobered her slightly and she quickly gathered her things as he stormed his way out through the pavilion exit.

'Now that was bleddy stupid,' Old Betty shouted above the music. 'You'll not get off scot-free for a trick like that, my girl, you mark my words.'

As she scrambled her way out after him, Mary-Jane and John looked appalled and clung to each other like limpets.

Hannah made it even worse, rushing up to her, saying, 'Leave him for a bit, yeah. You know how he gets when he's had a skinful.' Her breath was sour. As if she knew more about Sam than Christie did – he was *her* bloody husband!

'Stay away from me and stay away from him!' shouted Christie. 'I'll bloody kill you if you don't stop sniffing round him. Hear me?' and she pushed Hannah hard and fought her way out of the pub to the ironic opening chords of 'Don't Look Back in Anger'.

And then—

Christie is now on her kitchen floor, sitting awkwardly, slumped against the oven. Confused. Trying to work out how she got down here.

Sam stands over her, gesticulating with a bottle of Corona, spitting with anger. 'I will fucking kill you, hear me? Another stunt like that? I. Will. Fucking. Kill. You!'

But she can't compute the words because from upstairs, comes the wail like a smoke alarm, 'Mummy-Mummy-Mummy!'

She tries to get up but falls again. She tries a second time – she has to get to Tommy and the baby. No, the baby is still at Emma's, the twins and the baby are at Emma's . . . And, clumsy with alcohol or . . . she lurches up and forwards to the table, misses, bringing the tablecloth down with her, smashing two plates, the small vase of holly and silver ornaments she'd arranged in a moment of seasonal optimism, and the half-pot of homemade strawberry jam she'd put out ready for the morning.

Another wail from above.

She feels sick as she stumbles away from Sam, who has a livid red handprint across his cheek, and she clambers up the stairs, the swirly pattern on the carpet making her feel worse, his threats following her.

And as she sits on her son's bed and hugs him and tells him

not to worry – Mummy and Daddy are just messing about, it's all okay – she bites back her shame and rage and guilt.

And if Sam shouts up the stairs, 'I will kill you!' one more time, making Tommy flinch and cower into her, she will run downstairs and grab the heavy dolphin-shaped doorstop and she'll smash his bloody skull in.

St Mary's School

Miss Bevan said her story was lurid. Gwyn thought that was a good thing, but the teacher's face told her it wasn't. She looked it up later. Lurid *means shocking and sensational. Gwyn still thought that was a good thing.*

'I applaud your imagination, Gwyn, but the assignment was to write a story that showed the true nature of the Scilly Isles,' said Miss Bevan.

'It does!' insisted the child.

'I'm pretty sure there's no evidence of werewolves here.'

Tamar Searle laughed, and Miss Bevan did that head-cocked-to-the-side thing, as if Gwyn was simple. It felt worse when Miss Bevan pretended to be kind.

'It's a metaphor. Obviously!' said Gwyn.

Tamar Searle rolled her eyes.

'The werewolf only attacks women, like those who were attacked on Tresco, and I bet the one who's still missing was attacked too and—'

'In that case, the story is simply in bad taste,' said Miss Bevan.

'But—'

'No. That's enough. Please sit down, Gwyn.'

Gwyn hates Miss Bevan.

26

Kit

'You are best off out of it, darling. She behaved like an *animal* yesterday. The language!'

Beatrice has declared herself appalled at the scene in the bar last night. She has branded the barmaid *bad news*. But Kit and Hannah never stay mad at each other for long and they had a lovely making up session this morning.

'We've not split up. Anyway, she said you and Charlotte were being rude about her in the loo,' says Kit. He knows this will rile his mother. You could accuse her of mass murder, but do not ever say she is *rude*.

'We were *joking*,' simpers Charlotte, fluttering around the kitchen in the background.

Beatrice lays her perfectly manicured hand on Kit's arm. 'There was no malice intended. She took it the wrong way.'

Kit simply couldn't believe Hannah's hysterical accusations of what transpired in the toilets. He's sure there must have been some drink-fuelled misunderstanding. There's no way Charlotte would have threatened to glass anyone – it's not in her vocabulary. Of course when he suggested as much that night, Hannah went ballistic.

He sticks to what he considers are the facts. 'Char posted that unflattering video of her dancing. That wasn't intended as a joke.'

'She obviously doesn't have a sense of humour,' sniffs Charlotte.

'Hannah has a great sense of humour, but she isn't on social media. Your *joke* was wasted.'

'Who's not on Insta?' says Charlotte, genuinely bewildered.

'Anyone not desperately invested in what people they've never met think of them,' he snipes.

'Anyway, darling, I think enough is enough, don't you?' interjects his mother.

'Yes I do! It's half-eleven in the morning and you're already drunk!'

'Kit, darling, it is almost Christmas,' protests Beatrice, in an attempt to reclaim the moral high ground, 'and I'm only a tiny bit squiffy, which under the circumstances of *my husband's death* is not a crime in any—'

'More than a tiny bit, I'd say.'

It riles him how she has chosen to cope with the bereavement. When he's with her she takes up so much emotional space it's as if there's no room for his own grief.

Beatrice scowls at him. Her heavy scent of musky Velvet Rose & Oud turns his stomach.

Charlotte pipes up with, 'It was embarrassing, Kit. She looked like a lap dancer. At her age! I can't understand what you see in her. She's just a gold digger.'

He ignores the irritating whine in her voice, and says, 'Charlotte, will you please go away. I'm trying to talk to my mother.' The girl is practically a stalker. Every single party he goes to in London, bloody Charlotte turns up.

Charlotte pouts prettily, grabs her fake fur coat and flounces out into the garden, aggrieved.

Kit sighs heavily and sits across from his mother. God, she looks awful. In this tastefully arranged kitchen with ornaments of pale blue wooden fishing boats perched on the windowsill and prints of pretty sailing vessels on calm blue seas adorning the walls, his mother is a total wreck. Her hair a bird's nest, puffy eyes, splotchy skin. She may have been crying.

Before his father died, Beatrice wouldn't have been seen dead looking like this. She had always prided herself on being smartly turned out, even around the house.

But since the funeral her drinking has got totally out of hand and her standards have slipped. When his father was alive it would be a few glasses of wine with lunch, cocktail hour, perhaps another bottle of wine with dinner. Drinking was just one of the many ways his parents avoided the deep chasms in their marriage; one of the few hobbies they shared. Both were jolly drunks, the life and soul of every party.

Now Beatrice can turn on a sixpence. She can be an ugly drunk. If only his father were here to help him—

As soon as he's had this thought, Kit feels his face redden because tears threaten, as they often do when he thinks of his father.

'What is it?' he challenges his mother, who's looking at him belligerently, dark circles under her eyes giving her a haunted air.

'Be kind to Charlotte. The poor thing is a bit wobbly at the moment. You must see she still has a huge crush on you, darling.'

Kit shakes his head.

His mother finishes her drink and says, 'She would be far more suitable as a partner.'

'She's much too young—'

'*You're* much too young!' she counters. 'Anyway, Charlotte's right – what have you got in common with a barmaid?'

'Don't be such a snob,' he snaps. 'I've got a damned sight more in common with Hannah than *that* bloody show pony!' He indicates outside where Charlotte is pacing and vaping. 'Don't think I've not noticed how you're trying to play matchmaker with me and Charlotte. Why have you invited her here again? For Christmas!'

'Her father's just announced he's remarrying. Her mother's distraught so she's gone to stay with Amanda in Barbados for Christmas and you know Charlotte doesn't get on with Amanda. Poor Charlotte just needed cheering up, darling. I thought we all need a little cheering up.'

'But I'm with Hannah. You've not given her a chance.'

'It's just a fling, darling—'

'She's my girlfriend.'

'Girl!' scoffs his mother.

'She's good for me.'

'Really.'

'This is getting us nowhere. It's got nothing to do with you who I see.' He knows he sounds petulant.

'But it has got something to do with me when I'm the one bankrolling this *dalliance*,' snaps Beatrice. 'It is time you knuckled down to make something of your life rather than running away to an island every five minutes.'

'It is not a dalliance!' He's raising his voice. His bloody mother always has this effect on him. As soon as his dad's affairs are sorted, he won't have to crawl to her for handouts. She's lording it over him while she still can.

'It's hardly love's young dream though is it?' she laughs. 'The woman's over thirty for God's sake.'

'Past her best breeding years?' he mocks.

Beatrice sighs, stands and strides to the fridge, grabbing the chilled vodka bottle, proceeding to make herself another elaborate Bloody Mary, as if a dash of tabasco can disguise the underlying problem.

'You don't think you should rein it in a bit?'

She ignores him.

He slams his hand on the kitchen table. 'For fuck's sake, Mother!'

She flinches and Kit feels ashamed.

It's pointless trying to have a conversation when his mother is so closed off to any *real* discussion, and he's getting angrier by the second.

'I'm off,' he announces.

He leaves his mother marinating in vodka, retreating by the front door, so he doesn't have to see Charlotte's sulky face and hungry eyes.

27

Charlotte

She is mortified.

Earlier this morning Beatrice had sent her to the shop for milk, announcing *an unfortunate spillage*. Her godmother had knocked over the milk bottle with shaky hands, and Charlotte felt she had no choice but to minimise the situation by replacing it as soon as possible.

She was about to apply her make-up when Beatrice said, 'Chop, chop, darling! This coffee won't make itself, will it?' and Charlotte had immediately scampered to the shop, for she is the guest, although she rather feels like one of those *companions* of a bygone era, sourced via the small ads in her grandmother's *The Lady* magazine.

Still, it's better than facing the emotional warzone of her own family right now. If she'd spent Christmas with her father and his fiancée, her mother might implode. And she couldn't face her mother's . . . everything.

On the way down to the store Charlotte's stomach plummeted to see someone she thought she knew approaching. She tilted her head down and imagined wrapping a cloak of invisibility around herself. For two or three awful seconds she believed it was one of Golly's chums, but as the man neared, she realised it was just a random stranger.

She managed a swift 'good morning' without further interaction, turning as if to take a photo on her phone.

Charlotte is used to this evasive action – scuttling around corners in the local Planet Organic if one of her neighbours is shopping at the same time as she is, crossing the road and pretending not to see an acquaintance. For a woman who spends *an awful lot of time putting herself out there* as Kit once mocked, she is adept at making herself disappear. Especially, crucially, if she is not feeling her best; if her face is pasty and naked without the aid of cosmetics and ring lights, if her eyes are bloodshot from an unfortunate binge and purge session.

She had still not managed to put on her face after her return with the milk, and of course Kit popped round then, unannounced. Damn.

As Charlotte strides up and down the garden she watches him while appearing not to – taking swift sips of his beautiful face. From her peripheral vision she sees him disappear from the kitchen, and she hears the front door close behind him.

Her mood darkens.

Despite Beatrice's enticements to spend Christmas and New Year with her on Tresco, and her assurances that her son was on the cusp of dumping that ghastly barmaid, Kit has shown not one iota of interest in her since she arrived. Charlotte has made it pretty obvious that she's available, without appearing desperate, but now she's losing hope.

There'd been Golly's jewellery line launch party three weeks ago in her London club, when Kit gave her that lingering hug, and Charlotte had hoped it might develop into a kiss. But when she nuzzled into his neck, he'd pulled away, laughing, as if her affection was a joke.

She'd attempted to drag him up for a dance at the pub last night, but he'd smiled and shook his head. But then he'd danced with the barmaid, if that awful woman's flailing about could be called dancing.

And there had been the confrontation in the toilets, which was rather terrifying, truth be told. There was a savage look in the barmaid's eyes, as if she'd rip your head off or something. Even Beatrice was shaken.

But then she had been delighted to witness the very public spectacle of the hideous Hannah taking it out on Kit – shouting and gesticulating wildly – surely he wouldn't forgive that! Yet now Charlotte herself is being blamed for the incident along with his mother. Most unfair.

And the way Kit has just dismissed her, as if she were an irritating fly – *Will you please go away. I'm trying to talk to my mother.* Enraging!

Charlotte's thoughts suddenly turn to the large slab of cheese in the fridge. And she knows where the Ritz crackers are in the cupboard. No! She mustn't! She is all too aware that no matter what she eats, it will not stuff down these uncomfortable emotions. It is a terrible habit.

*

146

She has totally failed at not eating since she's been here. No discipline, that's her trouble. She'd scoffed two scones when Beatrice took her for a cream tea at the garden café yesterday afternoon. Two! Slathered with cream and huge dollops of jam oozing out of the sides like a popped pimple. Charlotte downed them both like she was a starving wolf.

She instantly felt so panicky she couldn't wait until they got back to Falcon, and she had rushed to the café toilets. It was a risk. Someone might have come in and heard the awful retching noises. When she got off her knees and left the cubicle, she had to lay her head against the cool tiles by the side of the sink as she washed her hands, feeling dizzy and tearful. It took her a few minutes to reapply her concealer and lipstick, then she sucked a mint and braced herself to face Beatrice and the other customers.

Charlotte pushes back her hair, which is blowing every which way, and marches to the bottom of the garden and back again, hoping the brisk sea breeze will blast away those awful memories, scour the shame, and that the activity will get rid of some excess calories.

Beatrice is a feeder. She provides huge servings of yummy food, and then merely nibbles, pushing things around her own plate, claiming the Bloody Marys are *the equivalent of soup, darling!* Unless they're planning to welcome a rugby team, her host has grossly over-catered for the festive season.

The tempting slab in the fridge is a Cornish Yarg. There's also a mild soft goat's cheese, a huge wheel of camembert, fresh bread and unsalted butter. . .

Charlotte takes another inhale of the cotton-candy-flavoured vape – a festive way to kill oneself – and exhales on a long sigh. She really believed she and Kit might have something special. Their paths keep crossing at various social occasions in London, which is hardly surprising as they have so many chums in common, but mightn't it be fate? Couldn't it be the universe's way of saying they belong together?

Thinking about Kit is making her stressed. Perhaps she should try to book a massage at the island spa.

Beatrice gives her a wave through the kitchen window. Beckoned, Charlotte goes inside.

'A drink, darling?' says Beatrice.

Charlotte shrugs off the pink fake fur. Empty calories, alcohol, but still. It has been a challenging morning.

'Oh, go on then,' she replies.

Much later, after she has finished a significant portion of the cheeses, plus the whole box of Ritz crackers, Charlotte escapes upstairs to stick her fingers down her throat to rectify the latest binge. She knows she'll ruin her teeth if she carries on like this, but she can't see another way out of it. She crawls to bed with bloodshot eyes.

Then in the dead of night she is tormented by fevered dreams. She lies in bed terrified, immobile, as her nemesis creeps into her bedroom . . . Hannah sliding her fingers around her neck, choking her, and Charlotte tries to fight back, but she's too weak to prise the fingers off her windpipe, which is hurting now, aflame, until the deep rage suddenly spews out of her throat and a torrent of hot acid splatters the barmaid's face, dissolving the features until all that is left is a horror.

28

Mary-Jane

The wind picks up as they leave the harbour. Mary-Jane sits and turns her face towards it, blinking hard and swallowing back tears as she watches St Mary's recede. Her phone buzzes. John again.

He kissed her tenderly on her forehead when he left for work early this morning. He's texted four times since – hearts, kittens, *I love you* – and it is barely midday.

His love has never been in doubt.

He will bring home flowers for her tonight, something unpronounceable and unseasonal from the garden greenhouses. He will tell her how much he's missed her, and he will mean it. Usually, if she's at work, he will pop in to see her in the garden café at lunchtime; then they will walk home together after she's cleaned the tables and washed the mugs and cake plates, and he's finished his day propagating or grafting or cataloguing or whatever – his vital, important work, as opposed to her menial job, dishing up cream teas to ancient day-trippers. It is his expertise, knowledge and passion that has brought them here for a year at least.

'The Abbey Garden!' he'd enthused. 'What a gift!'

She was nervous that the job was too high profile. Risky. But he reassured her as he so often did, saying, 'Sweetheart, they will only want photos of my work, not this ugly mug.' He smiled and added, 'Remember we are under His protection. Always.' He rubbed the softness of his beard into her neck until she shivered.

But she isn't sure anyone is protecting them, let alone the old God of their childhood. She hasn't been at all sure for a long time.

She tried to pray this morning before she got the boat over to shop at St Mary's. Failed.

John must know or at least intuit this sea change within her, although he's said nothing. Would he forgive her if he discerned her dissembling? She used to think he would forgive her anything, but she cannot see how his unconditional love might encompass her new doubts.

She can no longer forgive herself.

Tonight, he will smile and kiss her belly, her breasts, her eyelids, her lips. And she will respond because she cannot help but do so. Because she is weak. Because she knows no different. He is the only man she has ever loved. And she cannot help but love him, just as John can't help but believe, fervently, obsessively, that this is *right*.

As they make love, her body will betray her as it always does, moaning and squirming and pulling him deeper inside her, while her mind crawls away somewhere else entirely, into the darkness.

All of this is her fault. She has to finish it.

She has no idea how to do that.

A cry above her. She looks up, envying the seabirds soaring unburdened, buoyed by air currents. The souls of dead sailors some believe, although others say they're no better than winged rats. Scavengers, cannibals. A strong sense of direction, birds, but no moral compass. Only doves are blessed.

She has a vision of swiftly standing, hauling her legs over the edge of the boat and hurling herself into the wintry waters—

No. There are too many people on board. She would be saved. Her body would be saved. There will be no salvation for her soul.

But she has no idea what else she can do.

The wind needles her cheeks.

Today she slipped into the tiny church on St Mary's for privacy, to think. Our Lady Star of the Sea Catholic Church. She closed her eyes, but two loud voices ruined the moment.

'Oh!'

'How cute!'

Visitors always shatter the peace on the islands.

She did not have time to gather her thoughts.

In the church, alongside the tealights, there was a sign saying, *Please wait at least five minutes after applying hand sanitiser before lighting a candle.* It made her laugh out loud because she is wicked. She hides it well, but she knows her true nature.

Last week she sent away for a pregnancy test, having it delivered to the café rather than their home, telling her fellow workers that it was a surprise Christmas present for John.

In the toilets at work, she sat jiggling her leg as she waited to see which lines might appear. She hunched her shoulders against the chill and the foreboding, feeling sick when she thought of what might happen next.

Negative.

She was so relieved she might have given thanks then, but she found she could not. She wrapped the packaging in a carrier bag and walked swiftly up to the dump in her lunch break to dispose of it.

As they forge towards Tresco the wind snatches at the spray and flings it in her face. She bows her head as if she's praying now.

She is not praying.

29

Hannah

As he tackled his second coffee of the morning, Kit said, 'Look, I'm not her keeper. I can't help what Charlotte does.'

'She's being a total bitch,' replied Hannah, clattering around the kitchen in Guillemot. 'Apart from saying she wanted to smash a glass in my face that night in the pub, she's now going round calling me a gold digger. Alison heard her mouthing off and told me.'

'You don't really care what people call you, do you?'

'But it's a thing, isn't it? You're rich. I'm not. People will think I'm after your money.' She sighs. 'Everything's easier with money.'

'Not everything, no.'

She and Kit had made up several times after that stupid fight in the pub, but Hannah has still not entirely let it go. Both of them had drunk too much on Oasis night and she'd lashed out at him rather than decking his mother and bloody Charlotte.

She feels a bit stupid for that. Mind you, he'd questioned the truth of what she said had happened in the loos, she'd started hitting him, he pushed her away and Sam had to drag her off before she went for Kit again.

No one likes to be called a liar, even though he didn't say that in so many words. But taking bloody Charlotte's side!

She poured milk into her own coffee and softened a little. 'I wanted our first Christmas together to be just the two of us.'

'I know. But Mum didn't tell me she and Charlotte were coming until the last minute. I didn't think she'd want to be here without Dad. I thought she was going to be away with her friends. If I'd known we could have gone somewhere else.'

'No, we couldn't, Kit, because I'm working. I can't take time off over Christmas – it's too busy in the pub. It's fine for you because you don't have a job.'

'That's not fair.' He looked so sad she felt a bit guilty. 'I am looking,' he said, coming over to hug her by the sink, nestling into her hair.

'I know you are. But until you have something lined up, there's no way I can risk my job.'

'Always practical,' he smiled.

'Someone has to be,' she replied.

It irritates Hannah that Kit has no idea of what it's like in *the real world*, as she puts it. He might say he wants a job, but it isn't essential for him in the same way as it is for her. There's no real urgency for him to find work. And if they are to make a go of it together – and he swears he wants to be with her, to make a life with her – they need a proper plan.

When Kit tells her he loves her, she believes him, but she's not willing to give up what she has here if there's nothing for her workwise on the mainland. She doesn't want to be a kept woman, his pet.

It has taken her by surprise, falling so hard for Kit. It has obviously shaken him too. It was immediately apparent to both of them that it was much more than sex. And while the sex is the best, after six months it's never *just sex*, is it.

Fired up by the absences, she always wants him, and it's obvious that he can't get enough of her. The advantage of a long-distance romance is that there's never enough time to get bored.

But she worries about the fantasy future together. He's at a different stage in his life. Will the relationship burn itself out? She needs a safety net in case it doesn't last; she needs to be sure she can support herself if it all goes tits up.

Sometimes they argue about this, but then they make up in the usual way.

After his caffeine fix, Kit left to go for a run and while he was out, Hannah read the tarot. She uses the cards to get clarity; she uses them as a crutch. She's concerned that they no longer offer her comfort. They've been so gloomy recently. She does a spread for herself and another for Kit, in the same way that she reads their horoscopes every day. The cards keep turning up the Major Arcana: the Tower, never good news; the Moon, signifying dark powerful influences surrounding them both; and you don't need much skill to divine that the Devil doesn't mean a lottery win.

Hannah's not one for running but perhaps she should go out

for a walk. She needs to do something as she's getting antsy. She's working tonight and she and Alison are still at logger-heads due to her behaviour at the pub during the live music set. Kit now jokingly refers to their argument as Fight Night, but her boss was less amused.

She has to admit that things had got out of hand. Hannah can't cope with alcohol like she used to. Always a disadvantage, the female liver. She was still evilly hungover when she popped into the pub to retrieve her purse the following morning.

'Consider this a formal warning. I'll be putting it in writing,' said Alison.

'I didn't throw the bloody pint at Sam,' Hannah protested.

'But you're always somewhere in the middle of it, aren't you?' challenged her boss. 'A trouble-magnet. It's bad for business, you know that.'

'Did Queen Bea complain?'

'If you mean Beatrice Wallace, no she didn't. She didn't have to because I saw what her face did when you started having a go at her precious son. What was that about? You can't treat punters like that!'

'It was my night off,' replied Hannah, sulky. 'Anyway, they started it.'

'Beatrice and Kit? How did they start it?'

'No, Beatrice and Charlotte. In the loos, they were slagging me off big time. Charlotte threatened to glass me – don't look at me like that! That's what she said! But sorry. It won't happen again.'

'No, it won't!' said Alison, giving Hannah a dressing-down

for several more minutes before stomping away to sort out the cellar.

Hannah puts the tarot cards away in their special box and decides to go over to St Mary's to get some shopping at the Co-op. She puts on her jacket and walks down to the quay, a crisp, breezy, blue-sky day helping to blow away her dark thoughts about bloody Charlotte and bloody Beatrice and stop her worrying about Alison's foul mood.

She doesn't have to wait long before the boat approaches and the engine chugs into reverse, churning water into foam. As it pulls alongside the stone steps, passengers prepare to disembark. Hannah notices that Mary-Jane, sitting alone, doesn't make any attempt to move. She looks ashen. Ted the boatman jumps onto the quay and starts helping the day-trippers across. The steps at New Grimsby are steep and slippery, while the average age of the tourist knees alighting them is fifty-plus.

Hannah nods hello to a couple of returning visitors as they climb up.

When she gets on the boat she goes over to Mary-Jane to ask if she's okay.

Mary-Jane flinches as Hannah approaches. She looks around as if she's not sure where she is, and whispers, 'Sorry.'

Hannah tries again: 'Aren't you feeling well? Shall I give you a hand?'

Mary-Jane nods. Hannah dumps her bag and helps the woman to her feet, gently guiding her off the boat.

'Shall I come by later to check on you?' asks Hannah.

Mary-Jane gives a watery smile. 'No, it's fine. John will be back at lunchtime. Thank you.'

Hannah smiles to see Bobby pedalling frantically towards the quay, his little legs going ten to the dozen. They won't wait – tides wait for no man.

They're about to cast off when Bobby abandons his bike by the wall. No one could mistake it – rainbow stripes and neon pink LEDs in the spokes which make it look like a fairground ride in the dark. He dashes down the steps and leaps across at the last second, making his way through to settle by Hannah. It's the first time she's seen him since the argument with Kit.

'I hear you were providing some of the live entertainment in the pub the other night,' he says, raising an eyebrow.

Of course he's bloody heard. Hannah groans.

'Alison's on the warpath,' he says.

'When is she not?'

'Look—'

Hannah interrupts, 'I'm sorry, but I don't need another *bad for business* lecture, okay? It wasn't me who threw a pint! All I did was shout at my boyfriend. There was a bit of pushing and shoving. That's hardly a hanging offence, is it?'

Bobby leaves it a few seconds, then asks, 'What's the problem?'

The boat pulls away from the quay, heading over to Bryher before it returns to St Mary's.

Hannah considers.

Some days she's just a little irritated by Kit. For instance, he's always *there*, whenever she finishes work, waiting for her. It's a tiny thing that now grates, like a single grain of sand in your shoe – almost subliminal at the time, until, the next day, you've got a great bloody blister. His attention used to feel flattering . . .

She also envies his freedom to come and go as he pleases: that he might take a day in the garden reading or painting; that he can choose to eat or drink wherever, whatever, and not worry about the bill; that he can choose to buy a shirt, a painting, a flat, a home . . .

Then, like the tide rushing in, she loves him so much it hurts. But if he hugs bloody Charlotte one more time . . .

Her conflicting emotions are too hard to explain. Instead, she says, 'They were bitching about me in the bogs, Beatrice and the goddaughter. She has the hots for Kit, if you haven't noticed. I heard them slagging me off and I took it out on him. I know, I'm a numpty. Shouldn't have. Are you going to lecture me like Alison?'

'Is there any point?'

'Not really. It's done and dusted now.'

Bobby shakes his head.

Vlad comes out of the wheelhouse, where he's been chatting to Ted the boatman, and sits by Hannah.

'How's it going, young sir?' asks Bobby. Vlad looks a little wasted and more than a little glum. 'Not so festive, hey?'

'About right, mate. I want to be somewhere warm for Christmas; on a beach sipping a cocktail, not freezing my bollocks off with a batch of bloody pensioners – no offence.'

'None taken,' laughs Hannah.

She leans back and watches the gulls circling above as Vlad looks at his phone and Bobby starts eating his egg and cress breakfast sandwich. 'Might be a relative, that egg,' she jokes, nodding to the gulls.

Bobby doesn't smile.

She asks, 'What's wrong?'

'Don't get on the wrong side of Alison,' he advises, taking another bite.

Hannah sighs. 'I've already apologised.'

'You know that pub is her life. She will not take kindly to anyone upsetting guests and risking profit margins.'

'She spent about forty minutes telling me as much.' Vlad rolls his eyes in sympathy. 'But Kit's forgiven me.'

'I bet Alison hasn't. I don't think you're taking it seriously enough,' continues Bobby, removing a piece of cress from his teeth. 'You know her background?'

'I've heard, yeah.' According to the rumours which circulated when she first arrived, Alison is related to a variety of East End gangsters, including, possibly, the Kray twins. But then everybody from the East End claims the same.

'If you keep pushing it, she will kill you.'

Hannah laughs. An expression passes over Bobby's face which suggests she shouldn't have.

30

Beatrice

She cannot sleep. She's been tossing and turning and hitting her pillow in sheer frustration. Then she remembers Charlotte is in the bedroom next door and feels foolish.

She finally drops off around two but dreams she's on fire and awakes soaked with sweat and regrets. She has to get up and change her nightdress. Beatrice is sure the stress of Henry's death has precipitated these awful symptoms.

She goes downstairs to make a cup of tea and ponder her overwhelming sense of sadness. Her son has refused to spend Christmas Day with her!

'I am not leaving my girlfriend to sit and pull crackers with you and bloody Charlotte. We have plans.'

We!

'But this is the first year since your father—'

'I am very well aware of that,' he snapped. 'Which is why I want to be with Hannah.' More quietly, he added, 'I need to be with her.'

It stung. But not so much that she'd actually invite the barmaid.

The compromise was that he would pop round to drop off his mother's present on Christmas morning. She suggested he come for drinks after lunch, but he refused.

'We'll be going for a walk then.'

She almost suggested she could join them but guessed she wouldn't be welcome.

Since he moved into his father's pied-à-terre in central London and started practically commuting to the island every few weeks, Beatrice has hardly seen Kit. She misses him.

And then all her chums had bailed for various reasons, so she now faces the prospect of dealing with Charlotte by herself. The poor girl is not coping well with her mother and father's divorce. Rather than pick a side for the festive season she was keen to escape. Beatrice felt she had done a kind thing to invite her here. But she guesses how Christmas Day will go. The girl will stuff her face and then spend half an hour in the toilet throwing it all up again. As bad as Princess Diana!

Beatrice intends to spend as much time as humanly possible in the Old Ship. She might sing carols; she might read alone in her room; or she might howl at the bloody moon!

31

John

The flower is not one of the showy plants which bloom rarely, cossetted by the gardening team, attracting keen botanists from far and wide, but it is amazing, nonetheless. The Canary Island bellflower. Oozing with nectar. The island is exalted for these winter blooms, priding itself on dashes of colour all year round. English exotica.

But even in this small unpretentious blossom, John sees God's hand at work.

How can people believe in Darwin? Infinite *mistakes* could not create this single wondrous flower, let alone the embarrassment of delights to be found here in the gardens. Who could not see a grand design behind it all, the hand of the Father?

He sings softly to himself, 'Shy little flowers in hedge and dyke that hide themselves away, God paints them though they are so small, God makes them bright and gay.' An old English hymn. John has always been the Anglophile. So thrilled to come over to work here.

He says a silent prayer of thanks and straightens his back, tight from so much bending and carrying and digging, pausing to appreciate the surrounding beauty.

On the Middle Terrace he takes in a long, satisfied breath. Still ablaze with colours, this place. From all over the world, these blooms – from New Zealand the bright red *Clianthus puniceus*, the lobster claw; from South Africa the vibrant orange phallic spikes of the candelabra aloe, the strumpet relative of aloe vera.

Perhaps he loves his flowers too much. It is almost sinful.

He could stay here on the island forever. The small fly in the ointment is Mary-Jane. He's worried about her. A sadness has descended upon her, although whenever he asks, she claims it's nothing.

This fear is indulgent. He must trust in the Lord.

Of course, her delicate pale face is even more beautiful when she seems sorrowful. He's seen the way people look at her, the way men smile at her; he's seen the way Thor from the shop gazes at her—

Suddenly his own face is aflame. A hot wave of fury and jealousy. How dare that youth think of his Mary-Jane like that! Thou shalt not covet!

No!

No.

He takes another long breath. Looking down he sees the bloom he was holding is crushed and shredded in his palms.

The Sea Wall

*In the old days, women would stand here by the sea wall as their men
set off. They steeled themselves against savage winds and biting cold
as their sons and husbands and fathers and uncles launched their
fishing boats into the treacherous waters.*

*Worry is always etched onto the faces of those left behind. Those
with brine in their veins know that the denizens of the deep demand
sacrifices. Prayers are to be given up and offerings made to keep loved
ones safe. If a virgin can be found to sacrifice, all the better.*

Bobby shivers in the night air.

*Three days and three nights. When will they stop searching? When
will the police drift away? So many questions, so many rumours, but
precious few answers.*

*He's heard all the theories: a lover's tiff, a suicide, a drunken acci-
dent, a murder. She might have got a canoe and made her escape, or*

run off with a French sailor, but after more than seventy-two hours, most people think she's in the sea.

'Goodbye and good riddance,' slurred one of the teenagers in the pub last night, desperate to appear edgy, desperate for attention. When Alison told the girl to leave, shouting at her to show some respect, she laughed. 'Too soon?'

The gig crew might lose sponsorship. Bobby can't imagine Ophelia Gin will want to be associated with an island where women drown.

Missing, presumed drowned.

He wonders how long the fishermen's wives stood here and waited, peering into the darkness, hearts clenched by fear, waiting for men who never returned. How long can hope survive before it too goes under?

32

Alison

Nurse Kelly has come across to The Old Ship on her day off and is now perched on one of the stools at the bar, chatting to Alison. The seat is a little high for comfort, but Kelly likes that it makes her legs look longer.

She watches Alison work. The bar manager is always impeccably turned out, like Peggy Mitchell used to be.

Alison and Kelly have forged a deep friendship in the trenches of the menopause.

It's the 11 a.m. coffee rush and both barmen are down in the pavilion doing their best barista routine, drawing hearts and flowers in froth, flirting for tips, which are usually excellent at this time of year. Meanwhile Alison serves the occasional Buck's Fizz or freshly squeezed orange juice at the top bar, for nothing celebrates the birth of the baby Jesus like mid-morning alcohol. She's on her own until lunch, so the chat with Kelly is snatched between serving customers and clearing up after those who can't be bothered to return their glasses, because that would just be too hard, wouldn't it.

The Christmas tree winks at her in the corner. The needles are a bugger to get out of the carpet, but thankfully that's the cleaner's problem. Every time the pub door opens, a blast of icy air reminds those inside that, while things might be cosy and toasty here in the pub, the elements outside remain intent on destroying human life.

Alison is often stressed at this time of year. There are high expectations of communal goodwill at Christmas and she's never sure she can deliver. The masses, in determined high spirits as they flock to the Old Ship after feasting on an embarrassment of dead animals, require an atmosphere of hardcore *festive joy* while their bellies struggle to digest the riches within.

How times have changed from when families living on the isle of Samson were removed for their own good, malnourished, starving, trying to survive on a diet of limpets and potatoes.

The bar is frenetically busy during the holiday season. Until it isn't. Which is almost worse. At some point soon enough Alison will have slow days and slow nights, after which she will go to bed alone.

She doesn't want to think about that so she pours her friend another drink and Kelly starts confiding in her, telling her how she's worried about her cousin. She always calls the lad Alec rather than the ridiculous *Thor*.

'He'll be on his own for Christmas. Made it clear he didn't want to spend it with me. I reckon the poor sod will spend all his time holed up in his bedroom.'

'All kids do these days,' says Alison.

'But he's not a kid anymore,' sighs Kelly. 'You'll keep an eye out for him, won't you? He's a strange one, I know, but then, who isn't? I'm sure he could make friends if he put in the effort. But of course, anything I suggest is ignored because I was never young, was I?' She shakes her head.

'No need to worry,' says Alison. 'He seemed happy as Larry at the sing-along the other night.'

As she sees it, part of her job as bar manager is to offer advice and support to her customers, provide a motherly shoulder to cry on, a listening ear, soothing words when required. Alison is the modern equivalent of the village wise woman. Otherwise, as a woman over forty, she might be labelled a witch.

So she doesn't like to worry Kelly by telling her that two of the chambermaids were making fun of Thor on singalong night and that he stood by himself as he always does.

To cheer herself up, Alison says, 'Any gossip?'

Kelly leans in to whisper her latest juicy titbit – there's a chap staying over at the Star Castle Hotel on St Mary's who's just been admitted to the hospital after accidentally *falling on a lightbulb*, which lodged you know where.

'Is he an illuminati?' snorted Alison, and the two women cackle gleefully.

Their laughter is interrupted by Mrs Dalton from Room 14 – a regular guest at the inn at this time of year. Around the corner, they hear her loudly announcing to the receptionist on duty that there has been *an incident.*

'There was no mattress protector. I would strongly advise you to use them!' Mrs D's voice has the resonance of someone used to breeding and training gun dogs for several decades. 'Small accident, I'm afraid!' she booms.

The last thing Mrs Dalton sounds is afraid.

Alison smiles. The nasty chambermaids will have to deal with that.

Mrs D, now assured she will be furnished with a mattress protector, comes through to the bar carrying the source of the accident, kissing the dog tenderly on the nose. The animal has produced so many excellent pups, her bladder issues are excusable.

Mrs Dalton bids a cheery farewell to all and sets off to see her other dogs – the ones who now work for the island's game-keeper – a song in her heart and a packet of dried liver treats in her pocket.

Later this afternoon Kelly is planning to catch the air bus over to Land's End, then via slow taxi and slow train make her way across country to visit family and friends in the Midlands. Alison will miss her. She has a stocktake to sort, and a barman to bollock; she needs to bring up more sherry, organise the mulled wine, then supervise the Secret Santa for her staff.

'Do They Know It's Christmas?' plays over the speakers.

Of course we bloody do, thinks Alison.

33

The New Year Party

Outside the community centre, just beyond the piss-poor pools of light generated by the energy-saving bulbs, some of the island's youngsters have paired off to fumble in the bone-achingly cold darkness – an almost heroic endeavour, although they do not feel the chill, fuelled as they are by booze and hormones.

Inside, Charlotte is dancing to 'The Power of Love'. She has reached the misty-eyed and wobbly-lipped stage of the evening. Bobby, encased in a Union Jack suit that is straining along several seams, is clasped to her bosom as the pair shuffle around the dance floor. The throng of sweaty swaying bodies emanates a miasma of lust, nostalgia and Lynx Africa.

A human-sized banana, a rather frayed jellyfish, and a septuagenarian Indiana Jones stand shoulder to shoulder waiting to be served at the bar hatch, where Hannah is busy dispatching orders. Joyce from reception asks for a WKD, which Hannah gives her, knowing full well it's for her son, Robin, who's only fourteen, but, hey, it's a party. Joyce has come dressed as Cleopatra, or she might just be wearing a very bad wig with very bad eyeliner. Lounging against the wall with three other nerdy boys, Robin has come as a robin, wearing brown trousers and a brown jumper to which he's simply attached a big red circle – both lazy and impressive.

Most of the party crowd are in fancy dress. Half of the *Czar* gig crew are butch bearded Spice Girls, wearing the sort of shoddy cobbled-together garments which would make Ru Paul weep. Kit is a rabbit in tight white jeans and a white T-shirt, plus bunny ears, a bunny tail, and a giant inflatable carrot. Hannah is a sexy vampire in a red basque.

Vampire is a popular choice of costume, serving for both Halloween and the New Year party. Vlad is playing up to his nickname, sporting a black cloak and a trickle of fake blood down the side of his mouth. His own impressive canines mean he doesn't have to bother with fake teeth. There are two other sexy girl vampires, but Kit has assured Hannah that she is by far the hottest.

The young begin enthusiastically bopping along to 'Dancing Queen'. Those over thirty, having danced to this track many more times than they have had pay rises, are a good deal more jaded.

Maisie Willis from Sanderling is dressed as a Scilly bee in a jolly homemade yellow and black striped costume. Her mother has been a regular at this event for many years – her Dalek, fashioned around her wheelchair, won the fancy dress prize last year. Maisie has shared the terribly sad news that her mum is too ill to visit this time with anyone and everyone who cares to listen.

The state of Edith Willis's health, given her age and size, is no surprise. What is more notable is that her daughter seems to have bravely put her own sadness behind her. Maisie is now in full celebratory mode, dancing wildly and knocking over drinks with her frenzied bee wings. Such is the healing power of alcohol.

When she finally takes a break from dancing, Maisie stares hard into the eyes of any man of a certain height, hoping to see the visitor from the bathroom again. It is most disconcerting for those impaled by her searching gaze.

The DJ (Jeff from the kitchen team) announces the midnight countdown will commence in two minutes. Hannah leaves her post behind the bar and comes round to the dance floor to hug Kit. He kisses the top of her head. The teens reassemble indoors, hit by the blast of moist warm air. Cove Shiles is proudly sporting a red mark on his neck, while Amber Roskruge giggles as she cleans the steam from her glasses. The still-singles, and unhappy couples, eye potential new targets.

There are whoops and laughs as the countdown begins. Hannah and Kit shout out the numbers along with the crowd, and at the gongs, party poppers are released, and somewhere outside, even though there's supposed to be a ban on them, a firework is set off. The gamekeeper's dogs crack off in reply.

Belying the underlying pathos of the words, 'Auld Lang Syne' passes in a blur of sticky hand-holding, lurching and screeching, and then mass tonsil hockey commences.

Sam, absolutely off his tits, swoops in, grabs Hannah and gives her a big gropey kiss. Kit smiles. There are no hard feelings. He is sure of Hannah. He doesn't like to think of himself as the jealous type.

Not so Christie, who sees this, of course she does, because she's never allowed to have one single night where she can just enjoy herself, is she? She shoulders her way through the crowd into the shock of cold air outside and marches home without her coat, so fired up is she by alcohol and fury.

Alison, who's dressed as Bonnie (as in Bonnie and Clyde, although there is no Clyde), notices Thor sloping around the peripheries of the hall with a face like thunder. He's taken off his weird horror mask to wipe his sweat. She gives the lad a peck on the lips, and a 'Happy New Year!' But when he tries to slip her the tongue, she pushes him off with her plastic machine gun.

'I don't think so, Al,' she warns. 'I'm old enough to be your mother!'

He moves in again.

'Cool it, son,' she smiles, not unkindly, but he's wounded by the word *son* and angered that she's called him *Al* rather than Thor.

There is more umbrage in the corner by the toilets when Farmer Michael (a caveman) gives Fiona from the gallery (a Daryl Hannah-esque mermaid) a lingering kiss. The farmer's wife (a Viking warrior) would very much like to fillet Fiona with the horns of her helmet.

The notes of 'Come on Eileen' signal a return to manic leaping about on the dance floor.

Thor does not dance. He skulks by the toilets. Old Betty tells him to take off his Freddy Krueger face mask because he's frightening the smaller children. He mutters, 'Stupid old cow,' stomps into the cloakroom, and thrusts the mask into his sports bag, alongside the ceremonial dagger, nunchucks and balaclava.

Kit grabs Hannah and pulls her in for a kiss. He licks up her sweaty neck, and she shudders.

'Is that a naughty twinkle I see,' he enquires. 'Shall we christen the back room?'

'You leave my twinkle out of this, I have to get back to work,' she laughs and kisses him again.

Kit bought her loads of Christmas presents: earrings, chocolates, champagne; a cashmere jumper not unlike one of his mother's, but it was so soft she didn't mind. Her favourite gift was the bunches of local scented narcissi. He'd placed them all around the cottage and the smell was intoxicating, filling the rooms with the early promise of spring.

Before Hannah can make her way back to the bar, Emma's youngest, dressed as a small shark, runs up to her and she swoops him high, making him giggle with delight. Kit's heart feels like it might be executing a small somersault. One night they'd talked about having their own child. 'One day,' she'd said. He could see it now.

His daydream is abruptly interrupted. With a feeling approaching dread, Kit notices Charlotte heading towards them, followed by Beatrice. While his mother is dressed simply as a Greek goddess, Charlotte is dressed to kill. She's supposed to be a belly dancer or something, diaphanous wisps of pink and gold material barely covering her bony body and pneumatic chest (which she once informed him was *an investment*). He's seen her snapping herself alongside a plethora of characters throughout the night because she means him to: contorted into a provocative pose with one leg up against the predictable pirate, kissing fat Elvis (Big Bob), pouting alongside a

Poundland Madonna.

Charlotte's progress towards Kit is halted when Thor intercepts her. She stoops to reward him with a kiss, but then there seems to be a small altercation and she pushes him back. Unaware of this, Beatrice almost skips towards Kit, knocking Hannah out of the way as she launches herself at her son, grasping him around the neck, planting a big sloppy smacker on his cheek.

'Happy New Year, darling!'

'Happy New Year, Mother,' he replies.

Beatrice fusses over her boy, readjusting his giant rabbit ears and vowing, 'It will be a better year this year, just you wait and see. It will be—'

'Happy New Year,' says Hannah, in the spirit of the season. This takes some effort. It was recently reported back to her that, during the Boxing Day pub quiz, in answer to the question 'To whom, or what, does the whore of Babylon refer?' Beatrice, playing on Colonel Blimp's team, had laughed when Charlotte shouted, 'Hannah the barmaid!'

But now Beatrice swoops her into a moist embrace. 'Oh, Hannah, darling,' she coos, 'you make my boy happy!' There are actual tears in her eyes. 'You make him soooo happy! Thank you, darling. Thank you!'

Kit mouths, 'Off her head.'

Hannah is unable to disentangle herself.

'I always wanted a daughter,' slurs Beatrice, smiling lopsidedly, stroking Hannah's hair.

Charlotte arrives looking livid.

'Happy New Year, Char,' says Kit, planting a small kiss on her sticky lips.

'Happy New Year!' she replies. The kiss is obviously not enough, but then, neediness and anxiety can never be sated.

As she's finally released from Beatrice's arms, Hannah says, 'Happy New Year, Charlotte.'

Charlotte has her fingers linked behind Kit's neck. She has no intention of letting go, but she manages to turn and face Hannah. 'Just go away,' she snaps. 'I'm talking to Kit.'

'What—?'

'Leave us alone! GO AWAY!' shouts Charlotte, sounding like a toddler having a tantrum.

Hannah looks to Kit, but he just shrugs his shoulders, managing to disentangle himself from Charlotte's embrace.

'You're, you're . . . *disgusting*!' spits Charlotte.

'You . . . what—?'

'Charlotte!' gasps Beatrice.

'Charlotte!' warns Kit.

'But she is! She's old and disgusting. What do you see in her?' wails Charlotte. 'Leave him alone! Just leave us alone!'

'Perhaps you should leave before someone drops a house on you,' counters Hannah.

'Who do you think you are, some, some . . . bloody *siren* luring him onto the rocks?'

Hannah looks genuinely confused. 'What, like, NER-NER, NER-NER?' she asks, making the noise of a police car.

Kit snorts. He places his hand on Charlotte's shoulder and starts to say, 'Ignore her, Hannah. She's drunk, and—' but Charlotte slaps his hand away, looking furious, snarling, 'She just a basic bitch.'

Hannah's face turns deadly. 'I'm warning you—'

Charlotte tries to slap her. Hannah sidesteps. 'That's the

only chance you'll get. Come for me again, Charlotte, and you'll regret it.'

'Just stop! All of you!' shouts Kit.

He suddenly feels exhausted by it all. None of them will see reason. He makes his excuses, forging his way to the toilet, leaving the women to it.

After several seconds of belligerent eyeballing, Hannah turns to leave – Charlotte's not worth the trouble – but as she makes her way back to the serving hatch, there's a sharp pain in her leg, like she's been stabbed in the soft spot behind her knee, and suddenly she's tumbling forwards, landing heavily on her right hip.

'WHOA!' comes the whoop from several bystanders. It wouldn't be the first time Hannah has fallen over drunk. But that is not what's happened.

As she scrambles up off the floor, helped by Vlad, Hannah sees wisps of pink and gold chiffon hastily disappearing back into the crowd. Beatrice has turned away to chat to Ted the boatman and seemingly hasn't even noticed the incident.

Hannah decides to say nothing to Kit because she doesn't want to spoil his night further, or cause another row, but she will have a bruise from the kick for more than a week.

34

The Shoot

Ragnor, Valiant Conqueror of Daisy Dell, made his third visit to Tresco six months ago. Raggy is one of Mrs Dalton's top sires and the latest litter has been a splendid success. One of the pups in particular has already shown great potential and may even be part of the shoot next year, although most dogs take two years to train.

Today, the experienced gundogs will be unleashed on the unsuspecting pheasant population of the island, bred for the sole purpose of mass annihilation by chums of The Family – a seasonal bloodbath much enjoyed by those lucky enough to be invited – the upper echelons of society. Indeed, even royals sometimes grace the island with their presence at this magical time of the year. When that happens, everyone is expected to be on their best behaviour – smiles, bowing, scraping, limited eye contact, et cetera.

It is exhausting.

Vlad and Sam are acting as beaters this morning. While not directly responsible for the feathered carnage, they are morally accessories after the fact. Vlad hates it. As he half-heartedly whacks the bracken to send up the birds he thinks, *flap away little birdies, save yourselves and flap away.*

The men put aside any moral concerns and queasiness for the extra cash in their pockets. No women are invited to be beaters, and few would stake a claim to feminism for this particular event. It's an early start followed by a hearty breakfast hosted in the Flying Boat Club for those who can stomach it.

Someone double-barrelled laughs like a chainsaw, another discusses seed money for his daughter's cupcake business, while a newly minted couple are flirting over their guns, discussing American politics.

'They let absolutely anyone have weapons over there. Any Yank can buy a gun,' the gentleman pronounces, going on to mansplain the Second Amendment. 'They shoot the police, they shoot each other, they shoot anything that moves!' There is no sense of irony when his female companion agrees that this is 'so stupid', smiling tweedily, before blowing apart one of the birds fleeing for its life.

The gulls circling high above are dispassionate. While not classified as raptors or birds of prey, they have been known to eat one of their own and they remain untroubled by the pheasant carnage below.

Vlad, for all the jibes focusing on his carnivorous fangs, is so horrified by the splatters of blood and feathers, the whisper is that last year he crept out of his digs in the middle of the night and, aided by wire cutters, let baby birds out of their pen. Allegedly. Sadly, the creatures have brains the size of an orange pip. Several of the liberated blundered into the waiting jaws of owls and rats. Others stayed just where they were, the perceived safety of their pen the only thing they had ever known.

Some islanders experience a similar sort of stasis, while others resort to various forms of escapism.

Thor isn't the only one who spends his leisure time online. Ted the boatman is very active too. If they only knew their neighbour's secrets, they might have a real-life friend.

35

Thor

How silently, how silently, the wondrous gift is given.

Thor is furious. He is raging because he can't get rid of the bastard earworm from the carols still being played over the pub's sound system. He's raging because of the hangover. He's raging because he was pushed away by that disgusting old crone Alison, and pushed away by the hot blonde, Charlotte, who thinks she's it, and even by Mary-Jane from the café, who dresses like the girl next door, but he bets she's well dirty beneath those high frilly collars. The New Year party was rubbish. And he's raging not to be at the shoot – he volunteered but wasn't chosen to be one of the beaters this morning or tomorrow, and now he has nothing to look forward to.

The Christmas period is not Thor's favourite time of the year. He would rather scoop out his eyes with a spoon than return to Dudley. Seasonal memories are difficult. One year he might receive a present, and they'd have a proper meal with crackers and paper hats, the next, his mother might stay in bed all day, Thor left to his own devices, watching television until someone came round to find him eating cornflakes straight from the pack because there was no milk in the flat. A destabilising time, Christmas, the dead days between that and the New Year party, and the grim prospect of another year just the same as the last.

His cousin Kelly had made a fuss, trying to persuade him to come to the mainland for Christmas with her.

'I don't want you spending all your time on your computer playing games by yourself while I'm away.'

To some extent that is exactly what Thor has done. But they're not the sort of games she could ever imagine.

'Please don't make me!'

He types his reply, *Don't make me ask again.*

'But, Loki!'

It is four in the morning, a time for moths and bats, the glow from Thor's computer the only illumination in the room.

Don't answer me back! Do you want me to go? You don't care for me at all! I'll go!

'NO!'

Then do it!

He pauses. Sometimes, he's discovered, staying silent is more persuasive. He waits one long minute before he types, *I'm leaving.*

The girl on the screen yelps, 'No! Please don't go!'

She is grizzling now. Large mud-brown eyes pleading with a chat box on her own computer in her own small, sad bedroom.

Thor says nothing. The girl opens the can of cat food, seeming to heave at the smell.

Do it! Prove you love me! types Thor. *What are you waiting for?*

BDE666 came up with this idea when Thor told him this one was a vegan.

The girl scoops out a spoonful of the gloopy meat and jelly with her fingers, hesitates, trying to sniff back tears, and then finally puts it in her mouth. She gags.

Good girl. What does it taste like?

Loki, the persona Thor has fashioned for himself during this particular online game, does not generally appear on screen. He types his demands, the camera always off, his rectangle a gaping black hole.

'Horrible,' sobs the girl *Loki* is currently bullying. Her nose is reddening. She looks ugly; uglier.

If the girl doesn't do what he demands, *Loki* disappears, won't talk, won't play. For days.

If this girl, or any of the others, say they don't want to do the bizarre and horrible things Thor asks them to do, he will say, *You'd do it if you really cared about me.* He abandons chats with anyone who doesn't give in after four sessions. Plenty more fish in the ether.

He picks freaky sexy images from all over the world for his alter ego, creates bios which gush over Marilyn Manson, Armie Hammer, manga, Cronenberg, Von Trier.

I need to know how much you love me. You need to show me. Please!!!

It starts innocently enough – a request to see them in their underwear, *So I can see you whenever I'm lonely*. Easy compliments.

He swears he will never share the images. *They're just for me. Something special. You're special.*

Eventually, *Loki*, or one of his other alter egos, will start asking, pleading, begging Cat Food Girl or one of the others to go topless, to strip completely. *Show me! Please! Pretty please!!!*

Loki might confess, *You're the only one I can share things like this with. I don't know what I'd do without you! I'm a freak. Please don't hate me. You're my only friend in the world.* And then the clincher, *I love you!*

And these bodies on the screen felt loved and seen and needed and special and so they might say, *You're not a freak!* or even better, *I love you too.*

And when they did what Thor wanted they were rewarded with, *You're so beautiful!!!*

Baby steps, pushing further, asking for more each time. And as Thor drinks alone in his fusty bedroom, in the small cottage, on the tiny island surrounded by miles and miles of nothing, these *friends* across the world in their own lonely bedrooms perform for Thor because they love him.

And if this girl had said, 'No I can't do that!' *Loki* would sulk. Or *Loki* would tell her that, unless she complied, the sordid images from their last session would be shared with all the other men he chats with online: *Maverick, Uzi, Trumper, RedPill, Van Damme, Wolf.* These men have a huge library of images between them.

But *Loki* has used the word *love*. And that usually hooks the isolated souls who haunt these reaches of the virtual worlds.

Although sometimes, if these *friends* really thought about it, the word *blackmail* might come to mind.

Thor smiles to himself. The feminists all bang on about their independence until it comes to something like this, and then they start bleating about being *coerced* and forced into things against their will. Prick-teases the lot of them. If you didn't want it, you wouldn't go to those hotel rooms in the middle of the night – summoned by the producer who could make you a star; the footballer who could buy you nice things; the group of lads on holiday who were only having a laugh.

Thor is planning for the day when he and one of the more . . . *biddable* of his online friends will be together properly, in real life. Then he can do whatever he likes with them.

The girl on the screen is sitting with her flesh goose pimpled, shivering as she eats cat food, smearing the brown sludge on her body and then crawling for the camera. And a part of her heart must break because, surely, deep down, she knows this has nothing at all to do with *love*.

And while the urge for these nights – the craving to debase and ruin another human being – is irresistible, Thor is soon bored. At first, it's like leaching a boil, scratching an itch, but the relief soon passes. He needs to do something more. This is not enough.

He slams the computer shut without saying goodbye.

He goes to his window and opens the curtains. The sky is disturbing. Some say it's dust from the African desert. Whatever it is, the moon hangs blood-red over the sea.

He wonders about something more intense – getting his hands on someone in real life. But that will have to wait. He needs a proper plan.

He considers putting on his black leather mask with the zip for the mouth. He might switch on his own camera and message the fat one in Canada – she's always around at this time.

Thirsty bitch. He has an idea what he'll get her to drink.

The ear worm torments him, *Above thy deep and dreamless sleep, the silent stars go by.* He yanks his curtains shut again.

IV

May, Before the Storm

36

The Old Ship and the Cow Shed

The rumour started when Nurse Kelly popped in for a swift drink on the Sunday. Both Kelly and Alison faced a busy week ahead. No one gets much time off during the gig championships, least of all Alison, what with the invasion of crews from all over Cornwall and beyond: groups of fit young men and women, for some their first time away from home; teams of veterans mourning the prowess of their youth, desperate to settle old rivalries; fans of the racing, fans of the celebrating, fans of the commiserating. Winning! Losing! Alcohol! What could possibly go wrong?

But before that, there's a different event to toast. 'You didn't hear it from me, but a new arrival might be on the way,' whispers Kelly.

'Who is it? Who's up the duff?'

'No, I can't possibly tell you who it is, that would be unprofessional,' declares the nurse.

Someone on Tresco is all she will reveal, adding, 'You know her very well.'

That's hardly a clue. Alison knows everyone.

'Let's wet the baby's head,' Alison whispers back, mouthing, 'Cheers!'

'Let's have another in case it's twins,' giggles Kelly.

'Any bets on triplets?' laughs Alison.

Old Betty comes in to celebrate something else. She's been *up to the big city*, by which she means Truro rather than the capital, and she's been given a clean bill of health from the hospital check-up over there. She mouths the word *breasts*.

As Alison serves Old Betty, Kelly goes on to tell them about one of the builders who'd come to that week's drop-in clinic at the community centre.

'The poor lad was convinced he had, as he put it, *cock cancer*,' she whispers. 'Beside himself he was. I had to nag him into letting me see it, because of course he wanted *the male doctor* to do it. And he did have a lump under his foreskin. But do you know what it turned out to be when he finally let me examine him?'

Alison shakes her head. Old Betty shrugs.

'It was a piece of sweetcorn! He'd been eating pizza in bed, probably had a fiddle while he was at it, and a bit had got lodged there! Bloody sweetcorn!'

The women chuckle.

Alison notices Thor gawping at Charlotte, who's over for the gig weekend, staying at Falcon with Beatrice Wallace. The girl looks as if she's stepped out of the pages of a fashion magazine. The poor lad looks mesmerised.

Alison gives the news of the pregnancy no more thought, but the next night, she notices Hannah isn't drinking. No beers before her shift begins, no vodka added to her juice, no shots after she finishes.

She watches the barmaid closely. Are her cheeks fuller, a little rosier? Is the skirt, always short, always snug, pulling even tighter across her belly? When was the last time she took a cigarette break? Come to think of it, has she smoked at all over the last week?

Alison is not the sort to jump to conclusions, but she makes a perfectly natural deduction based on these observations.

Kit, sitting on a bar stool, beams at Hannah for the entire evening. He appears ruddy-faced and chipper, so Alison guesses he either doesn't know yet, or he's young and stupid enough to be happy about it, bless him.

Over the next few days this *information* escapes and runs free.

When Bobby next pops in for a burger on his way home Alison might mention this juicy piece of information, knowing he will only take it as a logical supposition rather than gospel, and that he's unlikely to spread it further. Alison isn't one to gossip, but this is a word to the wise – Bobby needs to be forewarned if one of the experienced staff is likely to leave him in the lurch. However management might frame it officially (according to the law of the land), privately there is a resigned weariness if staff disappear on maternity leave. Within a small team, resentments can brew.

Alison might also say something to Emma as she wrangles her kids and Christie's lads into a booth to shovel piles of chips in their faces. Emma is looking after her friend's brood yet again, because Christie is 'under the weather', and Alison can guess what that means. Emma runs the island's Starfish Playgroup, and she will appreciate having a heads-up that there might be another mini member joining in the not-too-distant future, because their grant might be cut otherwise. Few seem to be breeding on the islands right now. 'Don't tell another soul,' whispers Alison.

However, Emma might say something to a few, indeed all the other mums over the course of the following week as they drop off and collect their kids, plus those who come to the meeting to plan a tea party at the community centre to keep the little ones out of the way of the main gig-race celebrations in the pub, which get a bit lairy at this time of year, sometimes slipping into total carnage.

Never have so many eyes scrutinised Hannah's belly.

'She's got her claws into that tall visitor from Falcon . . .'

'Could be anyone's though . . .'

'Do you reckon she'll leave the island . . . ?'

By Thursday morning, Hannah is confused when Farmer Michael insists on taking the two heavy shopping bags from her as she's on her way back from the Co-op on St Mary's, saying she's looking *blooming*, telling her to take care of herself.

The rumour continues worming its way around the island.

*

On the Thursday lunchtime, Beatrice Wallace has managed to secure a much-needed massage at the island's spa. The tittle-tattle in the Cow Shed, as it's locally known, is seeded by Emma's friend Sasha, who does most of the beauty treatments.

Sweet Sasha pauses while browsing online bargains from ASOS to tell the massage therapist, Jason, the latest. He isn't the best masseur, but Joan, spa owner and reiki master, has already departed to make the epic trek up to see her family in Liverpool – unwilling to deal with gig-week chaos, thank you very much, for Joan no longer drinks and is thus an anomaly.

Jason, whose ambition is to work on a luxury yacht (being obsessed with *Below Deck* as he is), has no idea who Beatrice is in relation to Hannah, and later that afternoon, in reply to Beatrice's languid 'What's new around here, darling?' (asked with zero interest, but it's only polite to chat to staff), cheerfully chirrups the gossip that has thrilled him – Toff from *Made in Chelsea* has been spotted at the Hell Bay Hotel! – before casually unleashing the grenade, 'Oh, and the barmaid's preggers.'

The body beneath his hands stiffens.

'Which one?' asks the client, a Mrs Beatrice Wallace from Falcon – the notes say *demanding, but tips usually good.*

'Hannah,' replies Jason, kneading the client's rigid shoulder muscles.

Mrs Wallace sits up suddenly, spilling her towel onto the floor, saying she feels faint. Jason has to hurry and fetch her a glass of cucumber water.

There is no tip.

37

Kit

They've had their first big argument, over something really stupid – a row about poker nights with the boys. He wanted her to give them up.

Kit has rented Kittiwake for two weeks (his mother and Charlotte having claimed Falcon yet again), even though Hannah had told him she'd be too busy to spend much time with him until the gig championships were over.

They'd had a lovely romantic reunion, just the two of them snuggled up in the cottage, they'd played *Cards Against Humanity* with a group of gardening students in the pub yesterday afternoon, and he planned to take her fishing after the big gig weekend ended and it calmed down a little in the bar.

But yesterday teatime they'd squabbled and now she's gone missing.

He'd woken around five to find she wasn't next to him, she wasn't outside in the cottage garden having a morning cigarette, and she isn't answering her phone.

Last night's poker game was being held at the worker's cottage Vlad shares with Isak Mensah. Everyone is very careful not to say 'black Isak', one of only two black workers on the island. Although the other Isaac, Isaac Kaplan, is never referred to as white Isaac, and no one has to be at all careful about that.

Stretching and quickly pulling on his jogging bottoms and a T-shirt, Kit makes himself a large mug of Cornish coffee (which is a thing), and pops his head outside, deciding he'll need his windbreaker if Hannah doesn't return soon and he has to go looking for her. The sky looks unsettled despite the sun, and the wind has an edge to it.

He makes another coffee – he can't function without a certain degree of caffeine, but who can – and tries her phone again. Nothing.

There is still dew on the hedgerows as he walks down towards New Grimsby, birds already trilling. Spring is his favourite time on Tresco. The season is in full blowsy bloom, trumpeting lush green Thomas Hardy vibes, bursting forth with pornographic vigour. Poppies and bluebells and lilacs and tulips compete for attention, pumping out scents that cry, *Choose me, choose me! Pollinate me, baby!* In Farmer Michael's hives, the queens pimp out their worker bees to do the business.

Kit sneezes.

The row was all his fault. He's been unreasonable.

Hannah works bloody hard, and he admires that about her, but, God, she likes to play hard too. Of course, he did the same at uni, but Hannah is still at it, even though she's older than him. And it will be pretty full-on in the bar this weekend. How will she cope if she starts exhausted and hungover? He's worried about her. It's easier to tell himself that than acknowledge the deeper fear that she's not as committed to the relationship as she was at the start.

'You've got to grab life by the balls!' she'd laughed when he first suggested she take it down a notch, perhaps cut down on the drinking and smoking. Early last night, when he repeated this apparently unreasonable suggestion that she reel it in a little, she accused him of nagging, and amiably told him to fuck off.

'But I thought we could go to the outdoor theatre tonight,' he said, hurt.

'Why? I've already seen one play,' she quipped.

'It's *A Midsummer Night's Dream*.'

'Isn't it always.'

'Don't you want to do something together while I'm here?' He sounded needy to his own ears.

'Look, I arranged this poker game long before you told me you were coming over this time,' she protested. 'Not all of my life revolves around you, Kit. It can't. What would I do then when you aren't here? I'm not going to dump my mates whenever you click your fingers.'

Eventually she said he could join her at the poker game, but the way she said it suggested that she didn't really want him there.

As she dressed for her night out without him, pulling on her favourite tiger-print leggings, he'd sat on the bed and tried to get back in her good books by talking about her coming to the mainland so they could be together properly.

'You need a job first,' she said, as she always did.

'I think I know what I'd like to do,' he replied. 'I want to paint.'

'What, like a painter and decorator?' she asked, surprised.

'No. An artist.'

She rolled her eyes. 'It's a nice hobby, Kit. But how are you planning to make a living out of that?'

'I don't need to make much,' he said, annoyed because she wasn't taking him seriously. And it rankled, her constant harping on about money, insisting on paying her way.

'It's like saying you want to be a pop star or an astronaut when you're a kid,' she continued, shimmying into her tight gold lurex top. 'How many people can make a living being *creative*?' She said the word as if it was ludicrous. 'Your mother will probably cut you off if we move in together, you know that. You'll need a proper income.'

It hurt because what Hannah said was true. His father hadn't left him as much money as he'd anticipated. Stocks – as bad as roulette.

He sighed. The list of what he didn't want to do grew longer by the day. Before Hannah, he'd considered volunteering abroad, building a school perhaps, somewhere in Africa, but she wasn't at all keen. 'We need some form of security,' she argued. 'You've had your gap year, it's time to grow up.'

On this single aspect, Hannah and his mother agree.

He finds he is now marching down to New Grimsby, immune to Nature's flirtations, his dark thoughts ruining the morning-has-broken atmosphere.

He yanks at a blade of grass, tries to make the wild bird call Hannah showed him, fails. He flings it into the hedgerow, and kicks a sapling, startling a pheasant who does its best Roadrunner impression.

Yesterday, Hannah suddenly announced, 'My mother had such a small life. I want to travel, see a bit of the world. Visit New York, work there perhaps.'

She's mentioned it before. Yet this time, her tone suggested she might be considering going alone.

'What about me?' he asked.

'Come with me, if you like,' she said, as if she could take it or leave it.

He felt a little pathetic when he asked, 'You don't want to be with me in London?'

'I've just got to live a bit more before settling down. I want to live as much as I can, you know?'

You couldn't miss that about Hannah. It was there in the way she danced. Sometimes it was sexy dancing, more often just free and silly and wonderful – like a child really *goes for it* until the years exact a self-consciousness.

She didn't give a hoot if she looked cool. She didn't care if she wore something fashionable. Charlotte was all about the latest trends – the right parties to be seen at, the right clothes to be seen in, but Hannah wouldn't recognise a *hot new label* if her life depended on it. Charlotte once paid £400 for a pair of designer sunglasses and bragged about it on Instagram. Hannah wears a tatty old pair someone left behind on the bar, and she still looks great in them.

He stops a moment to gaze out over to Bryher, which is looking very comely in the early morning light, then he walks round the back of the Old Ship and up the steps of Vlad and Isak's Hobbit-sized home. He knocks softly. There's no reply so he quietly opens the door and finds Hannah on the battered sofa immediately in front of him, entangled with another body.

It takes a moment for his eyes to focus, the dimness of the interior a stark contrast after the brightness of the sun. Hannah doesn't seem to be wearing all her clothes. He recognises Vlad, similarly topless, and sees his legs are hooked over the arm of the sofa and the rest of him is splayed across Hannah's lap, his head lolling close to her naked breast. In other circumstances this might have made Kit think of *La Pietà* but right now art is the last thing on his mind. He is immediately and murderously furious.

'What the actual fuck?' he demands.

Vlad smiles, his eyes still closed.

On the coffee table in front of them, playing cards, a small pile of cash, an overflowing ashtray and an empty bottle of vodka are abandoned. Cushions are strewn across the carpet.

Kit grabs Vlad's arm, and pulls violently, spilling the youth onto the floor.

'What's up?' he groans.

'Hannah!' shouts Kit, shaking her.

She squints up at him and grins.

'Hannah! What the fuck are you doing?'

Her lack of reaction winds him up further.

'Strip poker, man,' slurs Vlad from somewhere near Kit's foot.

Isak appears from his bed in the next room. He is wearing ironic Spider-Man pants and nothing else. He yawns luxuriously and says, 'Oh . . . hello, Kit.' One of the young buff sailors from the big yacht mooring off Cromwell's Castle emerges behind him in a dressing gown several sizes too small.

Kit shouts, 'Hannah, get some fucking clothes on will you!'

She remains unfocused but reaches forwards for her cigarette packet. She croaks, 'Hi, honey, you're home!' sounding terrible as she laughs, precipitating a coughing fit.

Kit grabs a towel from the tiny bathroom, which is barely bigger than a wardrobe, and throws it at Hannah.

'Cover yourself up.'

'It's cool, man,' says Vlad. 'It's just a game.'

Hannah attempts to light a cigarette dangerously close to her hair. Kit snatches it from her.

'Get dressed. Now!'

She doesn't protest as he helps her into her hoody and shoes, which thankfully are slip-on sandals. He does not attempt the bra.

'Lenses,' she croaks, and he grabs her contacts from the bathroom, then drags her outside without saying goodbye, and slowly steers her back to Kittiwake. She tries to hold his hand and, petulant, he keeps snatching it away.

Caning it is Vlad's forte and Hannah is easily led in these circumstances. Or perhaps Vlad is the one being led astray by her. And she's back smoking again. Kit had managed to persuade her to stop, or at least cut down. She's had a hacking cough for weeks, her voice rough and crackly when they called each other each night they were apart.

She turns her face up to the sun and lifts her arms to the sky.

Kit is appalled by the burning feeling twisting his guts. The early workers and walkers beaming in the morning sunshine seem to mock him and it takes a great effort to say, 'Good morning.'

When they reach the holiday cottage he suggests Hannah take a shower.

'Are you coming in with me?' she asks. The walk seems to have brought her round.

'No.'

'Stop sulking. There was no harm in it. I drank too much, that's all. If this is going to work, you have to trust me.'

'I'm not sulking,' he says sulkily.

She walks upstairs, tossing, 'I don't like possessive people, Kit,' behind her.

For a second he feels a surge of anger so powerful he struggles to stop himself running after her, grabbing her by the shoulders and shaking her hard.

Instead, he sets his jaw and leaves her to her shower. Then, afraid of precipitating another argument if he stays, he trails back down to the pub for breakfast, shocked by how wound up he feels.

38

Charlotte

Beatrice sits on the bench in the immaculately groomed garden tackling her brunch – a very small portion of scrambled eggs and smoked salmon, a very large Bloody Mary – wearing an oversized sun hat that makes her look like Little Bo Peep. She turns up the volume on the music player so her classical music executes a passive-aggressive battle with the teenagers in the neighbouring garden, who are already smoking weed and playing gangsta rap – keeping it real, these *Baby Gs*, living it up in their parents' island crib, hailing from the hood of Chalfont St Giles.

Charlotte calls a farewell from the kitchen, keen to get away from Beatrice for a little while – her godmother has been so snippy-snappy with her the last two days. She gave Charlotte such a chilling stare when she accidentally called her *Bea* rather than Beatrice last night, Charlotte thought she might turn to marble.

She prefers it when Beatrice is in her maudlin mood – the widow proving the adage that misery loves company. And lashings of wine. She wonders if she and Bea are co-dependent.

Yesterday, she had shown her once-possible mother-in-law (in her mind at least) some old posts of her with Kit at one of Golly's shindigs. Charlotte became quite misty-eyed reliving these glory days when she and Kit seemed so much closer – oh to be twenty-two again, rather than a world-weary twenty-three.

Beatrice asked her why photos of Charlotte posing alongside her son were so popular *on the internet*. Why did young people want to look at other people's photos? However, she did say Kit and Charlotte made a very nice-looking couple. A *rather suitable couple*, as she put it.

Last night, when they popped to the pub for a quick drink, *early doors* as Alison describes it, Charlotte and Beatrice were met by much merriment – singing and dancing and a non-official party in aid of heavens knows what. They were both shocked (and she was secretly thrilled) to see the dreadful Hannah with the young heliport worker, Vlad. She sat on his lap and gave him a big kiss before draping herself around his neck like a kerchief. A few minutes later, the pair skipped off into the night with a couple of other young men, chanting, 'Poker! Poker! Poker!'

Charlotte can't wait to break the news to Kit.

Her campaign to woo Kit away from the vile barmaid means that, even on the off chance of meeting him, she always aims to appear in public looking her very best. Today, as she walks down to the Old Ship, she has her hair in an artfully messy ponytail, and she wears a pair of spray-on black leggings (circa *Grease*) and a pink Bardot top (circa whenever Brigitte Bardot wore it). She leaves her matching bubble-gum pink fake fur coat open, so her cleavage is on display, even though she is freezing. Charlotte's unnaturally low BMI means she has precious little insulation, although she is adamant she does not have bulimia – she simply makes herself sick on occasion, to expel any excesses. Anyway, being overweight is surely worse for one's health.

Now she sweeps into the pub, pausing on the threshold to make her entrance, and although no one looks up, she is rewarded. For here he is! Kit!

He looks grumpy. Squished in between Big Bob and a random visitor, his shoulders are slumped. Good. His face implies all is not well in his relationship.

Big Bob gets up to go to the bar and Charlotte makes her move.

'Hi. Can you budge up so I can sit?' she asks.

The place is already rammed so it's a valid request. Beatrice warned her it would be hectic during the gig championships.

Kit sighs, but she will not be put off. There is no sign of the awful Hannah. Perhaps she isn't working today, and the gods are on Charlotte's side.

Kit reluctantly makes room for her. He greets her but does not enquire after her health or offer to get her a drink, so it is left to her to open the conversation.

'Will you be watching the gig racing from here or are you going out?' she asks. She has heard that keen spectators hire boats to keep track of their favourite crews on the water.

'I'll stay here,' he replies. He angles round to face her and her heart leaps, but the set of his mouth deflates any hope. 'Tell me, why are you here yet again, Charlotte?'

'Your mother invited me. *She* enjoys my company, Kit. And

it's a world championship, isn't it? Like Oxford and Cambridge. I wouldn't miss that.'

'Gig racing is nothing like the Boat Race,' he snaps.

She bravely attempts to brush off his bad humour. 'Anyway, yesterday they were saying that Daniel Craig might be making an appearance.'

'What, in his submarine,' he sneers. 'Or is he aiming to land a sea plane at the start line?'

'You can mock me, Kit, but I'm reliably informed that Phil Mitchell from *EastEnders* is a regular visitor on the Scillies.'

'Wow.'

His attitude riles her. If there is to be neither kindness nor politeness, she will go straight for the nuclear option.

'You do know your cruddy paramour was snogging the face off one of the chaps from the heliport right here last night.'

'Yes, I know,' says Kit, refusing to rise to the bait, refusing to look at her, doing his absolute best not to believe her.

Charlotte pauses, stung with his attitude. She considers before deciding she might as well throw in another barb. 'Is it true?' she asks.

'Is what true?'

She leans in. 'She's trying to trap you by getting pregnant.'

'She's *what*?'

'Your mother told me. Everyone's talking about it.'

'About Hannah?'

'Is it even yours?' snipes Charlotte.

'She's not pregnant.' He laughs at this desperate attempt to goad him, as if the idea is ludicrous.

'Are you *sure*?' smiles Charlotte, lethally.

Kit snaps, 'Oh, I can see why my mother likes you, Charlotte.

You're as vicious as she is.' He finds he is raising his voice.

'So you trust her, do—'

'SHUT UP!' he shouts, apparently surprising himself as much as Charlotte by the volume. 'Yes, I could bloody wring her neck sometimes, but . . . Look. Please get out of my face, Charlotte.'

She places her hand on his arm, 'Kit—'

He brushes her away. 'What the hell do you think's going to happen here? You think I'm going to dump Hannah for *you*?' he sneers.

Charlotte's glossed pink lips wobble self-pityingly.

'It will never happen. Just stay away from me and stop bad-mouthing my girlfriend!'

Charlotte reaches for him again, but he knocks her hand away.

'I'm warning you—'

He gets up suddenly, upending his chair and stalking out the bar, abandoning both Charlotte and his jacket.

Over at the bar, spa masseuse Jason says to Alison, 'Ooh – this is better than *The Real Housewives of Cheshire*!'

Charlotte is shaken. She doesn't move for a moment, pretending to study the line drawings of notable Tresco workers past and present, which adorn the Old Ship's walls. Her mind immediately goes to the big box of chocolates sitting like an unexploded bomb back at Beatrice's. No, she mustn't! She finds herself sliding her hand into Kit's jacket pocket. She takes something, stands on shaky legs, then heads out.

39

Thor

It is a demanding time in the Island Shop. Customers who can afford to buy bottles of wine that cost more than he earns in a week still manage to be obnoxious, grumpy and dismissive. Plus, Thor is bored out of his mind.

As jobs go, working in a shop isn't as entertaining as his former employment – killing cattle at St Merryn Meat's slaughterhouse. But even that – the animals' terror, the piss and shit and horror, the thrill of delivering the bolt to the brain – all that initial excitement dulled with repetition. And he lost that job because he slept in one too many times.

That had been the death knell for his relationship with his sort-of girlfriend of the time, Kirsty. It was a half-hearted arrangement on both sides. They spent a lot of time sitting in the same room ignoring each other, him on his computer, her on her PlayStation. They didn't share a bed.

After the split, he had nowhere to stay and there was no way he was going back to the Midlands. He saw the position of shop assistant on Tresco advertised in the Bodmin Job Centre (crap wages, but accommodation included), so he came over here.

He's not been with anyone since Kirsty, not properly. There was that one girl, over here on holiday, but that had only been the one night and he hadn't pushed it. A kiss and a bit of a fumble. And then there was that flirty guest – the woman with the mad Mallen streak of white hair, who looked well dirty. He'd been sure she was up for it, but nothing happened.

His online *games* help pass the time, although he can't get off on them in the same way now. It's too easy. But today is his day off and he has plans. New horizons. He is heading up to the North End, where he will hunker down low, hidden by the gorse and bracken and boulders. Then he'll wait and see who takes his fancy.

Thor's bedroom is sparse. All his special things – the World War II memorabilia his dad collected, the treasure trove of women's underwear he stole from washing lines over on St Mary's when he first arrived, the special toys he's ordered online – they are stashed neatly away in the locked suitcase under his bed.

He dresses in the camouflage combat kit he ordered from the Preppers army surplus place on the industrial estate in Newquay. He puts his balaclava in his sports bag. He's taking the meat cleaver that he bought in the kitchen supply shop in Truro. And then he might . . . He has to adjust himself at the fantasy.

If he's lucky she will scream like the gulls above.

If there's no one up at the North End who catches his eye, he might saunter down to the Old Ship, sneak in through the back door, creep upstairs and hide until she finishes, and then he'll take a blade to that jumped-up barmaid, Alison. She thinks she's *it*, flirting with him, leading him on, then pushing him off at New Year. He thought she'd be gagging for it. The old bitch should be grateful at her age. But when she serves him now, it's like she doesn't really see him.

He'll make her see him tonight.

He lifts the huge watermelon he brought home with him from the shop yesterday, hefting it into the postage-stamp-size back yard, where he carefully balances it on top of the five old supply boxes he'd stacked earlier.

He takes the meat cleaver he keeps hidden in the bag beneath his bed, sizes up the trajectory, pulls back, then swings. The slice is satisfying. The top of the watermelon hurtles away, exposing juicy red flesh.

He guesses a skull would be harder, the brain greyer.

You have to make your own entertainment here.

40

Maisie

'Do you want to go for a walk, Mum? It's brewing up a storm, but you won't mind that, will you? Vile weather suits you right down to the ground, doesn't it, you old hag!'

There is no reply, just a lovely velvety quietness. Such a blissful peace after her demands, the incessant *Maisie, will you just . . . I need a hand . . . Maisie, Maisie, Maisie!*

Maisie takes one more swig of wine straight from the bottle, just to wind her mother up, and puts on her walking boots, steeling herself to battle the elements.

Then she grabs her mother and rams her deep into the bottom of her rucksack.

Maisie has decided to go for a long walk and then scatter her mother's ashes off a cliff. They never did much walking when they came on holiday, even before the wheelchair. They'd often meander round the Abbey gardens. More recently, it was Maisie's job to push her mother round, with her cooing over the pretty plants.

'You're so knowledgeable,' one or other of the gardeners would say, fussing round the marvellous Edith Willis, Our Lady of the Flowers, while Maisie had to stand there smiling sweetly, bored out of her skull, knowing the workers were only doing it because fawning over punters is part of their job.

'It's so sad,' is all anyone says to her now.

If they see her sitting up at the Old Blockhouse they might think, *Oh, poor Maisie is sobbing*, but really she's laughing her tits off!

'So sad . . .'

But it's not. She wants to shout from the hilltops, 'It's a liberation!'

Months of washing her mother's rotting flesh and wiping her lardy arse. Bedsores stink. And Maisie was forced to kneel at her mother's feet like she was the Buddha, struggling to bind her weeping calves and ankles.

A waterproof is necessary today. Gloves too.

Maisie sets off.

They lit a beacon on Tresco for the Queen's Silver Jubilee. *Too bad I couldn't have thrown her on it*, thinks Maisie; *it would have saved the cost of the cremation.* And there was so much tallow on Edith, the fire would still be going to this day!

A couple of hikers hurry past and Maisie turns her face away so they can't see her giggling. Then she sits for a moment on one of the many benches around the island to look out to sea. The sun is too brilliant against the darkness of the sky to the west, where the storm is gathering.

Maisie places the backpack on her knees. It weighs surprisingly little. She could hardly believe it when the urn arrived – so much smaller than she'd imagined. She unscrewed the lid, peering in nervously, as if the spirit of Edith Willis might re-materialize like some evil genie. She dabbed in a finger. The ashes were scratchy, not powdery as she'd assumed. Was it bits of bone? Or was it just *her*? Perhaps the remains of good souls were softer. She licked her finger and thrust it back into the urn, then put some of the ashes on her tongue. They were hard to swallow, but Maisie was determined to eat at least a bit of her mother, so she did.

She made herself a cup of tea afterwards.

She will fling what's left of her into the sea. She will wave her off and then whoop in celebration along with the gulls.

The only trouble is, Maisie has been distracted and sat too long. An ugly weather front is hurtling towards land, and she suddenly realises she is chilled to the bone.

And when she finally makes it to the path that leads up to the North End, other walkers are there, some heading to the top, others hurrying down and away from the threatening rain. So many visitors over for the gig racing. It is like the bloody M1 near the bottom of the cliff today.

41

Mary-Jane

At the beginning of the week she felt her larynx tightening, the familiar choking sensation, and her voice totally disappeared, as it regularly does.

She saw what her boss's face did. One of the busiest times of year with the gig championships and so many extra visitors coming over, and yet again Mary-Jane is useless. Struck dumb.

Any words she might speak are reined in. And what might those words be? 'Black or white coffee? Cash or card?'

Help! Make it stop!

The wind against the kitchen window whips up her fears until she can bear it no longer.

And those are the worst words, the ones she thinks but can never say to her ever-loving John; words which would be a dagger to his heart. *I can't bear it!*

Her predicament is beyond words.

When her fears were confirmed, it hit her low, sweeping her

feet from beneath her. She sat with her head between her knees until the faintness passed. She claimed it was a virus.

First thing tomorrow, she and John will travel to the mainland for his work trip to the Eden Project. He's excited to see the Horticultural Therapy project in the Outer Estate. She will accompany him. But she is dreading spending so much time with him in case he guesses her secret. And of course he'll guess.

Today she sits alone at the table in their lovely cottage while he is out at work. Their home is immaculate, just as he likes it. Polished, tidied, neat. It smells welcoming – notes of cinnamon and vanilla, lavender sachets amongst their clothes. There are posies in vases dotted around on the Welsh dresser, the windowsill, upstairs on the bedside tables.

The canker beneath is invisible.

Christie's ginger tom has visited in the night, creeping in through an open window, leaving her a gift – a small headless squirrel on the kitchen floor. The cat sees Mary-Jane as a helpless kitten. He is attempting to teach her how to disembowel prey, otherwise she will not survive.

Then, as Mary-Jane tried to make herself a cup of coffee after John left for work, the cafetiere exploded, sending boiling water through the cracked glass, scalding her hand. Bad things come in threes, although John would say that was a heathen superstition.

Mary-Jane stares at the room with unseeing eyes – her beautiful island home. Then she stands, attempting to psych herself up. She has hidden the leaflet Nurse Kelly gave her yesterday, pushed it deep inside the pocket of her coat without reading it.

She reaches in, feeling guilty as she does so, but she must

study it, it's her only way out and— there is nothing in the pocket. She was sure . . . She searches the other side, panicked now, pulling zips, rummaging through old tissues and a throat-lozenge wrapper.

The leaflet has gone.

Nurse Kelly popped in to check on her yesterday. She wasn't invited. Mary-Jane was both glad to see her because she cannot bear to be alone when John is out at work, and also afraid, because she had confided in the nurse about the pregnancy test. She had to tell someone, or it would drive her mad.

She is so foolish. After the scare a few months ago she should have taken steps to avoid this. But John is against any form of contraception, saying they should trust in the Lord, and fearful of him discovering her rebellion, she had failed to organise the pill or the coil for herself, so it is her fault.

She had gone to see Kelly in the drop-in clinic the nurse runs once a week at the community centre. She managed to tell her some of her worries, although she had disguised the exact nature of her concerns. She whispered, and the nurse told her not to strain her voice.

The risks were not so great, the nurse told her; it was not so uncommon within *certain communities*.

Mary-Jane shook her head.

All would be well, Kelly continued; Mary-Jane shouldn't torment herself. She should get some throat spray from the shop . . .

But then came the terrible thing. Kelly handed her the leaflet and said here was the alternative. She had done it herself when she was nineteen.

'It's not an easy decision,' said the nurse, 'but it was the right one for me at the time.'

Mary-Jane was horrified. She croaked, 'But it's murder!'

'It is not,' said the nurse.

'John would kill me if he knew we were even talking about this,' she mumbled. 'I can't do that.'

'It's your decision, not his,' said Kelly. 'It's your body. This has nothing to do with your partner, or religion, or . . .'

Mary-Jane realised then that the nurse was the serpent in the garden, hissing temptations.

The day after the clinic, Kelly stood in Mary-Jane's kitchen and smiled as if they were friends and asked how she was doing. Mary-Jane nodded and mimed that she was okay. Her eyes said otherwise.

The nurse sat, although Mary-Jane had not indicated she should do so, and she talked about *the options* once more. If Mary-Jane was dead set against abortion, she should go ahead with the pregnancy, have tests, try to put aside her worries. Marriages between cousins had once been common in royal circles, were still common within certain religious groups; she shouldn't worry so much. On and on the nurse talked until Mary-Jane could bear it no longer. She grabbed the piece of paper she'd used for her shopping list and scrawled down a single word.

The nurse stopped mid-sentence and the shock registered on her face even as she tried to appear professional.

Mary-Jane can't bear to be in the house with these thoughts any longer. She pulls on her padded coat, draws the hood tight around her face, and hurries out, desperate to escape.

Her peripheral vision is restricted, and she jumps as she hears, 'Aright, are ee?!'

Miss Elisabeth has come upon her from her own garden gate and Mary-Jane almost stumbled into her. She points apologetically towards her throat.

'Again?' says Elisabeth. 'You get a hot toddy down you! Some of Farmer Michael's honey will sort you right out. Scilly bees are the best.'

Mary-Jane tries to smile, nods, and hurries on. Her thoughts curdle like the threatening inky clouds above. There is danger in the air.

She hasn't decided, not for sure, yet she knows where she's heading, and she has a sense of what she intends when she gets there, if only she can find the courage.

Either way is a mortal sin. A murder. A suicide. She is caught between the devil and the deep blue sea.

She walks quickly, avoiding groups of tourists ambling towards the pub, perhaps seeking sanctuary from the rising winds currently doing violence to the treetops. She catches a whiff of ozone. Or is it sulphur?

She used to pray on her walks, but no prayers come to her now. There are no words of comfort when she most needs them.

For all things Mary-Jane usually turns to John. She has always done so; he has always been there for her. John is her guide, her protector; older and wiser and so sure of everything. But she cannot share these new torments, not with anyone, least of all him.

It is only a mile to the end of the island. It is not far enough.

Her legs strain as she tramps towards the cliff, damp under

her arms and between her breasts. It is a challenging walk and the weather is gathering its might, the wind stealing her breath as she reaches the sharper slope. She has to lower her head to forge against the mustering gale. The sky darkens further.

This is the wild side of the island, more exposed to the elements. Jagged crags and unforgiving fissures thrust and plunge in contrast to the gentle topography of the Old Grimsby end.

Mary-Jane clutches clumps of grass as she pulls herself upwards towards the steepest incline. As she nears the summit, she hears shouts, words snatched away by the wind before she can make them out. She pauses. Someone high above, their back to her, wearing a pink coat. Surely she's standing much too close to the edge—

A thought flings itself at her unbidden. She tries to force the image away, but it already has hold. Her secret might be safe, if only Nurse Kelly stood too near the edge of the cliff and took one step back. Or . . . one little push might do it.

Mary-Jane freezes, appalled by the evil in her mind, in her heart, in her belly.

She should fling herself into the psychotic waves far below her.

The Beach

May, After the Storm

She comes here to remember.

The wind snaps strands of hair in her face as she walks across the beach. She bends and stares hard at the sand, stooping to pick up a pretty shell that takes her fancy. A hobby from her childhood. So many happy memories here from the time when she'd picnic and play on these sands with her mother and father; their quintessential British holiday: hard-boiled eggs, salt in little twists of paper, throwing crusts to the birds.

Hers has been a life-long love affair with the island.

At Christmas they'd take their winter breaks here with candles and holly and carols in the church. That tartan dress she adored!

It is not the time to be indulging in such thoughts.

The gulls screech their disapproval. They sense her darkness.

She is not religious, but she feels observed here, judged by some . . .

presence. *She sends out a wish over the waves – for all her sins to be washed away.*

She comes here to forget.

Only three days ago, strangers walked here – volunteers grimly tramping onwards in the driving rain, searching the coastline, peering into the water, snooping into caves and crevices; hoping they would not be the ones to discover a battered corpse.

Some held prayer vigils in the church, although Old Betty said they would have been a damned sight more use if they'd been out with her and the others, combing the island, hacking through gorse, sodden gundogs yapping alongside them, heading back to the pub and community centre perished to the core – silver space blankets and free hot toddies provided to thaw them out.

Locals and visitors and police. Some went out in their boats, some posted appeals and updates on Facebook, Twitter, Instagram. They sent divers into the Abbey Pool, wading into the blackness and weeds and reeds and duck shit and rot and stink of the lake.

She pulls her pink waterproof closer to her neck and hurries back to the house.

Nothing has been found – not one single thing. Nothing will be found. The victim has vanished into thin air. All that is left now is a gaping silence.

42

Hannah

Hannah is in a foul mood. She's had to work three double shifts thanks to one of the barmen coming down with some god-awful bug that he'd better not have given her. She hardly had the energy for the poker party. Then things had got a bit out of hand and she's now hanging by a thread.

Of course, Vlad and his pals are so much younger than her and that stings, which isn't the only thing. She has violent cystitis – the honeymooner's curse. Too much to drink and too much catching up with Kit over the last couple of days. She'd not seen him for five weeks – the longest they've been apart.

When he's on the mainland, he calls her every day. He tells her how much he misses her. But this morning, he was furious with her, which isn't like Kit at all. He'd been ridiculously angry about the poker game, and then he'd stropped off while she was in the shower, leaving her to go to bed alone.

Now she's finally emerged, she'll have to go over to St Mary's at some point to get antibiotics. She can't wait for the doctor to come over – there's a vet on call here, but no resident GP. If she'd been a cow in distress she'd have got treatment quicker.

Last night she'd been necking cranberry juice and bicarbonate of soda like it was going out of style. Okay, there was vodka in it as well and they'd also done more than a fair amount of weed.

She'd laughed when Vlad asked her straight out, 'Not drinking for two are you?'

'Don't be stupid,' she'd replied. But then he'd told her that was the latest rumour doing the rounds, which was insane.

Kit had asked if she wanted children when they first got together.

'Not yet,' she'd replied. 'You need to be settled, emotionally and financially, before you bring a kid into this world.'

'We could have that,' he said. 'I'd look after you.'

It was so sweet she kissed him and said, 'One day. Perhaps.'

She saw what his face did. He'd obviously sensed her hesitation and seemed hurt.

'Look, it's a nice dream, Kit, but you need to make dreams happen. A dream is worth—' she snapped her fingers, 'fresh air. There needs to be something solid behind it.'

He came up behind her and said, 'Here's something solid for you!' and they'd laughed.

Afterwards, he said, 'Kit the drone – my only role to mate with the queen.'

'Do you feel used?' she grinned.

He looked like it stung a little.

But now she and Kit aren't talking, as far as she can make out. She sent him a text as soon as she woke up this afternoon, but he hasn't replied. Stuff him, then.

She glugs down a coffee and finishes what's left of the bread before walking down to the Estate Office to see if Bobby wants her to do anything for him before her evening shift at the pub. She is tasked with taking a batch of new crockery and ceramics to Hawk, Tern and Falcon.

The cottages all have a similar vibe – upmarket holiday chic. The colour palette consists of clean blues to suggest the sea, pale woods to evoke the beaches, plus a few individual prints of seascapes and the birds the properties are named after. The shipment of new plates, cups and vases had been delayed. It was all supposed to be done and dusted before the influx of guests for the gig championships, but it is what it is.

Hannah loads the golf buggy with the heavy boxes and as she pulls away, Bobby sticks his head out the office to call after her, 'Oh, and Alison needs to see you soon as, to reorganise the shifts for this weekend. She still needs you to pull a few extra to cover the illnesses.'

'I'll pop in after I've finished this,' she promises wearily.

The afternoon is wild. A gale is gathering strength and there's the smell of rain on the wind.

Hannah parks the buggy against the cottage wall of Falcon and hoicks one of the boxes onto her hip. She knocks as a courtesy, waits a few seconds, and when there's no reply, opens the back door. Her heart sinks to see Charlotte sitting slouched over the kitchen table. She looks up at Hannah as if she's come to steal the family silver.

'Alright, Charlotte?' tries Hannah. 'I've brought over the new place settings,' she explains.

'Should you be carrying that box in your condition?' sneers Charlotte.

Hannah bristles at the dig. She thought she'd put on enough foundation and concealer to disguise the ravages of the preceding night.

She bites back any comment, to keep the peace for Bobby and Kit's sake, and places the box on the counter.

'Is it even his?' hisses Charlotte.

'I beg your pardon?'

'You won't trap him like this. His mother will make sure he gets a DNA test.' Charlotte reaches for her mug, which very obviously does not contain a nice cup of tea and Hannah finally twigs what she's implying.

'You're off your head,' she laughs.

'And you're a fat, common whore, trying to drag Kit down to your level!'

The atmosphere coagulates. 'Say that again, and I'll wipe that smile off your face,' warns Hannah. She has an immediate urge to take the flower vase out of the packing case and fling it at Charlotte's head.

'We saw you all over that man last night! Kit was *thrilled* when I told him. And Beatrice can't wait to tell him about the other chap she saw you with after I'd left. One's a mistake. Two's a habit.'

Hannah recalls giving Vlad a kiss for his birthday. Later she kissed the sailor who is Isak's latest squeeze, not that it has anything to do with bloody Charlotte and bloody Beatrice Wallace.

'So what? Kit's cool with it,' she says, with a good degree more confidence than she feels. 'Anyway, what's it to you? Keep your nose out of my business!'

Charlotte's lovely face spasms with rage.

Hannah leaves to avoid a fight. She doesn't bother unpacking the box. If Bobby says anything, she'll tell him that it's above her pay grade to deal with drunk, aggressive guests. Unless she's behind the bar.

When Hannah pulls away on the buggy she passes Beatrice, who looks to be heading towards the Flying Boat Club. The filthy look Kit's mother gives her makes Hannah's spirits wither further.

After dropping off the crockery at the other two cottages, she dumps the buggy back at the office, and sends another text to Kit. No reply. Sod him then. She heads back home and sets about doing her laundry. And as she scrubs her smalls in the sink – the good bras and knickers that only come out when Kit's around – she can't help thinking how much easier life would be if bloody Charlotte just disappeared.

She thinks of hanging her handwash on the small rotary washing line in the yard outside, but it's blowing a hooley, so she loops it over the shower rail instead. Then she makes herself a cup of coffee and takes out her tarot cards. Her spread has nothing of note. The Three of Swords in her immediate present, obviously, signifying sadness, disappointment and miscommunication – because he won't answer her bloody texts! She shuffles again to read for Kit, cuts the deck into three, turns over the top one. The Fool again – a young man smiling as he steps off the edge of a cliff. It'd serve him right.

She makes another coffee, sits for a while, and finally, a ping. Halle-bloody-lujah!

Meet me up the North End. 4pm. I have a BIG surprise for you!

That's a relief. But she'd rather not traipse all the way up there because she's knackered and she feels the storm coming, a taste of rage in the air. The clouds scudding outside are now so low, they make her feel claustrophobic.

She types, *Why? Where are you? Can't you meet me back at the cottage?*

He replies, *Don't want to spoil the surprise!*

She's irritated. But . . . she'll be working later. She might not get a chance to make up properly if she doesn't see him this afternoon and she doesn't want to let it fester. It's a waste of their time together, especially as she'll now be working pretty much all weekend.

She sets off to the pub, planning to sort out the shift rota with Alison before she goes to meet Kit.

43

John

He has been betrayed in the worst way.

He finds he cannot concentrate on his work. His hands fumble and he is uncharacteristically sharp with his colleagues. He leaves the gardens with mumbled apologies, saying he's not feeling well.

The wickedness of Eve!

He fingers the creased leaflet he found in her coat pocket last night. It burns. Vile words spinning the lie that this is a *simple medical procedure*, as if you might be having a verruca removed. It is *safe*, they claim. You will only experience *bleeding* and *mild discomfort*. There is *little risk*. But what risk to the eternal soul!

The leaflet is pure evil.

And he cannot forget the hideous statistic – one in four women choose to have an abortion. This is Sodom and Gomorrah.

The father of the child has no legal rights. He has no say.

Yet . . . what if there is something wrong with the baby?

He shakes his head to rid himself of the thought. It is not worthy of him. Whatever the child is, they will love it. However it turns out it is God's will. Who is John to question that?

Who is Mary-Jane to question that? How dare she!

The gale is blowing straight at him, pitching the occasional splatter of rain into his face. He cannot see straight. He heads down the path towards home, taking the long way around the North End. He feels the need to rail at the tides and the wind and this entire wicked world, which has corrupted his sweet Mary-Jane. He needs to roar at the elements.

He prays for God to give him strength.

He had been looking forward to their trip to the mainland tomorrow morning. Now a hot bitterness has spoiled the anticipation.

He realises he still has the secateurs in his gardening coat. He should smite her for her wickedness. He should slice off the fingers of whoever gave her the sinful leaflet.

44

Charlotte

She hates the barmaid with every fibre of her being. So mortifying, Kit preferring *that* to her!

And it has been a terrible day already. When she got in after that awful confrontation with Kit at the pub, there was no sign of Beatrice – probably gone for a walk – which meant no one was around to stop her opening the artisan handmade chocolates made right here on the islands. She wouldn't have to steal them away and hide them in her room. She promised herself she'd just have a couple. Sea salt and caramel, her favourite. Thyme and rosemary? She might give that a miss. Ginger and cayenne? A definite no – it would burn on the way back up.

And she did only have a couple – although she had also poured herself a large measure of gin.

She'd pulled out Kit's phone. She shouldn't have taken it. She's a bad person. But she just wanted to get back at him, although she hadn't really thought of what she might do with it.

He'd not changed his code – his birthday. Not very secure. She scrolled through the images: a close-up of Hannah laughing; Hannah and Kit on the beach, his arm around her, her eyes scrunched up and her mouth wide open with joy; Hannah wrapped in a duvet, her shoulders bare, looking adoringly at the camera, or the man behind it. . .

She couldn't bear it.

Then the bitch turned up and Charlotte so wanted to hurt her; she wanted to hurt her in such a way that Kit would never look at her smug face in the same way ever again.

Now Charlotte thinks *fuck it* and opens the chocolates, eating on automatic pilot, stuffing them into her mouth, two at a time, beyond the point of registering any sweetness or unique flavours, beyond feeling queasy, revolted by the mush filling her mouth, disgusted with herself—

In the bathroom she heaves until her eyes water and her stomach convulses with pain. The taste of bile and acid and shame. When she stands she feels faint.

There is a packet of Cornish shortbread in the cupboard and two tubs of clotted-cream ice cream in the freezer. She has to get away from their siren call.

She grabs her coat and rushes out.

The force of the wind catches her, flinging her back against the door, and she falters. Her head feels separate to her aching body, as if it might blow away. Good. That's what she needs right now, to blow away all the bad thoughts.

She weaves her way along the path towards the wild side of the island, lurching upwards, stumbling against the force of the wind, blinded by tears. She doesn't care. Let it all blow away.

45

Beatrice

Beatrice returns from the Flying Boat Club via the shop carrying a loaf of bread, olives, two good bottles of wine and a fresh bottle of gin, which has been disappearing at an alarming rate thanks to Charlotte. She felt it would be bad form to buy alcohol by itself. She pours herself a small measure of vodka and puts on her music. Within moments she is lost within the aria. She turns up the volume, glad to be left alone for a little while. Charlotte will probably be gambolling around the island in her ridiculous shoes. In this weather! Who on earth wears heels here. She slips off her own flat sandals, folds her feet beneath her on the sofa like a little lamb, takes a sip of her drink, and closes her eyes.

This moment to herself sours when she recalls the incident last night.

She has to admit, the evening was a disappointment. And she'd caught Hannah cavorting with not one but two young men who very obviously were not her son. She'll have to tell him, although he might well shoot the messenger.

She and Charlotte had popped into the Old Ship for a couple of early drinks, where they found Hannah slobbering over the young man from the heliport. Beatrice was shocked. Charlotte seemed delighted. Beatrice left Charlotte to her G&T with an extra slice of schadenfreude, and she set off for her evening proper. At the invitation of Fiona from the art gallery, Beatrice had partnered the Colonel for the *mobile feast* – a dinner party staged around various homes. Those who live here, like Fiona, cook the courses they serve, while visitors tend to cater their contributions. Apart from the Colonel's Beef Wellington (provided by Organ Morgan the main chef) the fayre was wholesome but basic.

The final course was coffee and a cheese board served up at the farm. Beatrice had the impression that the farmer's wife would have been happier without the intrusion of guests, while Farmer Michael himself was merely showcasing his wares.

However, the Colonel was marvellous company. She'd been quite optimistic with the way things were going.

He told a rather amusing anecdote about one of his old chums who'd recently sworn off the booze. 'But then we had a night out at the casino and I'm afraid the poor fellow overindulged. He was worried about going home to the wife in the state he was in, because unfortunately he'd been a little sick down his suit.'

Beatrice applied her tinkly laugh. She had recently found herself in a similar state, not that she'd ever admit it.

The Colonel continued, 'I said he should tell the old ball and chain someone else had vomited on his suit, and to add plausibility, I suggested he claim his assailant had donated a twenty-pound note to have it dry cleaned.'

Beatrice nibbled daintily at her cheese.

'When he arrived home, my friend pre-empted his wife's rage by telling this tale, adding, "Look in my wallet if you don't believe me. There's the twenty pounds the man gave me."'

The Colonel chuckled and continued, 'The wife checked, and said, "But, darling, there are two twenty-pound notes here," and my chum replied, "Ah. That was from the other chap who shat in my trousers."'

The evening ended early as the farm, necessarily, had an early start. After their coffees, the Colonel suggested he accompany Beatrice back to the pub. Invigorated by the blast of fresh air after the humid farmhouse kitchen, Beatrice had felt giddy and reckless. At the stile over the first field, she flung her arms around the Colonel's neck and reached up to kiss him.

She was brushed away like a gnat. 'Steady on, old girl!' He laughed, to make it a joke.

She laughed back, although the rejection stung. The *old girl* stung more.

They didn't speak of it again as their torches led them back to the path by Dolphin Corner. And that might have been an end to it.

But then . . .

Then the shame crawled out of its hidey hole. Flinging herself at someone like him! Beatrice knew they called him Colonel Blimp behind his back. And while he was a rather excellent raconteur (entertaining everyone with stories from the Christmas shoots with the royals), while he was tall (thank the Lord), looks-wise he was no great catch. *Nothing to write home about*, as her mother would have said.

The first thing they saw as they entered the pub was Hannah draped across one of the French sailors, a huge shaven-headed creature with a neck as thick as one of the barmaid's thighs. Hannah was laughing loudly as the brute gnawed at her neck and the Colonel turned to Alison and said, 'Oh, to be that young man! Beguiling creature, young Hannah.'

And to rub salt into the wound, as he carried their wine over to a free table, she heard him muttering to himself, 'The full gravy, that girl.' He was positively salivating.

Beatrice had to stop herself grabbing Hannah and dragging her off the young man. First the heliport worker and now this! How could she humiliate Kit like that!

Hannah seemed oblivious to Beatrice's presence. She disappeared with the sailor a few minutes later. Alison said they'd only come back to the bar to grab another bottle because the poker party had run out of vodka.

Beatrice had sat rigidly alongside the Colonel, simmering.

Back at Falcon, she had a restless night, punctuated by images of her own lost youth when she herself had flirted with many unsuitable men. She dreamt of the fights with her husband, the man who had stolen so much from her – the years when she was desirable, the years when she was confident, the years she had some self-respect.

She woke in the early hours hot with humiliation.

No wonder she needs a drink.

46

The Old Ship

The bar is awash with outrage. Housekeeping have not shut up about it. Before skedaddling over to Penzance on their boat this morning, the guests in Razorbill had a party last night. Now the cleaners are refusing to touch the place. Someone has apparently urinated in a saucepan, and that's the least of it. The sofa has been damaged by cigarette burns, glassware's been smashed, most of the windows have been left wide open – in this weather! – and to literally top it all, one giant human turd sits languishing aloft the golf buggy parked at a crazy angle outside the timeshare property, taken, to add insult to injury, without being signed out at the Estate Office.

'How the bloody hell did it get up there?' asks Alison.

'Must've chucked it out the bathroom window,' guesses Bobby. 'But we'll never know for sure.'

The holidaymakers, first-time visitors, will be hit with a hefty penalty charge for their misdemeanours and forfeit both their deposit and any chance of staying here again. Unless bookings are especially dire.

There has also been outrage on the water – Mark Pender caught a crab during the St Agnes Down, which caused chaos, and the first race of the championship to finish in St Mary's Harbour with a shouting match. Bleddy stupid mistake. Cost the *Czar* crew a win.

'I thought they were racing, not crab fishing,' whispers one of the guests from Puffin. He is informed that 'to catch a crab' in this context, means, in technical terms, someone has 'totally fucked up their stroke, totally fucked up the flow, and totally fucked their crew'.

Spectators and rowers alike are spitting feathers over Mark Pender's cock-up.

In the worker's cottage several doors down from the Old Ship, Christie is also spitting feathers. Literally. The twins have had an epic pillow fight and their room now looks like a snow globe. If she believed in signs, the flurries of white feathers might signify a host of angels. Christie does not believe in signs. The day has served to wind her up good and proper, starting earlier this morning.

Old Betty came round first thing to give Christie a big casserole dish.

'I'm having a spring clean. Don't be needing this just for me. Thought you'd make better use, and job's a good 'un.'

'Thanks, Miss Elisabeth,' said Christie, already on the back foot, already stressed.

The cat ambled over to wind itself against Old Betty's vari-cose veins. She dipped in slow motion to stroke its back.

'Oh, she's a sweetie, this one. Pretty girl, aren't you. Pretty maid.'

Tommy piped up, 'Please don't misgender our cat.'

'What you talking about, young 'un?' asked Betty, straighten-ing with attendant creaks and cleaning her glasses on the sleeve of her cardigan.

'We thought Tabs was a girl, but they're not,' said Tommy.

'We called it Tabitha at first,' Christie attempted to clarify. 'Anyway, time to get going, young man. The school boat's on its way.'

Tommy stomped upstairs to get his books just as the twins kicked off, fighting over who got to play with the build-your-own dinosaur.

'Ben. Ben! It's your brother's turn, let him—'

'Shut up, you!' shouted Ben as Dan screamed in frustration.

'You going to let that little *heller* talk to you like that?' said Betty, shocked. 'They're running rings around you, this lot.'

The cat, reading the room, departed.

By the time Betty left, Christie was seething. Judged for her parenting skills. Judged by her own bloody kids. Yesterday Tommy had a go at her for throwing plastic in the bin rather than the recycling, and even though he was right, she felt awful. She's all for saving the world but some days she's just too bloody tired to rinse out a yoghurt pot.

Just then, to add insult to injury, she noticed Hannah strut-ting by outside the window, pausing to stroke the cat who was parading up and down the garden wall.

'Traitor,' hissed Christie.

This afternoon she dumps the twins and Finn on poor Emma yet again. Sam swore he'd be home by lunchtime to provide cover, but there's still no sign of him and she needs to go out to get something for everyone's tea.

As she hurries to the shop, she stokes her anger at her bloody husband. This morning he'd apologised for staying out late last night playing cards at the poker night for Vlad's birthday, and he promised, yet again, to cut down on the drinking. He swore he'd pull his weight more with the kids. He hugged and kissed her, and she'd forgiven him, as usual, because she was desperate to believe him.

She called him an hour and a half ago, and he vowed he'd be back to help out as soon as he'd finished replacing the fuse box in Skua, but there's still no bloody sign of him.

In the shop Christie picks up two packs of fish fingers, and a bottle of cider for herself. By the till, Isak Mensah is laughing with one of the French sailors and a couple of the lads from housekeeping. She's exploring the ice-cream section of the fridge when she hears them talking about the card game and her ears prick up. It had been a great night, a fun night. Vlad apparently lost a week's wages. But when she hears the words *strip poker* and *Hannah* her heart plummets down through her knees to her boots.

She didn't know the barmaid had been there.

She abandons her shopping basket on the floor, not waiting to hear that Sam had already left by the time the clothes came off.

She strides to the Old Ship, guessing that's where Sam will be, hurtling through the door to the bar like a gunslinger. 'Where the bloody hell is he?' she demands.

'Sam? He's doing a job for me. Do you need him?' asks Alison.

'Yes I bloody need him!' snaps Christie, glaring at Hannah, who's with Alison on the other side of the bar.

Alison orders Christie to sit and wait while someone fetches Sam, who's working upstairs. The last thing Christie wants is to sit down or calm down, but Alison says, 'I do not want World War bloody Three in the bedrooms, you hear me? I've got guests up there. Get a bloody grip!'

A boisterous group of gig rowers arrive so Alison whispers to Hannah to go up and get Sam because she's too busy.

'I'll serve this lot if you like,' says Hannah. 'You get him.'

'If you start serving this lot, you'll be stuck here, and I thought you had to be off to meet Kit at four.'

'Okay,' says Hannah. Alison's right – if she's to make it up to the North End in time, she'll have to get cracking.

She hurries up the stairs, and when she enters Room 3, she can immediately tell Sam has been drinking by the way his mouth hangs slack, or he might be still leathered from the poker game last night. He's kneeling in the far corner, his tool belt by his side, hammering in tacks along the carpet edge. His movements are sloppy.

'Your wife wants you,' says Hannah.

'Is that so?' he says, ignoring the summons, continuing hammering.

'She seems upset.'

'See this,' Sam gestures to the floor. 'Like a woman, a carpet – lay it right the first time and you can walk all over her for the rest of your life. Proper job.'

'You're a pig,' says Hannah.

'You used to like it, a bit of rutting,' he laughs, and snorts.

'And I used to like playing with matches before I knew any better,' she replies.

'Want a replay?' he indicates the bed.

'Just fuck off, Sam.'

He'd not been this belligerent last night, probably because the other card players were her mates as much as his.

Sam gets to his feet, stretches and then lunges for her, grabbing her arm and slinging her round so she falls awkwardly on the mattress.

'You think you're something, don't you.' It's not a question. 'You couldn't wait for a bit of this.' He makes an obscene gesture.

'As I recall, the one night I spent with you, you'd drunk so much you couldn't get it up.'

He kneels across her, laughing and tickling her in a way that is in no way humorous.

'Get off me!' She wriggles and gasps, finally managing to roll away and push him off. She scrambles up off the bed and tries to leave, but he scuttles round so he's between her and the door.

'Are you going to scream?' he sneers. He takes one step towards her, half playful, half menacing.

She takes a breath. 'Sam. Stop it. This isn't you.'

He pauses a second, then lunges forwards and grabs at her arm, catching her breast. She slaps him as hard as she can.

He jolts back, rears up like a cobra and roars, 'I WILL NOT HAVE ANOTHER FUCKING WOMAN HIT ME!' and he launches himself at her. Hannah manages to step back and smash her fist into his face.

His shock gives her enough time to dodge round him. She legs it back down to the bar where Christie is still pacing.

'Where is he?' she demands.

'In Room 3,' says Hannah, aware that her hair's a mess and her clothes are rumpled.

Christie ignores Alison, mid pint-pull, calling, 'Don't even think about—' and thunders up the stairs.

Hannah reckons it's best to make a quick getaway, but Alison says, 'Finish this round for me, will you?' and she heads upstairs after Christie.

Hannah takes deep breaths in through her nose as she pulls four more pints on automatic pilot, until her heart calms.

Despite everything, she feels for Sam. The one night they'd spent together, he lay beside her and told her all about Christie. And he's never forgiven her for that – for knowing his secrets. He let the others gossip about his *fling* with Hannah, added fuel to the fire, joked about it, because that was easier than people knowing that they'd shared something more intimate than sex. He'd trusted her.

Ever since, he's hated her for what she knows, even though Hannah's never breathed a word.

The pub is heaving. Hannah doesn't recognise half the faces. There's already a party atmosphere which might well turn ugly later tonight. Something's brewing.

Alison comes back downstairs to a line of punters still queuing to be served. 'Don't know where bloody Sam's got to. Christie's up there prowling the corridors in case he comes back for his tool belt, but I'll have to let them get on with it.'

'Right, I'm off to the North End,' says Hannah, 'I'm late.' She wonders what Kit's *big surprise* might be.

'I'll be back for my shift later. I'll take your bike if that's okay. My brakes are knackered.' (Of course it's okay, Alison has never been seen on the bike that lives in the pub garden.) Hannah calls a cheery farewell.

She's barely got outside when her phone buzzes again. It's Kit. *Charlotte, darling, where are you?*

What the actual fuck? *Charlotte, darling?*

She's jostled by two rowers still in their kit.

If he's doing this to try and make her jealous, he's bloody succeeded. Or does he think he's meeting Charlotte up the North End?

Hannah is bloody raging.

A big group of spectators invade the pub garden. She wheels the bike straight through the middle of them, causing two to fling themselves out of her path, then she disappears, the crowd closing around her.

Neither Hannah nor Alison have noticed Sam sneaking down the back stairs. As soon as he heard his wife shouting for him he legged it into another bedroom to wait it out and avoid her. Now he slips into the gents, where he splashes his face with cold water, stares at himself in the mirror, and shouts, 'FUCK! FUCK! FUCK!' so loudly he terrifies one of the guests in the cubicle.

A couple of minutes after Hannah's left, Sam reappears and pushes his way through to the crammed bar, where Alison seems to be wrestling one of the rowdy spectators who's waving a pool cue above his head.

He shouts over to her, 'Where's your bloody barmaid?'

'Your wife is upstairs after your blood,' she shouts back, disarming the visitor.

'You after Hannah?' asks Old Betty, sitting expectantly, accepting offers of drinks at Table 1. 'She's just left – off to the North End.'

Sam does not buy Betty a drink. He immediately sets off after the barmaid.

47

Christie

She's sick of people looking at her with their heads on the side, as if to say, *Poor Christie. A dog's life, that woman. So much on her plate with the lads and that husband. The fights they have! Everyone can hear them. He cheated on her with the barmaid, didn't he?*

They think she's a victim, *poor, poor Christie.*

She is not a fucking victim. She is no one's fucking doormat.

She's the one who punches, throws things, smashes her fist against his thick head, kicks him in the balls. He's the one with the black eye, spit lip, bruised arm. Naturally, people assume he fell down while drunk, fought with the builders, hurt himself at work. But it was her. She broke his toe stamping on his foot. She fractured his little finger slamming a bottle of wine on his hand. He tries to push her off, of course he does, and sometimes he pushes her over, trying to get her away from him, get her off him, but he's never hit her first. He's never hit her meaning to do her serious harm.

Christie has three brothers. She grew up scrapping. She knows how to hold her own. She always hits first. She always means to hurt him.

He always bloody deserves it.

There's no sign of Sam anywhere upstairs. When Alison goes back to the bar, Christie sits on the bed in Room 3 for a moment to gather herself. She wants to hit him very hard right now, to do real damage – perhaps with that lamp on the bedside table there, fake art nouveau, heavy. Cave in his fucking skull.

Things are getting on top of her and they're coming to a head with her and Sam. She can't even trust him with his own kids, for Christ's sake! And she definitely can't trust him around bloody Hannah. She sees the way he looks at her, no matter how many times he tells her it was just the one night, nothing happened, he swears, they were both off their heads, as if that excuses it. When he stays out late, it's never anything to do with the barmaid – how many times has he told her that? He always has an alibi.

Liar.

He's pushed her too far this time. She is done. Strip bloody poker! He has put her through the wringer for the last time. Everyone will know about that by tomorrow. She can imagine the looks when that gets around the island. She would very much like to rip Sam's heart out.

But . . . she loves him. Always has. Always will.

Christie comes back down the stairs. A group of young French sailors are falling about, Big Bob leading them in filthy choruses of 'Mademoiselle from Armentières'.

'You've just missed him. He went to the bog and then left,' says Alison.

'He went after Hannah,' pipes up Old Betty. Alison flashes her an exasperated look.

'Where's she gone?'

'She said something about the North End,' says Betty helpfully.

'I'll bloody kill the pair of them when I get my hands on them.'

Christie hurries out. She grabs one of the bikes left outside the pub, battling the wind hurtling tiny needles of rain into her face. She puts her head down and pedals hard. She's so intent on what she'd like to do to her fuckwit husband and that little cow if she finds them, when she gets to the corner by the heliport, she doesn't immediately notice the figure in a pink coat. The woman steps out into the road immediately in front of the bike and Christie almost runs into her.

'Fuck!' Christie brakes sharply, shouting, 'Sorry!'

She is not sorry, she's angry with the stupid idiot. It's that blonde girl who's been staying with Beatrice Wallace. Charlotte, is it?

'No, it was me,' says Charlotte. 'I wasn't looking where I was going. I just needed to go for a walk, you know. Blow away the cobwebs.'

Twat. 'Not the weather for a walk,' snaps Christie, setting off again. If she doesn't find Sam on the path up to the North End she'll leave the bike at the bottom and climb up the rocks. And if he's up there with her, *Hannah*, she'll kill him; she'll bloody kill them both.

V

May, the Storm

48

Thor

She thinks she's it.

Thor's watched her strut around the island like she owns the place. When he serves her in the shop, when he stands close to her in the pub, her eyes slide off him like he doesn't exist.

She doesn't see him now because he doesn't mean her to. He presses himself flat against the rocks and watches.

They all think they're it, fucking bitches.

She's standing looking out to sea, her hair billowing behind her, like some stupid advert for some stupid shampoo.

He pulls on the balaclava, and creeps towards her, feeling like a lion stalking its prey.

He will make her see him. He'll show her – she's nothing.

He doesn't hear the first scream because the weather is too loud. He grabs her hair and jerks her head back, dragging her towards the leeward side of the cliff. Away from the worst of the wind he sneers at the usual pleas, 'No! Stop! Please!' They all say the same stuff on Pornhub. Boring.

He wrenches her hair tighter so he can twist her head round to face him, and he tells her she's *nothing*. He tells her he can do whatever he wants to her. He kisses her hard, and she struggles, her hands slapping at him – pathetic – but her teeth hurt his lips, so he pulls away and punches her in the face. Her legs fold.

Then he's standing above her and she's on her knees hanging by the hair in his fist which is good. Her face is a mess of snot and blood and tears. But something's wrong. It's not how he thought it would be. He thought she'd fight back more. He wanted her to fight him. Now he's not feeling it, no matter what he calls her – all the usual bitch-slut-cunt combos – no matter how much she cries and begs.

The rain starts thrashing down and he feels cold, so he gets on with it.

He swings her round and puts his knee on her back to force her down and tells her what he's going to do to her and how she's been asking for it, and he reaches across to his bag. He strokes the wooden handle on the meat cleaver.

She rolls over and puts up her arm just as he slashes at her, as if that could protect her. Stupid cunt.

He's just beginning to feel it, but to the right, there's a shout. Someone else is up here. Nearby.

Fuck.

He's pretty sure no one can see them, but—

She's not worth it. Quickly he punches her a few more times just to be done, then he grabs his sports bag and runs, leaving her curled in a ball like a stupid animal, the rain battering her body.

But as he runs, before he's taken off the balaclava, the other one sees him . . .

VI

May, After the Storm

49

Bobby

The phone call comes mid-morning, when Bobby is at a low ebb, the time he'd prefer a nap or a gallon of coffee, especially now with so many visitors clogging the islands for the World Pilot Gig Championships. So busy, so many demands, so much potential for mayhem.

An unfortunate night which started in the pub and ended with him back home, drinking alone, watching *Some Like It Hot* for the zillionth time; he finished off the Tarquin's gin as the storm battered his windows.

The news makes him sit down heavily in his office chair, alert now, but struggling as he tries to make sense of what he's hearing. The shock catches him hard in his solar plexus.

Police need details of the next of kin.

One worker in the ICU. One worker dead.

St Nicholas's Church

There is something of the kicked dog about the woman.

She has sat alongside The Family in the front pew, hunched over, but now she pulls herself up, squeezes back her shoulders, marches forwards. Some in the congregation hold their breath for her. She does not inspire confidence in those heels.

The impression is of a pigeon as she totters up to speak. Her legs are like Twiglets, her feet tiny, her chest ample. She wears a large black hat on unfeasibly blue-black hair.

She manages the small step up to the lectern, turns to the sea of unfamiliar faces, and unfolds two sheets of paper. She swallows, and then starts her eulogy.

It was explained to her that it is not a eulogy as such. She can say some words about her daughter and ask for the search to continue. That is all. But she has been missing two weeks already.

She reads slowly and surely in a strange accent. It is a brave thing to do, speaking to honour a daughter when there is no body to bury, and so many unanswered questions whipping up confusion and anger and suspicion. There is a great deal of sympathy from the islanders for this grieving soul – those in the pews silently urge her on while also praying that it will soon be over.

The mother fumbles her papers and one sheet flutters away from her hands. She takes a sidestep, lunging after it, and stumbles, grabbing the lectern to stop herself plunging forwards. There's a collective gasp as her hat comes loose and skims over the front pews like a mournful frisbee.

Two girls sobbing at the back of the church are shocked into silence. The police family liaison officer steps forwards to help.

Alison whispers to Old Betty sitting next to her, 'Enough Dutch courage to sink a bloody fleet.' Miss Elisabeth feels the comment and the swearing in church to be in bad taste.

Little Daisy, Emma's second youngest, sitting squashed alongside her mother on the hard wooden seat, wonders what it is like to die, to be no more. She will not be able to sleep tonight, for fear of not waking up again. She will wet the bed for several months. Emma will blame herself for bringing her today.

Kit is amazed the woman at the front has stayed upright so long. He is a total mess. He cannot get the image of his father's coffin out of his mind. He didn't manage a reading at his father's funeral. But this is not a funeral. There can be no funeral.

At some point, the organ signals it's over, thank the Lord and all the saints above, and the congregation scampers outside to freedom. They can finally breathe. The sun is bright and the fresh breeze playfully blows fluffy lamb-like clouds across the sky.

On the path outside the church The Family speak in hushed tones to their flock. 'Yes. Terrible business.'

257

Bobby affixes himself to the mother's side, steering her around to talk to islanders and a few guests who have come to gawk – no! – who have come to pay their respects; colleagues and friends who want to offer self-conscious condolences and share a few neutered memories. They do not speak ill of the missing-unofficially-presumed-dead, *so these are abridged, sanitised tales.*

They are careful not to mention the others – the two women who were attacked right here on this lovely island at the time she went missing. They do not want to add images of violence to the mother's burden.

Close up, people observe the mother's hollow eyes. She seems not to hear their words, seems more absence than presence. There are no tears, so some feel she is hard, unfeeling. Others declare her brave.

But her grief is so huge it is eating her away from the inside, like a cancer.

She is dazed. She did not notice the double rainbow the previous afternoon, the frolicking dolphin in the distance as she sat rigid as a figurehead on the boat over from St Mary's, the chirpy sparrow which alighted on her hand as she sat at a table outside the Old Ship.

Now people tell her things about her daughter and tell her nothing.

It is a tight-knit community here – she hears the phrase several times. It is meant to assure her that her daughter was cared for; people watch out for each other here, she is missed. But all this means to her is that the community might unravel a little, but then it will swiftly re-stitch itself around the absence, like a shroud.

The gulls call out their own praises and laments – boisterous, the souls of the departed. It is a more fitting farewell. They shit on the heads of the guilty and the righteous alike.

50

Beatrice

She's very cold. Every muscle in her body protesting. Her head screeching. She finds herself on the bathroom floor. God, how humiliating.

Somehow Beatrice manages to haul herself up to sit on the side of the bath. She leans over to turn on the sink tap, desperate to get water into her mouth as fast as possible. But when she tries to move her jaw, it hurts so much it feels like it might detach itself from her skull.

In front of her a tangle of wet clothes from yesterday, everything totally sodden right through to her underwear.

Thankfully, she appears to have managed to wrap herself in a dressing gown before, presumably, falling asleep here last night. It would have been unforgiveable if Charlotte had found her naked.

But when she eventually manages to pull herself to her feet and, with some trepidation, walks across the landing to

Charlotte's room, Beatrice finds it's empty. It doesn't look as if her bed has been slept in either. Where on earth can she have gone? Perhaps she got lucky. Perhaps she has plunged over a precipice in her silly heels.

Beatrice loads the washing machine with her soaking garments and hangs up her coat to drip dry in the utility room, every movement revealing more damage.

When she returns to the bathroom to run a hot bath, she catches sight of herself in the mirror. She is shocked by the state of her face. She rinses off the blood while she waits for the bath to fill.

As she gingerly steps into the warm water there is the sudden image of the man in the black balaclava – she gasps, slips and twists her ankle as she jolts down in the bath, splashing water everywhere. She recalls going over on that same foot as she ran down the path from the North End, terrified that he'd catch up with her, desperate to escape. God. The thought of what might have happened, what might still happen, makes her heave.

51

Kit

Kit calls into the pub to ask if anyone has seen Hannah.

'She didn't turn up for her shift last night and she's not here this morning, as you can see,' huffs Alison, frantic and flustered at the busy bar. 'She's not replied to my messages, and here's me, knee deep in bacon butties and coffees for the brunch mob. Tell her to get her arse over here as soon as you find her!'

'She didn't come back to the cottage last night.' Kit is fretful. He waited in for her, had a few glasses of wine, had a few more, but despite himself he fell asleep.

Yesterday he'd left his jacket here. When he popped back to retrieve it he'd thought his phone would be in the pocket, but it wasn't. He assumed he'd left it in the bedroom, but it wasn't there either.

He says, 'I still can't find my phone. Can you try calling her again?'

Alison clearly has zero fucks left to give, and too many

punters to serve. 'I don't care, Kit. And unless Miss Hannah is dying, or dead in a ditch, she's out on her ear. I mean it. If she doesn't get here pronto, I'm done with her and I'm not bloody joking.'

Her face tells him as much.

There's no one home at Vlad's, so Kit walks round to Hannah's accommodation, not that she spends much time there when he's on the island. It's a glorious morning. The sea was insane with the storm yesterday afternoon, but it's now flat as a mill-pond despite the breeze, the water deceptively mild, harbour-ing its secrets.

Kit's knock at the worker's cottage is greeted with a 'Come in! We're indecent!' and giggles.

Hannah's two housemates are both sitting cross-legged on the sofa, their knees bumping. The windows have steamed up, presumably with a recent shower, and it smells of strawberry body cream. Molly is rolling a fat joint while Elle is dipping a slice of pizza into ketchup and they're watching an old cop series on the TV with the volume low. They're both wearing tiny bra tops and shorts.

'Hi,' they say in unison.

'What happened here?' he asks. The place looks like it's been burgled.

'We had to let the butler go,' deadpans Molly.

'Have you seen my girlfriend? She's AWOL.'

'No. Wanna join us for the breakfast of champions?' chirps Elle.

'No thanks. Could you call her? My phone's gone missing. She might have been trying to get in touch. And she needs to call Alison immediately.'

'Okay,' says Molly.

'And if you see her, can you tell her to come find me?'

'Sure you don't want to join us?' jokes Elle, licking her pizza slice in a pornographic manner.

'It's gone straight to voicemail,' says Molly.

The girls giggle as he leaves.

Kit walks up to the Estate Office. It's busy this morning; groups of day visitors are making their way to the good lookout spots to watch the gig racing.

There's a queue at the desk in the office, but Bobby is putting on his jacket, rushing to head out. Kit manages to grab him before he closes the door and ushers the visitors away.

'Hannah's gone missing,' says Kit.

'She'll turn up,' replies Bobby. His face looks ashen.

'Any idea where she might be?'

'No.'

'She's not at her place or Vlad's and—'

'Look, Kit, I don't know. I'm a bit busy with other things right now.'

'She's not at work either,' says Kit, following Bobby round to the cycle rack.

'That's Alison's problem, not mine.'

'She didn't call in sick. She might have been trying to get in contact with me but I've mislaid my phone. I thought she might call you.'

Bobby wheels his bike out of the stand. 'She hasn't. Look, Kit, old chap, I'm up to my eyes in it here. There are bigger fish to fry.'

'But—'

'Kindly fuck the fuck off will you,' says Bobby, straddling his bike and pedalling away.

'Do you know anyone else she might be with? Anyone she might—' Kit starts to run after Bobby, swerving around Old Betty, who's heading for the office, almost bumping into her.

She protests, 'Watch where you're—'

'Oh for Christ's sake,' he snaps.

As Kit rushes away, Miss Elisabeth is left fuming.

52

Bobby

After yesterday's storm, all was calm and bright as the helicopter made for the mainland. Mary-Jane and John left on the first flight this morning. John had a hire car waiting at Penzance and he was probably rushing to get to the Eden Project, keen to show his beloved wife the magic wrought within that old china clay pit, Cornwall's premier attraction, driving east into the sun's rays reflecting off wet, greasy roads. He had not driven for a long time.

He was killed outright according to the Truro police.

In the HR file Bobby discovered Mary-Jane had put John as both her next of kin and In Case of Emergency. Likewise, John has Mary-Jane listed. As soon as he's ditched Kit, Bobby pedals over to the couple's cottage, aiming to forage for more information. Several visitors remark on how he cycles by without so much as a 'Good morning!' Very unlike him.

It's been a while since Bobby was inside this particular

worker's cottage. Pretty matching curtains and cushions in pinks, blues and lemons. It's twee, a Cath Kidston wet dream.

He rootles through drawers – downstairs they're neatly packed with kitchen utensils and tea towels; upstairs, folded clothes and home-made lavender sachets.

There's a Bible on John's bedside table, an inscription inside: *To My Darling Boy, John. All My Love, Mom XXXXXX*. Bobby hasn't had much time for the book himself – hardly an ally, the Almighty – although Bobby always goes to the church services, just to be social, just to show his face. It would be remarked upon otherwise.

He finds the passports in a bureau on Mary-Jane's side of the bed – Mr and Mrs Smith. He recalls her saying in that whispery southern voice, 'Of course I took his name. We're old-fashioned, aren't we, darlin'?' He wonders if he remembers that because it was rare to hear Mary-Jane speak when the two of them were together. Compared with her husband she was the shrinking violet, a surrendered wife. He was the confident one – so esteemed by the garden team, so . . . *bumptious* is the word that comes to mind.

Bobby blushes to be thinking ill of the dead.

In Mary-Jane's neatly rolled underwear drawer, right at the bottom, he finds there's an old-fashioned address book with purple teddy bears on the front. It is something a teenager might have. He flicks through it. There's an address somewhere he's never heard of in Georgia, USA, and a phone number under M for Mom.

Bobby sits on the bed and steels himself. There is no rush to track down John's relatives – nothing to be done immediately, all too late. Informing them will be a job for the police. But

Mary-Jane's mother may want to get on the next plane over. Time may be of the essence. All he knows is that she's in the ICU. He's probably overstepping the mark, but surely the news is best coming from a *friend*, or at least someone who knows Mary-Jane as an employer.

He taps in the number. Waits, both impatient and reluctant.

A sleepy soft drawl on the end of the line, 'Hello?'

'Er, hello. I'm so sorry to disturb you in the middle of the night.' Is it night there? He is blurry on time zones. 'Is this Mary-Jane's mother?' He doesn't know Mary-Jane's maiden name.

'Sure is, darlin'. Who is this?' She sounds tipsy.

'My name is Robert Parkinson. I'm calling from Tresco, the Isles of Scilly, in the United Kingdom. Your daughter works for us over here. I'm afraid there's been an accident.'

'Oh lawd!' gasps the voice.

'She's in hospital in Truro. I can give you the number. I'm afraid we don't have all the details yet. A car crash I believe.'

'Lawd! Lawd!' exclaims the voice again. There's a shaky breath. Bobby frantically thinks of what is best to say next, but before he can say anything, the woman continues, 'And John? He was with her?'

He's not sure if this is his place to say. But it's too late now. It would be cruel not to tell her about her son-in-law. 'I'm so sorry. It seems he was killed outright.'

There's a blood-curdling scream, which skewers Bobby.

'NO!'

The invention of the telephone was an act of sheer torture for a circumstance like this.

Noisy sobs. 'When?' Gasps. 'How?'

Bobby swallows, his mouth dry, and says, 'It was earlier this morning, our time. I'm so sorry. I don't have all the details.'

There's a pause, then more strangled whimpers.

'John!' she wails. 'No!'

It jars that she seems less concerned about her own daughter. She hasn't asked about her injuries.

'I'm so sorry,' he offers. 'Would you like me to help you arrange a flight over here?' It's the least he can do. The Family will cover the mother's expenses and he's just about to explain this when there's a pitiful yelp of, 'My boy!'

Something nags at Bobby which he can't quite make sense of. 'My son!'

She must have been exceptionally close to her son-in-law, he reasons. Then he has a fleeting thought that she might mean this in a religious sense, because he recalls John being very enthusiastic in church – a bit too American with all the smiling and singing. But he feels the chill of the knowledge an instant before she says, 'Peas in a pod, those two. Always so close, my children.'

She continues talking, confirming the source of the shock spreading icy fingers across the back of his neck.

'Thank God she was with him. They sure loved each other, those two. Always so close. I'm glad he wasn't alone, you know?'

He's not sure what else he says exactly. He shares basic information – his number, the hospital's, the police contact. He disconnects.

Then he sits, winded as the information sinks in.

Mr and Mrs Smith, Mary-Jane and John, the *happily marrieds* – brother and sister.

53

The Gig Race

'DAB UP!'

Despite yesterday's brutal storm, the conditions are near-on perfect for the first outing of the morning, the Nut Rock Race. A beautiful day, clear water ahead. There are cheers and whoops from spectators and rowers alike, the atmosphere thrilling.

Coxswain Gill Pender, with her advantageous physique – body the size of a storm petrel, lungs the size of a beer barrel – braces, and at the signal shouts, 'STROKE!' and they're off.

Gill is peeved because Mary Enys was obviously on the piss last night, and nerves or no nerves, today is too important to risk. The five other rowers are taking up some of her slack.

Pilot gigs are heavy boats, with a history of rowing out in heavy seas to rescue ships in distress. The first gig to get to the ship would be paid. Money is on the line today, but more importantly, pride.

Gill urges on her girls, aiming for that moment when the

individuals blur into a single unified machine, powering the boat onwards. The Newquay crew are out on their right. The young Bristol rowers are showing their inexperience, already lagging behind.

They need to make a good showing today. They're in desperate need of a new boat, built to spec, which will cost upwards of thirty grand. They need to attract sponsorship.

There's no way they'll beat the American team – glossy-haired Amazonians who train on Power Plates apparently, with an actual sports psychologist making the trip over with them. But as long as they come second, all will be well. No one takes the Americans seriously. Gill is embarrassed to admit that she and some others started a rumour that the American women are all on steroids. By the looks of their shoulders, it might even be true.

'STROKE!' she screams louder, working at least as hard as the rowers. They just need to beat bloody Newquay.

When they finish there'll be a few pints in the Mermaid first, standing outside in the glorious sunshine, then it's over to the Old Ship, where you won't be able to get served for at least twenty minutes, so you need to get three rounds in at once. It will be heaving tonight.

The gig starts to pull ahead, and Gill is filled with a sense of wild joy.

She takes in a huge lungful of oxygen and screams, 'STROKE!'

The gulls wheel above, crying encouragement.

She's left the kids home alone for the first time today. Right now she guesses they'll be doing their hair and putting on too much make-up, because they're at that age, thirteen and fourteen, and in an hour both of them will be outdoors watching the races from the Tresco end. She's not worried though. Safest place in the world.

54

Emma

Emma is at the front door of the community centre ready to open up in preparation for the children's tea party this afternoon. The event is designed to keep kids and parents away from the pub, which will be rammed with visitors. It's also somewhere any islanders who are rowing or watching the races can dump their offspring while they get on with it. Emma doesn't need to use her key because Old Betty has forgotten to lock up again. That's not such a big deal because the bar is always secured by barman Will Ash (whose brain is several decades younger and a good deal more reliable), and booze is the only thing anyone might want to take. The Old Ship will be the focal point for most of the gig-championship partying, but there will also be a big do for the Tresco crews here tomorrow, so it's already fully stocked.

Emma doesn't immediately switch on the lights. Half the room is flooded with sunlight, chairs stacked neatly along the other side.

As her eyes adjust to the shadow bisecting the room she notices someone has left a large bag under one of the tables at the back. Why wasn't that cleared away? She'll have to have a word with Old Betty. Only, as she approaches, the bag moves.

For a moment, Emma freezes. It is only when her eyes make out it's someone lying in a contorted heap that she galvanises herself. She kneels to find a woman half-dressed beneath a pink coat, her face bloody and swollen, her skin perishingly cold to the touch. Jesus! She covers her with her own jacket, to warm her up and preserve her modesty.

Emma gently shakes her shoulder, and asks, 'Hello. Can you hear me? Are you okay?'

She is very obviously not okay.

Emma phones Vlad, who's one of the first responders on duty today, trying to keep her voice professional. 'Injured woman in the community centre. Possible hypothermia. Um. . .' She can't think of the posh word for bruises. 'Oh yes, contusions.'

'On my way.'

Emma feels sick but manages to keep it together to call the pub next. Nurse Kelly has let her flat on Airbnb for the gig weekend, a lucrative deal, and she's staying with Alison at the Old Ship for the duration.

Then she calls the police station on St Mary's.

While Emma waits for medical help, she gently rubs the woman's hands between her own to warm them up. The state she's in, she's obviously been attacked, so she tells her it will all be okay, and that help is coming – what else can you say?

Within fifteen minutes, Vlad and the nurse arrive, informing Emma that Sergeant Jack Moore is already on his way over from St Mary's.

Vlad stands to the side and looks away as Kelly does a pre-liminary check to ascertain they don't need the Air Ambulance, as far as she can tell. They'll travel over to St Mary's hospital by the jet boat, although they'll have to avoid the racers and spectators. There's a flurry of calls.

55

Kit and Beatrice

Kit is heading back to Kittiwake to see if Hannah's turned up there, when he spots Vlad driving a golf buggy towards him, a woman wrapped in a silver space blanket leaning heavily against the nurse in the back. She raises her head as they pass, and he realises it's Charlotte. He runs towards them, calling 'Charlotte! Charlotte!' and Vlad stops.

Charlotte's face is a swollen mess of cuts and bruises. She's shivering in violent spasms and her eyes don't seem to be focusing. Kelly hugs the girl to her side.

'Charlotte, what—? Are you okay? Is she okay?'

Charlotte says nothing. She closes her eyes.

'What the hell happened to her?' asks Kit.

'We're taking her to the hospital right now. Emma just found her like this,' explains Vlad. 'Have to get going.'

'Some madman attacked her,' says Kelly. The nurse looks upset and angry. 'She said it was somewhere up the North End yesterday. Police are on their way over. Check on Hannah and your mum!'

'Who? What—?'

'Now!' says Kelly. 'Make sure they're both okay!'

Kit leans in and asks, 'Charlotte, who did this to you?'

She whispers something that doesn't make any sense and Vlad says again, 'We have to get going,' and the golf buggy pulls away.

'Some man in a balaclava,' shouts Kelly as they pass. 'Some bloody madman is on the loose.'

Kit tries to make sense of this news. Who'd want to hurt Charlotte? He jogs up to Falcon, which is nearer than Kittiwake, and bursts in to find his mother splayed on the sofa.

'Mother. Mother! Mum!' Is she asleep or unconscious?

Beatrice hates to be called *Mum*. She stretches slowly. Everything is excruciating. She rolls over carefully, and he gasps.

'God, your face! What happened?'

Beatrice says nothing because she has no clear memory of what exactly happened, but she senses it's terrible, whatever it was. She tries to keep very still as everything hurts. Her son will accuse her of drinking too much and start nagging again. It is so wearisome.

But then she remembers, and she winces.

'Are you injured anywhere else?' His mother looks as bad as Charlotte.

Beatrice attempts to shake her head and winces again.

Kit kneels before her, looking so worried it brings tears to Beatrice's eyes.

Kit is shocked by his mother's display of emotion. 'Is it bad?

Where does it hurt?' he asks.

Her voice is shaky. 'It's nothing to worry about, darling. I'm just a little woozy.'

Speaking is a trial. Her jaw throbs. She is desperately touched that her son is so concerned.

'What happened?'

'I had a . . . tumble. Running. There was a man . . .'

'Were you up at the North End with Charlotte?'

'Why—?'

'Because I've just seen her. God! She's in a terrible state. They're taking her to hospital right now. A man attacked her up there yesterday!'

'A man. Yes. Couldn't see his face . . . I was so frightened . . .'

'Were you with her? Was it the same man? The one in the balaclava?'

'It must have been him. I was so scared . . .' Her son, her lovely boy . . . She pats his hand.

'Did you see Hannah anywhere up there?'

'No, darling.'

'Not at all yesterday?'

'No.' A shooting pain through her jaw makes her flinch.

'Where were you? What happened exactly? Could you tell who it was?'

Kit holds her hand. It hurts, but she doesn't pull it away.

'No, darling. No. He was wearing that thing over his face. But I didn't see Charlotte. I did go to look for her. I was worried because she was out . . . in that awful weather. But I didn't see her. Or Hannah. Did he hurt Hannah too?'

'Hannah's missing,' he says. 'She's out there somewhere and there's a madman prowling the island!' He bursts into noisy tears.

'It will all be alright, darling. I promise,' soothes Beatrice. 'But how is poor Charlotte? What did he do to her?'

Kit tells her the little he knows and then uses his mother's phone to call the Old Ship, despite her protests that she doesn't need help.

'But you do,' he says. 'And we need to warn people. He's still out there.'

When he's told Alison what's happened to his mother, and asked for medical help and police assistance, he makes Beatrice a cup of Earl Grey, spooning in some honey to help with the shock.

Beatrice considers asking for a little brandy but thinks better of it.

They wait for a first-aider to come round to check over Beatrice's injuries and for Sergeant Jack Moore to arrive from St Mary's.

And as soon as he opens the door, before the policeman questions his mother, Kit reports Hannah missing.

Omens

May, After the Storm

The first washed up on Porthcressa Beach. A dozen more in the following days – mangled corpses dotted around the island's shores; others spotted floating out at sea.

The wildlife team put on the protective gear that strikes fear into the hearts of visitors. Over the next two weeks, the apocalyptic white walkers will be spotted removing carcasses of more and more dead seabirds: fifty, sixty. The remains are sent on to Defra.

Bird flu. The word pandemic *triggers painful memories. Panic that it will spread to chickens, ducks, livestock. Dogs! Humans!*

'It's a curse,' pronounces Miss Elisabeth, 'It's the maid's revenge,' although no one listens to her.

Perhaps they should. Perhaps it is.

VII

The Accounts

56

Bobby

The pub is full to the gills, visitors and islanders gathering there for snippets of news, while also spreading rumours, sharing opinions, dissecting reputations. The music is kept at a low level as a mark of respect. Some are out searching still, but only in daylight hours. There's no hope now. She's been missing for days.

Bobby smiles sadly and shakes the hands of the new guests as they arrive, saying, 'Yes, terrible business,' and then he swiftly moves the conversation along. Tragic accidents happen everywhere where the sea adjoins the land, more so when alcohol is involved. The intimation is that only the drunk and foolhardy are victims.

And somehow, thankfully, the panic about the attacks flared, blazed, and is now already ebbing. It is now almost universally agreed that the man who assaulted Charlotte Howard-Dormer and Beatrice Wallace must have been someone over for the gig championships last week, who slipped away with the hundreds of other visitors. A one-off. It was not an islander; it couldn't possibly be someone who lived here.

Mercifully, the victims of the attacks only suffered *superficial injuries* according to police and both will be going home to recuperate. Bobby hasn't seen the women's faces, but even he wonders at the word *superficial*. It must have been terrifying.

Most people, including Bobby, think the barmaid's disappearance was an accident, an unrelated incident. They may never know.

Taking his drink outside to the pub garden to make the most of the sunshine, Bobby closes his eyes for a moment. He needs a few minutes to himself; a quiet pause where he doesn't have to manage the endless questions from tourists and locals alike. But there's no peace here on the island – the wind sighs, the birds cry, and the waves slap incessantly against the granite of the rocks and the concrete of the quay.

As if reading his thoughts, the sky above the sun umbrella is suddenly filled with a shriek as two gulls swoop, dispersing the smaller sparrows and thrushes mooching about for treats from the visitors who constantly ignore the signs not to feed them. The gulls settle on a nearby table, *hangrily* eyeing Bobby and the visitors drinking outside.

Bobby's taking the first sip of his invigorating G&T when Old Betty plonks her glass of half a Guinness on his table and plonks herself down next to him. She sets about cleaning her specs like she's scouring the roast pan.

'Have you heard the latest?'

'What?' asks Bobby, sighing heavily. There are so many theories swirling around at the moment and he's probably heard most of them, including the more flamboyant: Hannah was involved with international drug smugglers; Hannah took Kit for a mug and did a runner with that Frenchie sailor; Kit did away with Hannah in a jealous rage and covered it up by rowing out to sea and dumping the body; someone saw Hannah swimming over to the Eastern Isles; Hannah was spotted at Gimble Point, hovering over the sea in a halo of light, although that was probably a Brocken spectre, an illusion, a mirage.

Not a grain of actual evidence. Chinese whispers. He catches himself – is that racist?

Old Betty leans in to say, 'John from the garden and his Mary-Jane from the café? I heard they were closer than husband and wife, if you get my drift.'

'I'm aware of that. I was the one who had to inform The Family and the police.' Bobby feels responsible for starting this particular strand of gossip. 'I'd rather you not go spreading that around,' he warns.

'Please yourself,' sniffs Betty, getting up and flouncing away in a huff, although it is an incremental flounce, such is the state of her hips. 'You've opened a can of worms there. Now you have to lie in it.'

Bobby takes a large gulp of his drink. And blushes.

Unfortunately, after one or two drinks the night he discovered the *husband and wife* were actually brother and sister, he confided in Alison. He needed to talk it over with someone in order to make sense of it. He blames the shock for his indiscretion. He shouldn't feel guilty because Alison is obviously the source of this leak, but it doesn't sit easily with him. He should have known better. He trusts Alison, but she probably told someone she trusted too, who passed it on to just the one person, in strictest confidence, naturally, who passed it on . . . That's how it works here.

And there has been another worrying snippet doing the rounds. The vet has been shifting ketamine according to one of the chambermaids, who heard it from Isak Mensah, who has refused to reveal his source. The man has been asked to leave. Bobby thinks the fact that he didn't fight to stay says it all.

When this information spread, it spawned one of the more popular theories – that the barmaid slipped into the sea whilst off her head on drugs, although a few folk, like Kit, believe that whoever attacked Beatrice and Charlotte was also responsible for Hannah's disappearance.

However it happened, Hannah is now missing, presumed dead. Water closes over the heads of the drowned soon enough. *Put it out of your mind*, Bobby tells himself. Guests have shelled out for their holidays in paradise, and while they might pay lip service to the missing woman they still want to be shown a good time.

He's about to head to the bar for a refill when he pauses.

There's something else niggling at him. Before he came to the pub today he helped Fiona prepare for another gallery party. Something caught his eye and he's just realised what it was.

Fiona and her assistant were hanging a new work, a whimsical picture of sheep tombstoning off a cliff, so Bobby set about unloading crates of wine from the golf buggy, carrying them through to pile them in the store cupboard. He'd just noticed a glimpse of pink right at the back, but at that very moment, Fiona and her assistant both screamed. He rushed through to find the ladder had almost toppled, but luckily no harm done. He then had to take a call from The Family, so that had further distracted him.

It's only now he wonders if it could possibly be his own pink waterproof, mislaid months ago during an unfortunate week of advanced *tipsification* (one of many jokey words and phrases he uses – along with *sozzled, a little worse for wear, a tad out of it* – to make his drinking seem less worrying).

It is now common knowledge that someone reported seeing Hannah up at the North End on the day she went missing – arguing with someone who was wearing a pink coat, presumably a woman. If it was Bobby's own coat abandoned in the art gallery's back room, anyone might have used it. It is probably not the time to say he owns one, or to claim it.

He'll leave it where it is. Why would he put himself under suspicion.

He makes his way to the bar, where two of the mainland police officers stand drinking together – the one with the closely cropped grey hair, well-built, hard eyes, terribly sexy in that super cocky manner possessed by those in uniform, indeed most straight white men, and the woman.

They admit to Bobby that they are bewildered. They seem to be getting nowhere fast. This is like no investigation they've ever been on. Usually, the police are treated with suspicion; usually they have to work hard to prise information out of interviewees. But on this island they are welcomed. Drinks are provided and people are keen to engage them in conversation. There is not so much a reluctance to help as a tsunami of scandal and gossip and rumours, which only serve to muddy the waters. They talk and talk, these islanders – mainly the women, but men sidle up in the bar to offer opinions too – about the guests who were attacked, about the barmaid:

'Put it about a bit. . .'

'*Polish mafia . . .*'

'*She was a witch, that one . . .*'

'*I heard she did a runner with one of the sailors . . .*'

They have also interviewed dozens of islanders and visitors alike but they're still no closer to clarifying what happened.

57

Sam

'Yes she hit me that afternoon, gave me a right shiner.

'What did we argue about? You'd have to ask her. Oh no, you can't.

'No, I don't think it's a joke. I think she's a scheming little cow, that's what. She's disappeared somewhere with some bloke, not caring what mess she leaves behind. She'll have found some sailor boy and be off with him on his boat.

'No, I do not think she's come to any harm. She's a survivor that one.

'Yes, I know several people heard me threaten her at Vlad's on the poker night. I'd had a few. We all had. She'd taken a bloody great hunk of my wages, cunning little cow. It was a joke, what I said, about wanting to kill her.

'No, I don't make a habit of wanting to kill people – that's why it was a joke.

'Yes, after she hit me I went looking for her.

'I didn't go immediately, no. I needed a piss first.

'Up at the North End, yes. Old Betty, I mean Miss Elisabeth, told me that's where she was headed. I cycled up after her. I heard someone say later that she'd took Alison's bike, so I guess I would have got there around ten minutes or so after her.

'No, I don't know the exact time because I had no bloody clue I'd need to know the time, did I.

'No, I do not own a balaclava.

'No, I didn't see Beatrice Wallace or Charlotte what's-her-name.

'Christie? No, she didn't go after her as far as I know. If my wife was out searching for anyone, she'd be after me, not Hannah. She didn't find her, even if she had been looking for her. She'd have told me if she found her or if anything happened up there.

'Why did Christie have beef with Hannah? Oh, you've heard about that have you? She thought me and Hannah had a fling. We didn't.

'Yes, I might have suggested we did at one point. But we didn't.

'It was just a laugh, bar talk. Teasing. Hannah didn't mind. You can ask—

'Can't see that's any of your business what happened with me and her. It had nothing to do with this. It was well in the past, all that.

'No, Christie has never had a pink coat as far as I know; not much one for fashion, me.

'Yes, I said something like it was a pity that bloke with the balaclava hadn't found Hannah rather than those visitors he attacked, but I didn't know she was really missing then, did I? It was meant as a joke. Yes, another.

'Yes, I did see Hannah up there at the North End, very briefly that day. She was round the other side of the rocks, high above me. She was with someone. No, I don't know who. I couldn't make them out. I didn't see exactly what they were wearing, or if their face was covered. It was only a glimpse. They had their back to me.

'It was tipping it down by then, so I decided to get back home.

'Yes, just like that. Changed my mind. I hadn't got the right gear on to be out in that. I imagine anyone up there would hot-foot it down as soon as they could in that weather.

'No, I didn't go near her. I didn't touch her. I don't know what happened to her.

'Look, I didn't have to tell you I'd seen her, did I?'

That's what Sam told them. None of it was a lie.

He understood why he was one of the first people they wanted to talk to.

It was bloody freezing in the community centre, where the coppers had set up shop. He was glad to be out of it when they'd finished. He wanted to go straight to the pub, but he had to finish work first. And he'd promised Christie that he'd get back early today to tell her how the interview had gone.

There was stuff Sam didn't tell the police.

He could hardly tell them what he wanted to do to bloody Hannah. The little cow proper walloped him. She might have had his eye out when she punched him, and he was steaming. And he'd had enough of bloody women bloody hitting him, thank you very bloody much.

They asked if Hannah was with someone up there. There'd

been a witness who'd told them they saw her arguing with someone who was wearing a pink waterproof. And sure, Christie might have had one of them pink coats. She once said that she was going to buy one. But Sam never saw it, that much is true. He could swear on the bible about that.

As far as he could tell.

Because he couldn't see it. It's a condition. Bang to rights, protanopia. Christie would joke it was more to do with him being blind drunk.

She's the one who sees red. Vicious if provoked. But . . .

His bloody wife irritates the hell out of Sam. Nag, nag, bloody nag. But he loves her. He loves her with all his heart. The boys love her. She's a good mother. She'd never hurt the lads. And he couldn't risk her getting banged up and depriving them of their mum, could he?

So, just in case . . .

He didn't mention the other stuff. Her nasty streak. *She-Hulk*, his missus. Can lash out if provoked. Apparently, he's always provoking her.

So, he told the police she didn't have a pink coat as far as he knew. That wasn't a lie. It's the least he could do.

And he could hardly tell them that he might have done something to the bloody barmaid if he'd found her first, but someone else was doing it for him by the looks of it. On the rocks high above him – Hannah and someone else fighting up there. He couldn't see who it was. He only got a glimpse. Perhaps . . . it *might* have been Christie. Someone wearing a waterproof at any rate. But he legged it before he saw what happened. Deliberately turned away. He couldn't make out much because of the rain anyway. Mental it was, that afternoon. He got himself out of there as fast as possible. He couldn't afford to see for sure . . . just in case. Walked all the way round the bloody island and stood on top of Tommy's Hill watching the storm, the sea a huge churning mirror, until his ears screamed with the wind; until he was shaking and soaked and sober. Call him a coward if you like.

No one needs to know anything about that.

It's not that he's frightened of his wife, not at all. He loves her. She's a good mother.

58

Miss Elisabeth

'No, I don't want a cup of tea, thank you. Rubbish stuff from that bleddy urn here. Need a new one if you ask me, only the estate manager disagrees, penny-pinching so and so. I'd like to see him deal with all the complaints when we do the bingo and the tea parties for the—

'Yes. Back to the points in question. I don't have all day either.

'No, I wasn't on a walkabout that afternoon. Only bleddy idiots would be out galivanting in that. You could smell the storm coming in. And they were all caught out in it weren't they, Sam and Christie, and that John from the gardens – his missus, and Maisie Willis who used to come with her mother, and that blonde maid who was staying at Falcon and—

'No, of course I didn't see them all. I've not got eyes in the back of my neck. It's just what people have been saying in the pub, that's all. But I tell you what I think. I'd look to that youth from Falcon if I were you. Kit.

'Because most murders are committed by lovers, them's the facts. And it'd not be an islander. I'd lay my life on that. I know everyone who works here like my own family. Inside and out. Not one of them – couldn't be. Not even one of the young 'uns. Bound to be one of the blow-ins.

'Definitely not an accident, no. She was just too canny that maid, that's why.

'No, there's nothing *espercifically* he did that made me suspect him. But he was her boyfriend. I've seen all them programmes about it. Crimes of passion they calls 'em. Was always that way. And they'd had a big falling-out the night before, Hannah and her bloke, so they says. I saw some of that, what she was up to. Kissing sailors in the Old Ship. The usual. Then she'd been with young Vlad all night by all accounts.

'You can't teach a leopard new spots.

'*Her.* That's who I mean. She's the leopard. Always a bit of a wild child, Hannah. And so what? Enjoy yourself while you can, I says.

'That's sexism that, calling her *flighty*. She was just having fun.

'Jealousy. It's a pretty good motive, don't you think? Although it's not for me to tell you your jobs.

'Of course he'd be rushing round like a blue-arsed fly asking all and sundry if they'd seen her. That'd be a good cover story, wouldn't it? Of course he'd be out searching day and night. He did her in and then felt guilty, I reckon.

'He might have had a go at his mother too. No love lost between them pair. For all her airs and graces, I reckon Beatrice Wallace is a fall-down drunk.

'Listen. When you've been on this earth as long as I have,

young man, then you can tell me about *supposition* and *lack of evidence*. You get a proper feel for people, that's why. And Hannah was good as gold, that girl, and he was proper jealous, I could feel it and—

'Okay. Well, I'll be off then.'

Miss Elisabeth makes her way to the pub from the community centre. As she walks she thinks it through again. Ruminating, that's what she's doing.

Always made her awkward, people questioning her. Like her mother and father giving her the third degree if she'd been naughty. Long time ago now, all that.

He'd been very rude to her the day after they reckon it happened, the youth, Kit. He'd almost had her over, rushing by like that, running out of the Estate Office. Suspicious, it was. There was something wrong, she could tell. His face looked like bone. And no apology. He'd been up to something right enough. She could smell it on him.

And you should always trust your instincts. Miss Elisabeth used to watch all those programmes with them clever ones: Ironside, Miss Marple, Columbo, although he was a scruffy beggar. It's the hunches, that's what they call it.

The further away she gets from the community centre and the police and the questions, the better she feels. By the time she's rounding the corner to New Grimsby, Miss Elisabeth feels in a very good mood, almost skittish. A blooming magical day. *Proper ansom.* She could skip.

That bleddy C word. It required the trek over to the big city. Too busy, Truro. Turned out it was only a *calcified cyst* in her breast. *Non-maligernant* they told her. Nothing to worry about. Not the cancer. Thank the Lord. She'd written in the book in the church asking for prayers and it worked a treat.

It was a premonition of the cold breath of death, no more, no less. But she's prepared now. She has steeled herself.

The poor maid probably didn't have time to do that. Taken before her time. Still a lot to achieve. Lovely maid, Hannah. Didn't talk down to you like some of the bleddy young 'uns.

Most murders are committed by men – it was in all those programmes; them's the facts. Husbands, lovers, boyfriends. That's who they should be questioning, that tall lad, Kit.

His girlfriend, his mother, and the blonde – he did for them all, she reckons.

59

Charlotte

'I'd gone for a walk. The North End, yes. He came at me. From behind. And . . . And . . . he grabbed my hair. Utter bastard. He had a knife-thing. And. And . . . slashed me. Punched me. I was a mess. An absolute mess. He took my . . . my . . . knickers.

'No. Nothing more. He was disturbed.

'By a scream? A gull?

'He wore a balaclava. I'll have to wear a mask now. My face . . .

'I DON'T KNOW WHAT ELSE HE WAS WEARING!

'Sorry. I squeezed my eyes shut.

'I didn't see the barmaid. I didn't see Beatrice.

'There was so much rain.

'No, I didn't see anyone else. And . . . I can't remember how I got down to the community centre.

'He shouted at me. I can't remember exactly what.

'I DON'T KNOW WHAT ACCENT! HE WAS PUNCHING ME AT THE TIME!'

*

They tell her the injuries will heal and you'll hardly be able to see the scars. A few stitches. The swelling will soon go down. Mild concussion. Mild hypothermia. Small hairline fracture. That's all. She'll be released tomorrow. She can't wait to get away.

Mild. Superficial. No real harm done, they say.

She doesn't want to see Beatrice or Kit. She just wants to go, get as far away as possible from this godforsaken place.

She probes the puffiness of her lip with her tongue and explores the new contours of her forehead and cheek with her fingertips, although they tell her not to touch. She still can't bear to look at herself.

She does not like the police – they give her the ick. She told them she didn't need victim support as she has a proper counsellor back home.

There are things she didn't tell them.

These *superficial* injuries aren't the worst thing.

The words he said! They can't take them away. They'll never take them away. She can't repeat them. She can't tell the police what he called her.

You stupid fat *cunt.*

She shivers, although the hospital room is over-warm.

There's a big bunch of flowers from Kit, which make her sad.

She didn't tell the police that she'd taken Kit's phone. Petty. Not sure what she was thinking.

The police seem to think Kit might have had something to do with the other thing, Hannah's disappearance. Let them. She may have told them that his relationship with the barmaid was volatile. She may have mentioned that big bust-up between Hannah and Kit in the pub just before Christmas. Loads of witnesses to that. That wasn't spite on her part.

They asked if she'd ever seen him be violent. She'd shook her head. But she hadn't exactly said no. It was easy to look tearful – this whole horrible experience has made her tearful.

No. Kit doesn't really deserve that. She needs to give herself a talking-to. She needs to put the record straight . . .

Golly sent her a lovely message this morning. *The pain on life's journey is a precious gift.* It took her until this afternoon to realise that is true.

There is a silver lining. She has had so many likes for the shot of her bruised hand on the hospital bed. That post was one of her most popular ever! If only her parents had cared to comment. And she's lost almost three kilos already!

60

Maisie

'I'm so sorry. I'm using up all your Kleenex. It's just all so upsetting.

'I'd only gone up there, to the North End, to scatter my mother' s ashes. I'm sorry. I didn't ask if it was allowed. It's probably frowned upon isn't it, but it's hardly illegal, is it?

'No. I'll be okay in a moment. It's just a lot, you know.

'No, I didn't see anything suspicious up there. Nothing suspicious. No.

'I didn't see Hannah anywhere. I didn't see the guests who were attacked – the two women from Falcon, wasn't it? Poor souls.

'It's terrifying to think some madman was on the loose up there when I was out walking with—

'Yes, I did see Sam's wife heading that way. She cycled up to me and asked if I'd seen her husband. But I hadn't.

'Was there anything suspicious in the way Christie was

299

behaving? Well, she was shouting. But that might have been because the wind was so loud.

'I honestly can't remember what she was wearing.

'No, I didn't see anyone else up there.

'Yes, of course. I've seen the notices you've put up in the Old Ship, advising women not to walk or cycle anywhere alone. Isak Mensah is always kind enough to walk me back from the pub.'

Somehow she managed to answer their questions. Stuttering, garbling. She doesn't think she said anything incriminating but she must have looked guilty as sin. Of course she wasn't to blame for the attacks or for that woman going missing. But no one is entirely blameless are they?

She doesn't tell them that she saw *him* up there. At least she assumes it was him – the man wearing a balaclava, running across the path on the right side of the cliff, the other side to her. Someone else might have had a black balaclava, but she could tell it was the same man who was in her bathroom all those months ago. She just knew.

She didn't see the one he chose, Charlotte. Could hardly picture her.

She told the police nothing of that because she would very much like to deal with the situation in her own way. She can't wait to run into him again.

If she hadn't been startled by Sam's wife, she might have gone after him that afternoon, but Christie had come right up to her and shouted in her face 'Have you seen Sam?' She didn't tell her Sam had gone round the outcrop near the top a few minutes earlier, because Christie looked so furious. And Maisie likes Sam. He always helped her with her mother's wheelchair. The police didn't need to know he was up there. He wouldn't hurt a fly, Sam. Such a polite chap.

As she walks away from the community centre, almost shaking with relief, Maisie thinks of that afternoon again, wondering why the man in the balaclava chose someone else and not her? She'd thought they had a connection – she felt it the first time she saw him in the bathroom. If only he'd come after her. The thought was thrilling . . .

She imagined him taking hold of her arm and she would have whirled around and smashed her mother's urn into his face, splattering his nose across his features, the gristle and blood—

When she gets back to the holiday cottage, Maisie makes herself a nice cup of tea.

It is so restful here without her mother.

All night long that bloody machine – the Darth Vader breathing. *She* slept like a baby, but her mother's sleep apnoea kept Maisie awake hour after hour. She'd tried earplugs, but they made her itch and of course her mother refused to shut the bedroom door just in case she needed something in the middle of the night.

She always needed something in the middle of the night.

Maisie sometimes thought it must be what it was like having a newborn. Chance would be a fine thing. No time for relationships when you're a full-time carer. Precious little time to do anything except tend to *her* – the bloated queen bee. All Edith did was eat and grow fatter.

There wasn't enough physio in the world to help Maisie's back, screaming with pain as she struggled to lift and turn her.

She screamed internally with the lack of sleep.

That last night . . .

They'd already resorted to giant nappies – ordered specially from the chemist. And that still didn't stop Edith Willis bleating that she needed changing.

Maisie waited until her mother had fallen back to sleep.

Then she unplugged the machine and for an hour or more listened to the snores, loud as a pig's, on and on – and then the silence. And she counted the seconds – five, six, seven, eight – and then the gurgling fight for another in breath.

Her mother's huge breasts weighing heavy on her rib cage. Crushing her.

It had started to get light when Maisie decided she just couldn't stand it any longer. She gently removed the facemask from her mother's mouth and nose. Edith didn't wake.

She waited another half hour.

And then she held the pillow over her mother's face, pushing down with all her might until there was no more movement.

And no more sound.

61

Christie

'It looks bad, I know it does.

'I did go after her, yes, but I didn't find her. I had nothing to do with it.

'I didn't smash her head in and throw her into the sea, like you two seem to be suggesting, not to say I wouldn't have smacked her smug face if I had found her. But I didn't.

'Do I think someone did that? Throw her into the sea? How the hell would I know?

'I couldn't stand her. I'm sure people have told you that. It's no secret.

'She was all over my husband, that's why – everyone saw that; everyone will tell you that. But I didn't touch her.

'I cycled up to where the path ends then climbed the rest of the way up the cliffs on the east side. I saw Maisie Willis from Sanderling up that way, a couple of other visitors I didn't know, that's all. I didn't see the other two, the posh girl and Beatrice

Wallace. I didn't see Kit. And I didn't see *her*, Hannah.

'When it started raining I came back. It was bloody torrential. I didn't want to stay out in that. I saw a few walkers hurrying away from the North End when it started to really chuck it down. I didn't see who they were.

'Yeah, I did say I hoped she'd bloody drowned. That was the next day in the shop. I wouldn't have said it if I'd known she had – I mean, we assume she has, although some people think she's on a boat somewhere living it up.

'You'll have to ask Sam what he was doing up there. I'm not his bloody keeper.'

The trouble was, there was an eyewitness who saw the barmaid up there with another woman. Fighting. Someone who might have it in for Christie, someone who told them about seeing a pink coat. Perhaps they'd heard her say she'd bought a new pink coat – well, new second-hand from eBay. Pink and fluffy on the inside. She felt like a giant teddy bear in it, and she bloody loved it. She's guessing it's waterproof, but she hasn't even worn it once, so she doesn't know for sure. She's keeping it for best. That doesn't mean someone didn't remember her saying she'd bought it, though.

And what with Alison telling the police that she'd said 'I'll bloody kill the pair of them when I get my hands on them', and a couple of customers *corroborating* that, well . . . even though she hadn't been wearing it that day, she panicked.

Christie came home after the interview, and poured herself a drink and waited for Sam to come back. He'd been in to be questioned during his lunch break, but she didn't know how it had gone because he hadn't replied to her text. The twins and

Finn were over at Emma's again. Christie owed her friend a hell of a lot of babysitting to make up for it.

That day it all happened Christie remembers Sam coming home looking terrible. Soaked through, like a drowned rat, coughing up a lung. His eye was still puffy where Hannah had hit him. Christie had put on dry clothes by then, although her hair was still wet.

She could see why the police wondered if he'd had something to do with it. And he might have lashed out after Hannah provoked him, there was always that possibility. He might have snapped. But she'd told them she didn't think so. She'd said that if he'd cycled all the way up to the North End to find Hannah, he would have calmed down by the time he got up there.

When he came in after his interview he didn't tell Christie much, but he did say the police had asked him about a pink coat. Of course he'd remember that she'd said she was going to buy one because they'd had a row about it. He'd said she didn't need another coat and they needed the money for Tommy's birthday, and she'd said they'd have the money if he didn't pour so much bloody alcohol down his throat and, well . . .

He swore he'd not mentioned to the police that Christie had a pink coat, but she doesn't know if she believes him. Anyway, Sam wouldn't know a pink coat if it bit him on the arse.

When Tommy got in from school Christie collected the kids from Emma, made the tea, watched some rubbish on the telly, and settled them down to bed. Sam switched on the news and helped himself to a beer from the fridge and she put the plates in the dishwasher and wiped the kitchen down and set out the kids' stuff for the morning and started the ironing.

He went up to bed at some point.

When it was quiet, she snuck upstairs and took the pink coat out of the twins' wardrobe where she'd hidden it at the back, because if Sam had seen it, that would have started another bloody argument about money. What she'd planned to do was wait a while and start wearing it in a few weeks when she could truthfully say, *This? I've had it for ages!*

She took the coat to the bottom of the garden and rammed it in the old oil drum Sam uses to get rid of garden waste, and she covered it with old wood and rubbish.

Two days later, when Sam was at work, and Tommy was at school, she left the kids in front of the telly, went out and doused it all with a little petrol and burnt it.

And even if someone was spying on her, no one would think anything of a small garden bonfire on a grey afternoon even though all the wood was still damp from the storm.

62

Thor

He is shitting himself.

He hasn't been questioned yet, but that doesn't mean they won't ask him to come in. So many others to talk to first. A mass exodus to the North End by what they said in the pub last night. If they asked the blokes he shares accommodation with, they'd assume he'd been holed up in his room that afternoon playing games on his computer. They were both out at work when he got back. No CCTV anywhere on the island, only a couple of webcams live streaming nice views to lure in the tourists.

No one but the women saw Thor up there – as far as he knows. But then no one could see much at all in that rain.

Thor's made a point of joining the other volunteers out searching, but all the time he's been pretending to look, he's been worrying that the police might break into his room when he wasn't there, although they'd need a warrant for that wouldn't they, and on what grounds? He couldn't bear anyone poking into his private things – the images on his computer, his collections – although none of that has anything to do with the missing barmaid.

He saw some of what happened. They won't find her.

But he can never tell them what he saw – the barmaid and the other one – because that would put him up there at the North End. And he can't risk that. They haven't asked him though.

The blonde . . . she heard his voice. What will he do if she comes into the shop? He'll have to pretend he's sick. He can't risk her recognising him. He'll have to go into the back where they store the supplies to avoid her. He didn't think that part through. Should have stayed silent. But that was the best bit of it, shouting at her.

She was hardly worth the bother.

The other one, the older one from Falcon, she didn't hear his voice. He'd not shouted at her. What could she tell the police? Nothing.

The Old Ship is busy tonight, although most of the visitors who came for the gig racing have already left. The police can't question thousands of people, can they; they can't keep them all on an island, just in case.

There's gossip in the pub about the one in hospital. Thor's ears prick up and he moves closer, leaning on the wall at the back of Table 5 to listen as Emma tells one of the chambermaids the latest.

His cousin Kelly probably told Alison, who told Emma. Can't keep her mouth shut, Kelly.

She's on the mend, *Charlotte* – that's her name, not that he cares. A fractured eye socket was the worst injury, apparently. But the cut on her arm wasn't the only one they discovered on examining her – they found older scars where she'd been cutting herself.

Thor is surprised that his reaction to this news is something almost resembling pity.

63

Ted

'There's a tide table on the notice board if you want a look; most people have it on their phones now, but I reckon she'd have been swept over Samson way, if she'd gone into the water, that's my bet. That's where she'd wash up. Eventually.

'No, I didn't see a thing. I was out on the boat watching the gig racing.'

'A former penal colony,' said the younger copper, the one who googled *Samson*. 'An uninhabited island with breast-like mounds like the Paps of Jura in Scotland . . . large ancient burial grounds . . . bird sanctuary. . .'

Ted saw the way the older copper looked at him when his colleague said the words *penal colony*. Anyone who's got form gets a look like that. A million years ago now. He did six months for something and nothing – a row, a fight over some girl he can't even picture now, and they found a few drugs on him. Ted was only a kid himself back then.

He knew the copper's look well – it's the way his missus looks at him on the days he comes back from his special delivery trips over to St Mary's. His balls shrivel and curl back up inside at those looks.

He'd told the police he'd seen nothing. Couldn't risk them poking about and discovering his sideline. Couldn't have them rootling round his hard drive either – he didn't want anyone seeing the stuff on that. He'd assumed the influx of visitors out on the water for the gig races would be cover enough for his trip over to St Mary's that day. Hiding in plain sight. The storm was a bonus.

He only does a bit on the side and only for the big occasions like the gig championships, Christmas, summer. He carries it across, that's all. Doesn't make him a drug dealer as such. And there are a few bigger packages he takes across from the French yachts, but still, he's hardly Pablo bloody Escobar.

Someone else had reported seeing two women arguing at the North End – one in a pink coat and the barmaid. It makes sense of what he thought was the pair of them dancing up there. And if someone else had already told the police that, he didn't have to say anything, did he. He couldn't add anything more.

He couldn't tell them the other thing either because it was nothing, really. But . . .

He'd seen her in the pub earlier that afternoon, before he went out on his delivery. The one with the pink waterproof. He reckons it was her. Even though the place was busy, there was something about her face as she came in – it was like his own before he'd had the first couple of pints. She stood close to him at the bar and there was something about her eyes. Not like she'd go off on one like Christie, all in a flap, all hot-headed. No, this one looked . . . cold-blooded – a raptor. Bleddy chilling. But what could he say? It was just a hunch.

64

Kit

'I am aware that some people have said that, yes. I assume several more think it or suspect it. But I loved her. I would never harm Hannah. We'd been together almost a year and it was serious. We were planning a future together.

'I'm afraid we did argue that morning on the day she went missing. I was annoyed with her. They've probably already told you that they'd been playing strip poker.

'You'd have to speak to Vlad about that. She hardly "spent the night with him" in the way you're suggesting. Ask Isak, he was there as well. They played cards, that was all.

'I hardly think her disappearance would be anything to do with a poker debt of some kind.

'I don't know anything about Sam's argument with her.

'I did hear that she'd kissed one of the French sailors in the pub, yes. But I wasn't jealous about that. Not at all. She kissed a lot of people. It didn't mean that she'd run off with any of them.

You had to know her.

'I don't believe she would have "done a runner", as you put it. To teach me a lesson? I hardly think disappearing from the face of the earth is a normal response to one brief disagreement.

'She was used to drink. She was used to smoking a little weed. I never saw her do other drugs. I can't imagine that caused an accident. I just can't see her falling.

'What? No! She would never harm herself. Yes, we'd had an argument, but we hadn't split up, and she wasn't the sort of person who'd do that. No. Definitely not.

'What do I think happened?

'I don't know. I just don't know . . . just. Yeah. Give me a minute.

'I didn't go to the North End. I had no idea that's where she might be. I've no idea why she said she was meeting me there. When the storm started I went back to the cottage and waited. I assumed she'd be sheltering somewhere.

'I was on my own. I fell asleep after a bottle of wine. I started looking for her . . . the next morning. Hang on. I just need a second.

'I just . . . look, two women were brutally attacked that afternoon. My mother and Charlotte both up at the North End. And that's where Hannah told Alison she was heading. Surely that's the most logical explanation – whoever hurt my mother and Charlotte had something to do with Hannah disappearing.

'Of course, if I think of anything else . . .

'I won't be leaving Tresco, no. I'm moving into a room at the Old Ship until we find her. We have to find her!

'And you have to find the man who was in the balaclava. You have to!

'Okay . . . Yes. Please get in touch if there's anything else I can do to help. You can leave a message at the pub as I might be out searching. I seem to have lost my mobile phone.'

65

Beatrice

'I rarely go to the North End – it's a little blustery for me even on nice days. I usually go for a walk with Primrose towards Cromwell's Castle. No, that's not a person; Primrose is my dog, bless her. I didn't bring her this time. I'm not sure why I decided to go up there that day. I was out looking for Charlotte. But I didn't find her.

'Yes. I was alone when it happened.

'I'm not sure *where* exactly. I can't remember too many details. I was in the Old Ship earlier. I'm afraid I was a little squiffy. I lost my husband you see and—

'Yes. I can carry on . . . It started raining.

'He came at me from behind. I think the first blow caught me here, this bit of my eyebrow. You can see where it's swollen. It still hurts.

'I stumbled. Cut up my hands and knees.

'No. I didn't see the man clearly. I only caught a glimpse of the balaclava. I'm afraid I didn't notice what else he wore. It all happened so quickly.

'I pushed him off and he slipped and fell. That's how I got away.

'I remember running down and down and twisting my ankle a little and then I got back here. I fell asleep, or possibly passed out from the shock, I'm not sure. My son found me the next morning.'

She was shaking by the time the interview was over. Traumatic. It brought it all back – the storm, the screams, the shock of the balaclava – running and stumbling down and down . . .

She got away. Poor Charlotte didn't.

66

Kelly

'I'm sorry I've not been in to talk before now, but I've been so busy. Yes, quite a few more injuries to deal with during the championships, although most of them relate to the celebrations rather than the actual rowing.

'I didn't see anything of note that day. Nothing, really. I was in the pub most of the time.

'Was anyone behaving oddly? It was the pub! In the middle of the gig championships!

'I did go out for a breath of fresh air. An hour, at most. Before it started bucketing it down. There were so many people around that afternoon. Dozens of walkers I didn't know, probably just over for the day, sightseeing in between races.

'I heard Christie was cycling up in that direction at some point, but I didn't see her. And I heard one of the regular guests was there, the one whose mother used to come here, Mrs Willis. No, that was the mother; Edith Willis, that's it. I don't recall the daughter's name. The Estate Office will have it. And I saw *Mary-Jane* was heading up there.

'What do you mean, *how I say that*? That's her name – Mary-Jane.

'It's just . . . the woman's odd, that's all. But that has nothing to do with this, does it.

'Of course you could ask her if she saw anything. I've heard she's recovering well over on the mainland.'

After the interview Kelly heads back to the pub, taking the long way round. She's not on shift at the hospital until tomorrow and she wants to make the best of the good weather while they have it. She spends too much time indoors. Nothing beats sunlight to lift the mood.

She didn't say a word to the police about the other thing – the news that's been all around the island like wildfire. She's no idea how that got out, but it wasn't from her. That wouldn't be professional. Mary-Jane confided in her as a nurse. She couldn't say a word about that. It's like a confessional when patients talk to Kelly.

At first Mary-Jane had told her that she and John were cousins. Kelly had explained that there were some genetic risks if cousins had a child, but it was common in certain communities – Mormons, that sort of thing. But then, the day before the accident on the mainland, she'd revealed the shocker.

That single word scrawled on a piece of paper – *Brother.*

Jesus.

It took all Kelly's professional training not to be sick right then. And the woman was pregnant!

She couldn't tell the police that.

Kelly didn't really believe Mary-Jane had anything to do with the barmaid's disappearance. But if you can keep something like that a secret, *incest*, what else might you be capable of?

67

Mary-Jane

'Yes, I am still a little groggy. Yes, it is painful.

'He swerved. Something in the road. I didn't see what . . .

'The next thing I knew, I was here . . .

'Yes. Kind-hearted, my John. Probably a pheasant or something. My poor John . . .

'I . . .

'Oh . . .

'Oh . . .

'Oh. Oh. Oh . . .

'Water, yes . . .

'I can't talk about that. No. Please don't make me. How do you know? I loved him. He was my world! My *everything*. You don't understand. NO . . .'

'No, I'll talk about the other thing. I can't really tell you much . . .'

'I didn't see the other two, but I saw her up there. The

barmaid at the North End. I was going for a walk. Because . . .
I'm sorry . . .'

'No. I can go on . . .

'I didn't see the women who were hurt, but I saw Hannah.
She was up there arguing with someone. Another woman, I
think. In one of those pink waterproof coats. A lot of people
have them. There was a sale . . .

'I didn't see the other one's face. Her back was to me. I
couldn't see who it was . . .

'They were shouting. Fighting, I think. I didn't see anything
else. No. I had to get home, I . . . you see . . .'

She whispered her answers. The words made their way out soft
as a butterfly's wing, her breath fluttery.

The nurse stopped the interview when Mary-Jane had a violent coughing fit. The police left.

She didn't tell them what she saw next. She saw Hannah.

Until she didn't—

Mary-Jane had walked up to the North End to throw herself
into the sea. It was her only way out. But the two women were
already up there. They were arguing – the one in the pink coat
and Hannah.

Shouts. Crashing waves below. The roar of the wind. A tussle.
Then Hannah caught sight of her. It distracted her for a second.
She looked right at Mary-Jane like she could see deep into her
soul, opened her mouth as if to say something, and that was
when the other one lunged at her.

Mary-Jane heard the scream; hears it still.

Hannah clubbed with a hammer, a fight . . . and . . . then she disappeared.

The shock hit Mary-Jane so hard her knees buckled, and she plonked down onto a mound of vivid green grass, gasping. She couldn't make sense of what she'd just witnessed.

It was her fault. If Hannah hadn't turned to her. . .

And what if that woman came for her? Mary-Jane scooted round on her bum, fear scalding her throat. She managed to crawl on her hands and knees round the west side of the rocks, shaky, slowly hauling herself upright into the buffeting wind, and then she ran as fast as she could, until, somehow, gasping, heaving, she got back to level ground, rushing, blinded by the rain which suddenly unleashed in epic quantities, blowing horizontally, lashing her until she was inhaling rain, drowning in rain. She pushed on and on until she slammed the cottage door behind her.

And as she stood by the heater to warm herself up, trembling, horrified, she realised she had not wanted to die after all. She had run for her life.

But she couldn't believe what she saw. Impossible. It was a scene sent to punish her for her own wicked thoughts, the torment of the devil, a dumb show, a morality play. It wasn't real. It can't have been.

But, even if it had been real, what could she do? She told herself she could never risk going to the police. If the authorities got involved, her secret, John's secret, might come to light. Her thinking was a little unhinged.

There in her beautiful home Mary-Jane silently sobbed. She had contemplated suicide, and this torment was her just reward. There was no escape from the top of the cliffs. There was no respite from her many sins. She was skewered by guilt and shame. The pain in her body was nothing compared to that. She deserved her body's torment.

She was disgusted with herself. And the baby inside her would be a deformed monster and it would all be her fault and her just punishment.

And she had stupidly, recklessly confessed to the nurse, Kelly. The man she loved, had always loved, was her brother.

But now they know anyway. Somehow the police know. And she and John had been so careful.

This is her punishment too. Because she can never return to that beautiful island. She couldn't face anyone there now. Somehow they will all know, and they will all talk about her behind her back forever. And by now their mother must know too, so she can't go home either. She and John escaped here to get away from the gossip that had already started back there.

And she couldn't tell the police; she could never tell anyone what happened the morning of the accident, after she and John had crossed the sea in the helicopter and picked up the hire car and had the argument about the baby, about the abortion leaflet – which he'd stolen from her! going through her private things! – and he was shouting at her, despising her, blaming her for contemplating that terrible sin, and she had no voice to answer back, because John always knew best, knew everything, so she grabbed the steering wheel and pulled hard and they spun across the road, the windscreen glaring, and that's the last thing she remembered.

Until now.

Late that night, after the police and the nurse leave her to her broken bones and internal injuries, the IV-line tug-tug-tugging at her hand, and the noise and bustle all around her, there is a pause. And she feels such relief. And this is the worst of her sins.

The relief.

John saw the baby inside her as a gift, a confirmation that God had given their union His blessing.

But she knew the new life rooted inside her was no blessing. It was an obscenity.

And while she grieves for him, the man she loved, with all her heart and all her body, while she will miss him day and night, forever and ever, the thing she will never be able to tell anyone is that she is glad there is no more John. And she is glad there is no more baby. She is free.

The Sea Fog

October, After the Storm

It roils in across the black waters bringing a sepulchral breath that chills to the core – fog, the colour of sadness.

'Like a smoke machine,' says Vlad, who's already pretty wasted. His laugh is nervous.

The ethereal vapour shrouds the horizon within minutes.

The lads are making their way to the quay, where they have business.

Away from the music and shouts in the bar, it is peaceful here. The fog muffles sound – even the sploshing of the wavelets against the concrete is deadened. Then comes the first mournful boom of the foghorn from Round Island.

They settle with their backs against the quay wall and share another pre-rolled joint, the smoke billowing out to mix with the misty tendrils sneaking their way up the steps from the water.

Until—

They turn to each other.

'The fuck?' says Vlad.

'You hear it too, right?' asks Isak.

Higher pitched than the foghorn's doleful bass note, a faint unearthly wail.

Isak looks down at the joint. Is it laced with something else? He's pretty sure it's the same stuff they had last night, and it was well mellow then.

The keening comes again. Isak feels Vlad's arm brace against his own as they peer into the fog, trying to make out the source. The sound dies, then grows louder, closer, a sad-screechy-lowing. It seems to be inching towards them.

'No way, no way. I'm not here for this, mate. Sorry.' Vlad clambers to his feet, but stalls, then gasps, 'Fuck. Me.'

A shadow glides over the water, accompanied by the melancholy shriek. No – a figure.

'You seeing this?'

Indeed, Isak is seeing what he cannot be seeing. A long black cloak, a hood, a scythe. Crossing the Styx, it glides towards them.

'Mate!' shouts Vlad, dragging Isak to his feet, digging his fingers into his wrist so hard it hurts.

They are not the only ones witnessing the supernatural. Miss Elisabeth, whose cottage is the nearest one to the quay, observes the spectral vision as she's closing her front curtains. She does not bat an eyelid. If it's time, it's time.

'Mate,' croaks Vlad, trying to yank Isak away, but his friend is immobile.

'Isak! Vlad!' shouts Death. The accent is most definitely French.

'Jesus-fucking-Christ-I-nearly-shat-myself!' shouts Isak.

Behind Death (more commonly known by his given name, Hugo), Jean-Paul is attempting to play some form of bagpipes. Badly. They are members of the French crew from the big yacht anchored on one of the deep-water moorings off New Grimsby. Over to deliver a package. Isak can't remember the name of the other lad who's rowing.

Playing the bloody bagpipes to announce a bloody drug deal! Twats!

The exchange is brisk. Hugo clambers up the steps, hands a Jiffy bag to Isak. Vlad gives Hugo an envelope of money and he throws it down to Jean-Paul, who has mercifully abandoned his instrument – French bagpipes, the cornemuse; pure evil. The nameless crewmate turns the boat around and rows away. As they disappear, a few baleful notes start up again and recede with them.

Hugo joins Vlad and Isak as they make their way back to the Old Ship for the Halloween party. Vlad, once more exploiting his long canines, is Dracula, a single trickle of fake blood his only accessory. He doesn't even wear a cloak, which was mislaid last New Year. Isak is dressed as a devil, and as they walk, he whips the back of Vlad's legs with his forked tail, giddy with relief, the lads laughing too loudly and taking the piss out of each other. Hugo's scythe gets tangled in a tree's branches and they laugh again.

'Get me one in,' instructs Vlad, making a detour to stash the weed in the shortbread tin back at his Hobbit-house home. 'I'll be there dreckly.'

Party noises from the gathering reach him as he walks round to his digs at the back of the pub. Now he's alone, the maid comes to mind, as she often does. He wonders if it's true, that the veil between this world and the next is thinner this night, All Hallows' Eve. If it is, he wonders if Hannah knows how much she's missed; how much he misses her. He imagines his fingers reaching through the fog to touch

the ribbons of sea-jellied flesh which is all that is left of her now.
This joint has definitely been laced with something.

VIII

November, After the Storm

68

The Old Ship

A queasy pall falls over the island the day after the Halloween party. Revellers look like death warmed up, nursing tender heads and eviscerated wallets. November marks the lull, a time when this small community can take a breath before the Christmas rush.

Alison is down to her core staff, the same as everywhere. The seasonal workers have long gone and there aren't so many builders over this year either.

After the less than merry month of May, Bobby had confided in Alison on more than one occasion, admitting how worried he was that the bad publicity – two women attacked, another assumed dead – would affect bookings. Visitors come here to avoid those sorts of crime statistics, and the terrifying nights walking home alone those horror stories spawn, although the attacks on the island had been in broad daylight, hadn't they. Amazingly no one cancelled. August was busy enough. The collective unconscious seems to have labelled and filed the incidents away as a one-off, a freak occurrence, and both the attacks and the mystery about what happened to Hannah are now just that – scary stories to add a frisson to the gossip in the pub.

It is quiet in the Old Ship right now, but that's to be expected. Only a few hardy types come at this time of year – dedicated walkers, poets, that sort. Even so, Alison will have a steady night. The regulars are always in.

Ted arrives early. He tells Alison he's only stopping for the one as he still needs to do some repairs on the boat's handrail. But he's in a good mood because he's just heard his boy is planning on coming over with his girlfriend this Christmas. Staying a week. Might be proposing. Ted wants to make a good show of it.

He doesn't mention the special boat runs he'll be doing to make this possible.

Kit comes down from his room. He's been staying at the Old Ship ever since Hannah went missing. That's how they still refer to it, *missing*, rather than the more obvious *dead*. The young man has drawn into himself. He's aged in the last six months. He's lost weight and his muscles have hardened – including his heart.

'The usual?' asks Alison.

He nods.

To stop himself moping, Kit has been doing odd jobs to keep himself busy. This might take his mind off things, but it causes some hard feelings. He takes shifts here and over at the Mermaid on St Mary's; he's been helping the builders with the incessant painting of exteriors which will need to be done again next year, and the next, thanks to sea air and scouring winds; he's even picked narcissi, that back-breaking work in the fields on St Martin's. Unskilled jobs. But that work might have gone to someone who really needed the money. And no one here sees him as anything but a blow-in. He'll be gone soon enough.

Kit waits morosely at the bar as Alison serves him, doing her best to smile cheery encouragement, before he trails away to Table 2, taking both his pint and his miasma of sadness with him.

Last night's fog has now cleared, which means Kit's mother is coming over on the last helicopter today. It will be the first time Beatrice Wallace has met up with her son since she left the island after the gig championships back in May. Things have apparently been strained between mother and son, *since* . . .

Kit is finding life difficult. There have been many new lows. He misses Hannah so much it's a physical pain. He tortures himself with theories about what might have happened to her. And he's still furious when he thinks of some of the newspaper coverage, branding Hannah a *party girl*, as if that was a bad thing, as if that meant she deserved it – whatever *it* was. The local press was respectful, but the tabloids published quotes from people who claimed to know Hannah – tall tales about *drink* and *drugs* and *satanic rituals*. All total bollocks.

The press and the police seemed to suppose Hannah's disappearance was a separate incident to the attacks on his mother and Charlotte, but Kit finds that hard to swallow. Neither Charlotte nor Beatrice had given interviews to reporters, the statements the police gave to the press were brief, and their wounds weren't serious enough to warrant much coverage. How many women are injured every week, every day – dozens,

335

scores, hundreds? He was repeatedly told there was no evidence to link the attacks with Hannah's disappearance. It may well have been a tragic coincidence, but it would also suit the police to avoid accusations of letting a killer run free, wouldn't it?

Kit feels angry and exhausted in turns. Speculation torments him. He drinks too much and sleeps badly.

He is taking the first sip of his pint when Sam comes in, asks for a non-alcoholic Corona, and joins him. Sam has reined it in a lot lately. Alison jokes that her profits are way down.

He's had a shock, that's why. Christie chucked him out in May. It was the worst possible timing – like she believed he had something to do with the attacks or the disappearance or both. But she was adamant, despite the wagging tongues. Sam sees the way some of the locals look at him now, hears fragments of the whispers:

'Do you think he . . . ?'

'The wife always knows something . . .'

'He and Hannah, didn't they . . . ?'

'Reckon Christie did the barmaid . . . ?'

At first Sam slept over at Vlad's, because he spent his nights sleeping with one of the housekeepers, but she left mid-October. Sam then slept on Emma's sofa for a few nights, and he's been bunking down in the builders' accommodation for the past two weeks.

He can't go home. Not invited.

Sam won't push it. He sees the lads at teatime every night, minds them when Christie asks, then goes back to his single bed. You'd think his sleep would be more peaceful without the kids, but he still jolts awake at the slightest noise. Anyway, the boys have settled down now, according to Christie.

He worries about his sons . . . but, no, she'd never hurt them.

He and Christie tell people they're trying to work things out; they need a bit of space. The truth is they've talked about a more permanent split after the twins start school. To be honest, it'll be a weight off – they bring out the worst in each other, him and Christie. They both fell in love with the wrong person.

Sam leaves after just the one drink, then Ted comes across to sit with Kit, nodding a greeting. They make an odd couple, but they can often be found sitting together at Table 2 of an evening. Ted is a silent drinking partner for the most part, then, a few pints in, it's as if a switch has been flicked. He'll start talking, as much to himself as to Kit. Mulling things through. Only when he's not working, only when his counterpart is operating the boat service.

'Can't go to sea bladdered,' he'll say, and everyone will laugh.

He's on his second pint already. The boat repairs will have to wait.

'You planning on staying then, boy?' he asks Kit.

'Yes.'

There has been speculation about when Kit would leave – when the police pulled out, at the end of the season, at the start of November . . .

'Why?'

It's a simple enough question. Staying won't bring Hannah back. What's left for him here? Only . . . Kit feels closer to her in the pub than anywhere. And he just can't galvanise himself to go back to London.

He shreds his beer mat, staring at it like it might have the answer. 'I'm not sure.' He isn't up to sharing anything emotional right now. He can't imagine the boatman would be interested in that sort of unburdening anyway. Their conversations stick to mutually agreed parameters: sport, weather, work, the news. 'I like the sea,' he tries. 'I like the history of the place.'

'History!' Ted mocks him. 'A few years back folk here were *starving*. Eating seagulls. Probably ate each other.' Ted takes a long gulp of his pint. 'Wreckers and pirates and scum. That's us; that's our history. A bunch of alcoholics washed up on the rocks, that's what we are.'

Kit notices the time is later than he imagined and feels he should perhaps walk over to Falcon and check on his mother, who will have arrived by now. Since he decided to stay on Tresco rather than returning to London, Beatrice has accused him of neglecting her. She says she feels lonely.

But the prospect of seeing her appals him, so he orders another round for him and Ted.

They talk of safer topics – asylum seekers. 'I wouldn't fancy chancing it in one of those bleddy dinghies, even in the summer,' says Ted.

Another round.

They talk of Alison and Kelly deciding to share a worker's cottage together on Tresco, so Kelly can continue renting out her place on St Mary's and there'll be an extra bedroom for holidaymakers at the inn.

Another round.

'I miss her.' The reprise. It spills out. Kit thinks of her constantly. Sunny reminiscences. Grief.

Then abruptly, sickeningly, they are talking about the terrible time – the day Hannah disappeared. Kit obsessively worries at the sparse details of what is known, like picking at a scab, testing it again and again to check it still hurts, making it bleed: where she was last spotted, what he last said to her, what might have happened . . .

There's a long silence. Over in the corner, Vlad and a couple of the younger builders laugh. And Ted says, 'I think I saw her that afternoon.' Like it's an ordinary sentence.

Kit is suddenly alert. 'I was told only Sam and one other person reported seeing her. Did you tell the police?'

'No.'

He tries to keep his voice civil, can't. 'Why the fuck—?'

'I was on some business.'

'But—'

'Private business.'

Rather than raging, or even pushing, Kit waits. He doesn't quiz Ted about what kind of business that was, guessing correctly that would only make the boatman clam up. He takes another mouthful of his pint, desperate to know more.

When he can bear it no longer, he asks, 'Where?'

The boatman slowly rotates his pint glass. He says nothing for almost a minute, then, 'Up the North End.'

Kit feels both cold and clammy. He knows this is important. He needs details. 'On her own?'

'I was out on the boat. Didn't see much. Another maid with her, I reckon. The one in the pink coat.'

There was some debate about that pink waterproof. Sam told the police he saw Hannah standing with someone up at the North End, but he didn't mention a pink coat. Another witness apparently reported seeing a woman in a pink waterproof arguing with Hannah up there. Police told Bobby, who told Alison, who told Kit, that the coat might be something and nothing. Kit repeatedly asked the officers if they'd followed up on this information, but by then the police were irritated by Kit's constant questions. They had thousands of potential suspects who'd come over to the Isles of Scilly for the gig championships. What were they supposed to do – question every single one of the buggers?

Kit treads carefully with Ted. 'Sam told the police – he told me – he saw Hannah up there with someone else he couldn't make out. He was quite near to them. But he never mentioned a pink coat.'

'Wouldn't have seen it,' says Ted.

'But he saw them—'

'Can't see pink, Sam. Colour blind.'

Kit comes at it from different angles, trying to prise out another crumb – anything more that might explain what this means and how it might tie in with why and how Hannah vanished – but that's all Ted will say. The more he interrogates, the more truculent Ted becomes, and the boatman gets up and leaves before last orders.

Kit sits and stews by himself until his final mouthful. He says goodnight to Alison and goes upstairs to his room. Usually he'd read, but his eyes can't focus. He lies on top of the neatly made bed and his mind gnaws at the pink coat until, at some point, he falls asleep.

He wakes at three, four, gets up at six, drinks coffee until it gets light.

His guts churn. Something is needling him there, more than the hangover, something he can't quite place, floating around his peripheral vision.

Kit dresses in his running gear and heads out, setting off up to Cromwell's Castle, jogging through the back fields, eager to move his body. The day promises balmy weather and unparalleled views. These freakishly beautiful late autumn days are an example of the benign micro-climate that blesses the Scilly Isles. Or perhaps it's an example of global warming. The back of his neck feels hot within minutes.

A big group of magpies shouts abuse at him from a clump of trees as he passes. He pauses to stretch his calves and counts seven birds, but he can't remember the rhyme, or the collective noun. It's not a murder, is it?

Hannah was the one to believe in them, she looked for all sorts of signs; she read the cards, she trusted her dreams, her instincts, her gut feelings.

For all the waking hours he thinks about her, he can never dream about Hannah. He wishes he could sense her with him now as he runs, he yearns to feel her close to him, but she is nowhere.

After an hour or so, he decides he needs to return to the Old Ship for a shower and another coffee to steel himself before he sees Beatrice. Get it over with.

69

Beatrice

She is out early, walking, taking the air, looking for shells, enjoying the sunshine which has been all but absent on the mainland. She had an early night, and her head is amazingly clear. She very deliberately did not go down to the pub last night. She is determined to prove to him that she's turned over a new leaf. Beatrice cannot recall a time on the island when she has felt so positively perky at this hour.

'Primrose. Don't be a beast. Come here. Come to Mummy!'

The dog is savaging the remains of a sea bird.

Technically the animal should be on the lead, but there's no one around. If anyone challenges her, Beatrice will tell them, *I lost my husband recently.* Seventeen months ago – does that count as recently? Surely she still has a pass as a grieving widow. Silently rehearsing this imaginary confrontation, she huffs, *I am allowed to grieve for as long as I choose!*

A sensation washes over her – she is being observed.

She wheels around to find . . . nothing and no one, just a beautiful bay straight out of a holiday brochure.

This is why she can no longer drink – these jolts of paranoia. Well, a glass or two of wine with dinner if out with friends, just to be sociable, but she simply can't indulge to the degree she used to.

She turns towards the breeze to blow away the bad thoughts and shakes out her hair. It needs a trim.

Her friends supported this off-season getaway; her acupuncturist positively encouraged it. A return to her lovely holiday home on this lovely island is part of her healing process.

Primrose trots back to her, bringing a small piece of driftwood as a gift, and as Beatrice bends to stroke the animal she spots a cowrie shell. A symbol of wealth!

As she crouches to pick it up the feeling washes over her again. She shudders. There's a wave of dizziness as she stands, as if she is bobbing out to sea.

She looks round again, and this time she spots Kit heading towards her from the far side of the beach.

70

Thor

Yesterday morning he heard them talking about Beatrice Wallace coming back to stay in Falcon. The heliport workers were chatting about it up by the tinned goods. Thor moved to the shelves on the other side so he could hear better, pretending to price cans of tomatoes. He felt sick.

The men stood there for ages. The one with the teeth who they call Vlad said how much he missed the barmaid. Boring stuff. But then Thor heard, 'She's coming alone, Kit's mother. The husband died, didn't he. And that other maid who was with her last time, she wouldn't want to come back here, would she. Came off worse, didn't she.'

So he might be safe – for now. She's not been back to the island at all since the gig championships, the one who heard his voice. The blonde one.

That afternoon the old hag, Beatrice, came in to buy some extra provisions. He felt like throwing up, but he forced himself to stay calm as he served her. She'd not seen his face. She'd not heard his voice. And thank Christ she hadn't recognised him.

This morning, still buoyed by relief, Thor gets up early. The day after tomorrow he's off to the mainland. Saved up for a helicopter flight and everything. A real occasion. He can hardly wait.

He's meeting one of his online *friends*. He's booked a room in the Travelodge in Hayle. She wanted to go to the seaside, but he doesn't want to stay in Penzance just in case someone recognises him there.

She's taking the day off school.

He thought that might be a problem, but he's seen her with and without makeup, with and without clothes – she can look older if she wants.

That's not the main thing anyway. The young ones aren't always the best. This one is. One of the more docile ones. Cries a lot.

His bag is packed. Tripod for his camera phone. Rope and tape. Toys.

He pulls on his short-sleeved T-shirt because it's mild enough, checks himself in the mirror – it shows off his muscles and tattoos nicely. He'll treat himself to a breakfast at the pub before heading to the shop for his shift. He has something to celebrate.

He'll buy a knife on the mainland. He threw the meat cleaver into the sea.

71

Kit and Beatrice

She holds up her hand and calls out to him, 'Darling!'

Primrose barrels across the sand and launches herself at Kit's knees. He swoops her up, nuzzling her ears as she bestows delighted licks about his face and neck. He carries the dog as he walks towards Beatrice, keeping hold of her to avoid hugging his mother.

'Mother.' He carefully kisses her cheek.

'Dear God, you look like a navvy!'

He winces. How many seconds has it taken before he wants to immediately turn around and walk away from her?

She sees him tense and hastily adds, 'Only joking. It suits you, these muscles. This tan. A working man!'

They stand regarding each other warily.

'Do come back to the house, darling. Let's have tea or something. What time is it?'

He assumes the unspoken question – is it socially acceptable to offer him a drink other than tea.

Kit puts Primrose down and she hops up on her hind legs, executing a small circle on the sand accompanied by half a dozen delirious yaps. From the small dog's perspective, she has just been reunited with a brother.

'Oh, Primmy!' Beatrice claps in delight. 'Primmy Primrose Wallace, we should have put you in a circus!'

The dog trots ahead, head held high. But walking alongside her, Beatrice notices Kit's shoulders slump. He has never carried himself with any great confidence, her boy. Such a pity. Wasted potential.

Mother and son walk up towards the dunes and the holiday home, remarking on the warmth in the sunshine, if not their relationship. The gulls circle overhead like vultures.

Kit feels odd as they approach Falcon. He's walked past it most days, but this is the first time he's been inside the time-share for several months. When his mother opens the door, it is the same chic haven as always. Beatrice hasn't yet unpacked one of her bags, which sits on the kitchen floor, but she has made a start on the provisions.

'I'll take this up for you, shall I?'

'Thank you, darling. That would be lovely.'

Kit carries his mother's luggage up the stairs to her room.

She calls up after him, 'I'll put the kettle on!'

She has turned over a new leaf.

72

Bobby

Fuming does not cover it. Sam has just called to say a couple of visitors have reported seeing a golf buggy in the sea up at Old Grimsby. The husband and wife had been watching out for the seal who's been rootling around up that end, when they spotted it. It took Sam a good while to get the couple off the phone because they wanted to tell him all about the whale they'd seen the previous day.

Bobby mobilises Farmer Michael and his tractor then cycles up to supervise.

The bloody Halloween party! One of the bikes for hire has also been totalled. Insurance will sort out both incidents, although then there's the premiums and excess to worry about. It's one thing claiming for an accident, another to have to stump up for vandalism and sheer drunken stupidity.

Bobby is slightly out of puff already and he's not even half-way to Old Grimsby. Perhaps the sun is to blame. That and his recent indulgences. He's pretty sure he's become addicted to Troytown Farm ice creams. Lovely little business over on St Agnes. But he needs to cut down, otherwise it'll be Christmas, and no one denies themselves then.

He pumps his legs to power the bike up a slight incline. The sooner they get the buggy out of the water, the sooner they can see if it can be salvaged. Sam and Farmer Michael will do the heavy lifting.

Bobby is relieved that Sam has cleaned up his act in the past few months. He's much more reliable these days. He only wishes he could say the same about Christie. She seems to have embraced the levels of drunkenness previously exhibited by her husband. Alison is on the verge of banning her from the bar. And while it is sexist, it is somehow more disturbing to see a woman legless in public, although Bobby feels guilty for thinking so. He'd tell anyone who asks that he's a proud feminist. Causes should stick together – he's watched the film *Pride*.

As he heads down the track to Old Grimsby, he reminds himself that he needs to pop in on Beatrice Wallace today or tomorrow, although he'll most probably see her in the pub at some point. While she's assured him she won't be giving up any of her timeshare weeks, this is her first visit back since the unfortunate incidents. She sublet to friends over August, two couples and six teenagers; party people.

Buttering up Beatrice Wallace will be time well spent. He'll lend his support, ask how she's coping, listen to some of her woes and perhaps discuss the state of her son.

He will take gin.

73

Kit

The sun flooding Falcon's lovely kitchen is doing nothing to soften his mother's words. The morning has developed into that most awkward of things – a sickening heart-to-heart.

'I know you miss her terribly, darling. But girls like that are for flings, not for keeps. And I should know – Henry went through enough of them.'

This is the first time his mother has openly acknowledged her husband's serial unfaithfulness, the bloody great elephant in the room for so many years.

Beatrice stands with her back to Kit, making herself another cup of tea.

Kit consciously squeezes his shoulders down away from his ears as Primrose sits leaning against his ankle, unflustered by Beatrice's *revelations*. He has no idea what to say.

As she waits for the kettle to boil, his mother begins to take the remaining items from the provision boxes, putting them into the cupboards in a haphazard manner.

After this show of busyness, she suddenly says, 'Oh, before I forget, Charlotte sends her love.'

'Jesus Christ!'

The dog sits to attention, as if Kit has called her name.

'There's no need to be so touchy, darling. She misses you.'

'She's a bloody stalker. She DMs me every week!'

'She is a lovely girl. Why you two didn't get together is beyond me.'

'She was vile to—'

'The barmaid?'

'My girlfriend, you mean? Hannah. She has a name. Charlotte hated her.'

Beatrice pauses, then slowly moves towards him, a look of revelation painted across her face. She says, 'Have you considered Charlotte might have bumped into her up there? What if they had some sort of . . . altercation?'

'Are you insane? Charlotte couldn't knock the skin off a rice pudding,' snorts Kit. 'If there had been a fight, Hannah would have wiped the floor with her.'

'Yes, I'm sure you're right.'

Exasperated, he gets up to leave. 'I want to get out on the water this afternoon – make the best of the weather. It might be my last chance.'

'That's the ticket! Good food, good wine, and fresh air!' smiles Beatrice. 'All the soul needs.'

74

Bobby and Kit

By the time Bobby has overseen the removal of the buggy from the sea, cycled back to the Estate Office and dealt with a grumble about the degree of evening cloud cover, which has left a gaggle of stargazers 'extremely disappointed', Kit appears asking for his supply box.

'I'm after my sailing stuff. I just need to get out in the sunshine while we have it, you know.'

'Good plan. Have you seen your mother?' asks Bobby.

'Yes.'

'And? Is she well?'

'She is firing on all cylinders,' replies Kit, making a face which does not convey complete and absolute joy at the reunion.

'Of course,' replies Bobby, in a manner intended to agree with anything Kit is suggesting, while providing no evidence of actually siding with him.

'Will you do me a favour and take your mother's supply boxes over to Falcon while you're at it?' asks Bobby. 'Save me a job. We have a golf buggy free right now if you could run them up.'

While Kit is a little annoyed with this request, as it means seeing his mother again, he agrees. He tries hard to fit in with the community here. He occupies a strange position on the island – not exactly a visitor, not exactly a worker. Doing a favour for Bobby will go down well.

And he does feel sorry for his mother. It is true that he's been avoiding her. But, while grief brings some families together, sadly, theirs is not one of them.

75

Christie

She has overfilled her mug. Liquid is now dribbling off the worktop, down the cupboard door, and merrily dripping on the floor. Christie wipes up the mess, sips the top of the tea, even though it's too hot, and carries it over to the window to look out over the sea. Gorgeous sunshine today. She might take the twins and Finn out for a walk in a bit. Blow away this bloody headache, which has nagged her all day.

Dan and Ben are playing an elaborate game under the table known only to themselves. She shouts an 'Oi!' when it threatens to become murderous. She looks around the kitchen. The place is a bit of a mess.

She's a bit of a mess.

She'll have to get her act together later – Emma's two youngest are coming over tonight. It's payback time on the babysitting front. She doesn't really mind – a night in bingeing an entire drama series on Netflix will do her good. She likes the foreign ones with the subtitles which make her feel worldly and clever. She doesn't like the ones with weekly episodes as she can never keep the plot in her head.

She smiles to herself. A good session in the bar the other night – a bit of flirting and a lot of drink. So what? She's thriving! Even though she sees Sam every day she feels free.

At odd times it hits her again – Sam, the rows, the whole Hannah saga, but she refuses to go down that route again. She likes the feeling of calm when she's not having to think about where her husband might be and what he might be getting up to; not having to listen to people *telling* her what he's getting up to. She likes going to sleep without wanting to punch someone very hard.

Now people are talking about her rather than Sam – dancing with the hot builder at the Halloween party, singing along with Kate Bush, The Prodigy. Top night.

If Hannah had been there she'd have been all over the builders like a rash. She'd have been attracting all the attention as usual, with her mad dancing and that annoying laugh. It makes a change for Christie to be centre stage.

But as soon as she thinks of Hannah, the rage is instant. She sees herself punching the barmaid, smashing a glass in her face.

She's glad the bitch is dead.

The tea is still too hot. Christie burns her lip.

76

Beatrice

She is quite shaken after Kit leaves. Such a shame that their reunion was spoilt. Even though she is long gone the barmaid still manages to ruin things. His obsession with that woman! Whenever her name comes up – and her name always comes up – they end up arguing, or he becomes frosty towards her.

Every single time Kit phoned home he'd ask if she'd remembered another snippet about the man in the balaclava, convinced he had something to do with the barmaid's disappearance. And when Beatrice protested that she didn't want to be quizzed about that awful holiday *every single time I try to have a conversation with my son*, he accused her of being insensitive. He even accused her of being a snob!

And it wasn't as if she was prejudiced against her, not at all. She just knew she wasn't right for her boy. She had learned that the hard way, from bitter experience.

She hadn't intended to drink. She'd not even been to the pub, to avoid temptation, but the free sample of the Scilly Spirit gin is sitting there, just asking for it.

She feels rather guilty about throwing poor Charlotte under the bus, suggesting she might have had something to do with the *saintly Hannah* going AWOL. Kit didn't believe it though, so she shouldn't feel bad.

Her boy is grieving now but he will get over it. He will meet someone new, and he will fall in love again simply because he is young and foolish and sweet. Perhaps not Charlotte. Beatrice has rather given up on that front. She has come to agree with him that she is more than a tad annoying.

But he will find someone new. And in the future, she hopes he will eventually make her a grandmother. With a more suitable girl. Genes are important.

She will go and sit out in the garden in a moment. The Agapanthus looks rather magnificent. It is such a treat to see blooms in flower at this time of year. Her garden at home is rather bleak.

Kit's annoyed with her now. But he will thank her one day. He will realise that his mother would do anything for him.

She should have listened to her own mother. She warned Beatrice about *marrying down*, as she put it. 'Not people like us, darling,' was her verdict on Henry. (His family lived in a terrace house.) Some might think that's an old-fashioned concept, but it matters. It's a question of education, cultural acclimatisation, world views. Her son and a barmaid! Different species. What did they talk about? Crisp flavours? Dry roasted?

People like her darling husband only want people like her as some sort of trophy. But she was so ridiculously, shamefully in love with him, she refused to believe that those wild differences that had so thrilled her at the start of the relationship would lead to trouble later. It was so heady, so *passionate*. But then, inevitably, just as her mother predicted, she started to want more than he could give, and the trouble started. Not money – Henry provided well enough on that front – but her social life was severely curtailed. He upset several of Beatrice's friends. He insisted on paying for dinner with the ones he liked, ordering the most ostentatious bottles of wine that didn't actually pair, and it was so . . . *gauche*.

Yes to Ascot, no to Henley; yes to Wimbledon – but you should have seen his face when she suggested Glyndebourne. 'Why would I want to listen to fat birds sing?' he mocked.

Obsessive about weight, Henry, although never his own. If Beatrice have developed a paunch like his, she would not have heard the end of it. 'The balcony over the toy box,' he'd laugh. Always crude.

They drag you down, these types; stop you from reaching your full potential. He wanted her to go to the dogs for God's sake. Literally. And when she protested, he asked, *What's the difference between that and horse racing*? If you had to explain it, they'd never understand.

So naturally she wanted rid of the barmaid from the first day she learned about the fling. Horrid thing. She only wanted a meal ticket.

The ice cubes in her drink ping one of the fillings at the back of her mouth. Damn. She'll need to have that looked at when she returns to London.

She does feel for Kit, although he doesn't believe it. She hates to see him so glum. She would never shed a tear for that awful woman, but he has sobbed over her on the phone. As a mother that is hard to hear.

He might have believed he was in love, but the barmaid was only using him. She didn't truly care about him. The absolute show she made of herself, draped around the neck of that young chap from the heliport! They call him Vlad; she doesn't know his actual name. And then kissing that beastly French man, letting him paw her in public! Like a cat in heat.

Kit couldn't see it though; wouldn't see it.

And worse than the entire . . . *spectacle* that night in the pub, was her belly. Beatrice is sure, absolutely, sickeningly sure, that it was bigger, rounder than it was before.

And . . .

She places Primrose on her lap.

Of course she knew Henry was cheating on her. And yet she did nothing! Worse, she bought some awful La Perla underwear, got herself trussed up in it, and cavorted around the bedroom. It did the trick. Simple creatures, men. But afterwards, he got up, got dressed, and went out – straight round to one or the other of his little side trollops, she's guessing.

She should have bought Ann Summers.

All his lies. And she colluded. She wanted to believe him.

He swore it was work; he was always *away for work*. She was being *paranoid*, she needed *her head looked at*, she needed to keep her *fucking nose out of his business*!

And then, when she'd actually started to doubt herself – perhaps it was the nature of his job; perhaps he was working all hours – *to keep you in the fucking manner you're accustomed to –* the ambulance people found him in flagrante . . .

The barmaid was like that – as bad as Henry. She couldn't stand by and watch her ruin her son's life like her husband had ruined her own.

She is convinced that the conniving little cow got pregnant to trap her boy. Kit wouldn't have a clue, the silly sap. *Pussy-whipped –* Charlotte told her that expression.

Over her dead body would that woman join this family.

She could not bear to think of Kit going through the same crushing indignities she had suffered. And anyone could tell the barmaid was not the faithful type. She would have broken his heart, of that Beatrice is certain.

Perhaps she should have something to eat. She's not been drinking so much since her stay at the health spa. Her tolerance levels must have changed . . .

The last time she and Kit were here together back in May she had pointed out that a barmaid's salary wouldn't get him very far. She'd said something like, *I hope your love keeps you warm because you can't live on fresh air, darling.*

He'd countered with something along the lines of, *You always wanted me to step up, to take responsibility for my life. Well, now I'm going to!*

It was the first time Beatrice had heard him use the word *responsibility.* It made her feel sick.

He'd left without helping her load the dishwasher after that particular row. Stormed out.

Later that day she'd found his phone on the kitchen table . . .

77

Kit

His mother isn't in when he arrives at Falcon with the supply boxes. Neither is the dog, so they've probably gone out for another walk. To the pub he assumes. Without Beatrice's jarring presence, the kitchen is once more a peaceful oasis of pale blue walls and golden light. The view from the window promises a relaxing excursion on the water later, the double glazing filtering out the more homicidal shrieks of the gulls.

He opens the lid on the first of the supply boxes. His mother has packed sloppily. Two pashminas lie in a crumpled heap on top of her torch and walking boots. He removes items which belong downstairs and takes the rest up to his mother's bedroom. She has yet to unpack most of the luggage she's brought with her. Why does she need so many clothes?

The second box is much heavier. He guesses right – this is the one that contains the rest of her outdoor gear. He opens it, removing her wellingtons and a second, sturdier pair of walking

361

boots, putting them under the coat rack.

He takes out her bright yellow sou'wester and a large bobble hat, a water bottle, small rucksack – then he sees it, right at the bottom – his mother's pink waterproof.

Icy fingers of dread creep across his scalp.

78

Alison

Alison has just caught a couple of ramblers out in the garden, sitting there bold as brass eating sandwiches from two Tupperware containers they'd brought along with them. She politely challenged them, saying, 'I'm sorry, but you can't eat your own sandwiches here.' They looked at her, looked at each other, then simply swapped them.

It threw her. It was so clever she couldn't think of a comeback.

There's a new booze rep in today, a cocky young blade in a suit that would look at home in the audience of a darts championship. 'Lovely gaff you have here,' he enthuses. 'I've been in some right dives, know what I'm saying.'

'Really?' says Alison, already irritated by him. His aftershave is overwhelming, and to her exacting standards the bar is in obvious need of a spruce-up, so she feels a little embarrassed.

'Went to a pub yesterday and had a ploughman's lunch. The ploughman wasn't happy.' He laughs at his own crap joke, a high giggle that goes through Alison like cheese wire.

Sitting across on Table 1, nursing her half-drunk Guinness, Old Betty pipes up, 'Last week, we had a penguin come in here and ask if anyone had seen his brother, and I says, "What does he look like then?"'

She laughs until she wheezes.

Oh God, it's going to be like this, thinks Alison.

The rep and Old Betty josh until Alison interrupts to get the bloke back on track. They discuss the new concoction he's over here promoting – a sickly-sweet alcopop in a cartoon-like bottle that's supposed to be a lighthouse. After his spiel, the rep hops up on a bar stool and asks to sample the local gin.

'I never get high on my own supply,' he winks.

Alison hates winkers.

She joins him for a drink because she bloody needs one.

The rep witters on, 'You had that trouble over here a while back, yeah? The missing barmaid? The others? What's the low-down on that then?'

Her heart sinks. She talks in generalisations and drinks her vodka quickly so she can be rid of him. But when she offers him another drink, a kneejerk habit, of course he says yes. She could kick herself.

He grins, 'A man walks into a bar and asks the barmaid for a double entendre – so she gave him one!' That bloody giggle again.

Alison turns to adjust the optics to stop herself throwing the ice bucket in his face.

Not for the first time does she wish Hannah was still around, then they could cut this little prick down to size together.

Old Betty toddles up to the bar for another. 'I'll get that for you,' says the rep. 'Stick it on my card.'

'Thank you. I'll have the usual please, Alison.' Old Betty smiles with all her teeth.

Along with another Guinness, Alison puts through an order for fish and chips and an apple crumble. Serves him right.

'Hey, why does a barmaid wear fur-lined knickers?' asks the rep. Neither Alison nor Betty answer. 'To keep her ankles warm!' He's still laughing when Alison finally loses patience and tells the rep and his man bun to fuck off out of her bar.

79

Kit

He walks along the swoop of Appletree Bay, sea salt in the air, tears mixing with the rain on his face.

He's crying for his father. He's crying for Hannah. It won't bring either of them back.

A gull circles twice and plumps itself down on the sand within kicking distance. He is very tempted to do it, but he is not that man.

Other things he might do instead: drink the blue vodka, sleep with the new girl from the garden team, punch his mother in the face. He has to keep reminding himself, *I am not that man.*

He must swallow all of this, this . . . impotent fury. He will have to push it down to the deepest depths, leave it there, deny and ignore it until he can function. But if he pretends he hasn't seen what he has just seen he will never be able to look himself in the face again. The guilt will eat him alive. And he will have let her down. Hannah deserves better.

A small object on the foreshore catches his eye. So much waste thrown up by the sea, even here. For some reason he stoops to pick it up before he's processed what it is he's looking at. He brushes away the wet sand to reveal a tiny piece of Lego . . . a lifeboat, yellow as the gull's yolky beak currently taunting him with its calls.

He knows the story – a shipment of Lego somehow ended up in the sea in the late nineties, smashed open, and spewed miniature treasures into the waves. The irony was that so many of these pieces featured sea creatures and flippers and scuba tanks; a myriad of maritime mementos, which wash up on Cornish sands to this day.

Kit turns the Lego piece this way and that, considers throwing it back into the water. The gull protests. Quite right. Too much plastic in the oceans these days.

Hannah was his life raft. If he sinks now, he is not doing right by her; he needs to honour her by doing the right thing and then making something of his life. Be a man.

You have to grow up sometime, darling. How many times has his mother said that? Hannah probably thought the same thing.

If his body was lost at sea he knows what Hannah would do. She might grieve, but she would *live*. She would get on with it and live her very best life, wringing every experience out of it that she could.

But before Kit gets on with his life, he has a big decision to make, and he has never been good at making decisions.

The gull caws its disapproval and flaps away. The creature is part dinosaur, a winged lizard. Surely Kit is better than that; surely he's evolved.

But he is a coward. He would rather bury his head in the sand

and do nothing. What good would it do, telling the police what he thinks he knows, what he's just seen? It is not proof exactly, is it? And it can't bring Hannah back.

Can he betray his own mother? What sort of man would do that? Wouldn't it ruin her life even if there was an innocent explanation? He can't imagine Beatrice would ever speak to him again whatever happened, although that might not be such a terrible thing.

Could there be a benign account? He tries to make sense of what he's seen. But he can't.

He took his mother's pink waterproof out from the bottom of her supply box, turning it over, slowly examining it as if it might be radioactive. There was nothing on the surface that he could see, nothing in the pockets.

His shoulders dropped a little. It was only when he was hanging it up, the sun bright on the wall by the coat pegs, that he noticed the long dark hairs caught around one of the toggles right at the bottom of the coat. Three strands. You might mistake it for black cotton. Coarse hair, like the mane of a wild horse.

He stood there for several minutes, aware of little except swallowing the bitter taste in his mouth, before he put the coat back in the box, ramming the lid down tight, and then he sat at the kitchen table facing the door, waiting for his mother to return from her walk, trying to work out what he would say to her, trying to decide what to do, his legs vibrating, hoping for an explanation.

Beatrice eventually arrived, several gins or vodkas the worse for wear. As soon as he confronted her she started weeping. *How could he think that! How could he accuse her?* The cries upset Primrose, who started barking in distress. Then an all-out screaming match ensued.

'You have no idea how much I've sacrificed for you, you ungrateful child! Yes – you're still a *child*!' she spat. 'You have no idea! You tore me to pieces the day you were born and you're tearing me to pieces still!'

The rage he felt was blinding.

In the end he needed to get away from her because he feared what he might do.

He walked for miles, the sun beating down on his head, the breeze stiffening.

And then it started raining.

Whatever he decides now, despite everything, he does love his mother. He doesn't like her, but the basic unit of love is a given, hardwired, programmed from birth. What good would it do now, throwing her to the wolves? What would it achieve? But he needs to do the right thing, not just for Hannah, not to avenge her death, for that's not possible, not just to try and give Hannah's mother some form of closure, but for his own peace of mind.

He knows what Hannah would do.

He strides on, turning the piece of Lego over and over in his hand.

No one has ever made him laugh so much, no one has ever made him feel freer, more alive, than her. He always wanted to be a better man for her.

The shower is passing now. A shaft of sunshine rushes towards land, a laser through the cloud.

He takes out his phone, finds the number for the police station on St Mary's, peers at it.

It's at least another minute before he manages to make the call.

80

Miss Elisabeth

Miss Elisabeth pauses on her walk, watching the youth from Falcon down on the beach below her. He's hunched over, staring at his phone. Youngsters these days never look up; they don't see what's in front of them – the rainbow, the brilliant light slicing through the clouds. His head is bowed. He looks grief-stricken. She feels for him. She knows a fair few things about loss herself – her mother, her father, her baby brother, her friend Florence. You don't get to Miss Elisabeth's age without loss nibbling at the extremities of your life like moths in your woollens.

She wonders, did she do the right thing telling the police her suspicions about Kit? She's less sure of it now. He seems genuine. She can't take it back anyhow.

But she does know that the young man will heal. He will grow a brand-new heart, and the injured places will be more resilient this time – scar tissue and knitted-together bones are so much tougher than the originals.

Whatever happens, this island knits itself back together.

She thinks of Hannah. The waters have closed over the maid's head and her atoms are mixing in the deepest waters now; she is part of the mighty ocean.

Hannah once told Miss Elisabeth she wanted to visit New York. Perhaps parts of her will reach it, eventually. You can't fight the tides and the currents – you go with the flow.

Addressing nothing and no one, Miss Elisabeth says out loud, 'Well, time to get on.' She sets off towards the shop at a fair old clip.

The next stop from Tresco is the east coast of North America. You could row it if you were that way inclined. Some hardy souls have done just that, raising money for charity. Months at sea, thousands and thousands of nautical miles, one hell of a lot of nothing but the freezing Atlantic in between. Miss Elisabeth hugs her coat tighter around herself at the thought. She does not fancy so much nothing.

81

Beatrice

He slammed the door behind him. It felt so . . . final. He might never come back. And now she doesn't know what to do. But she knows where Kit got his temper and that language from – her husband. At a certain stage in the evening, Henry always had that whiff of violence about him.

Oh God – what should she do?

If only Charlotte hadn't left his phone on the kitchen table that day.

She knew his password – his birthday. He'd never changed it because he's a simple boy at heart, her son, a romantic boy at heart.

It wasn't as if she had a plan exactly. But . . .

She texted the barmaid from his phone: *Meet me up the North End. 4pm. I have a BIG surprise for you!*

She thought she might offer her money. Pay her off. Or warn her off . . . who knows.

When she popped round to give Miss Elisabeth their leftover

venison, she spotted the carving knife in her washing-up bowl. If anything were found missing from Falcon on the changeover day, the inventory would pick up on it; better to be safe than sorry. She'd only intended to take it for protection. The barmaid might go feral.

But it didn't matter what she had in mind then, because, in the end, she forgot to take it. She might have been a little the worse for wear. Stress.

She'd accidentally texted Charlotte from Kit's phone. She'd lost track of the time. When she realised almost an hour had passed, she had to rush to meet the barmaid up there.

She grabbed her waterproof and dashed out. The wind was extraordinary. It was only when she was about halfway there she remembered that she'd left the knife back in the kitchen by the bread bin.

But she had a stroke of luck. The builders who'd been working on Tern had scurried inside to shelter because of the weather, and she noticed one of their tool bags had been left just sitting there, wide open on the back of an old golf buggy. She helped herself to a hammer and a screwdriver. She's not sure why. They just took her fancy.

If it had been a fair fight, the barmaid might have hurt Beatrice – animal instincts, people like her. But Beatrice had surprise on her side.

Hannah was waiting for Kit at the top of the cliffs, looking out to sea like the bloody *French Lieutenant's Woman*. Hair whipping around her head like black straw. Fucking witch!

Beatrice crept up on her. Hannah sensed someone was behind her, and whirled round as Beatrice roared, 'LEAVE MY SON ALONE!

And she shrieked, 'Keep your fucking nose out of our business!' Beatrice can't recall exactly what she yelled next, but there was an awful lot of shouting.

She gripped the screwdriver in her left pocket and the hammer in her right. Deep pockets, those waterproofs.

And when she'd had enough – how dare that woman scream and swear at her! Who did she think she was! – she whipped out the hammer, and all of a sudden the barmaid turned, as if she'd seen someone, and Beatrice swung and caught the side of her face by mistake. If she hadn't struck the first blow, the barmaid would have gone for her, of that she is absolutely sure! It was self-defence.

The shock of the hammer blow made Hannah scream and step back. If only she'd have fallen over the cliff edge then. But she managed to lunge for Beatrice and hit her a couple of times, flailing, calling her all the names under the sun, terrible language, and she grabbed Beatrice's hair and managed to kick her. Beatrice felt no pain at the time but she was very annoyed.

She felt better when she stabbed her. The barmaid didn't see the screwdriver coming. She stopped hitting back after that. Three more swift jabs to the side of her ribs.

It was easy really. If the woman had been wearing an oilskin it might have been more difficult, but she only had a cheap windbreaker jacket, poor-quality material, which says it all really.

Beatrice considered one more blow to her repulsive gut, but call her sentimental, she couldn't, because if there was a baby it would have been partly Kit's.

The barmaid didn't scream again. Or if she did it was snatched away by the wind.

The push was easy because she didn't seem entirely aware

of what was happening by then. She was staggering. One small push for Beatrice, one giant push for mankind. Ha! How many other men had she saved by disposing of the awful woman?

She was a bloody wrecker, luring men to their deaths on the rocks. She was a bloody siren, and Beatrice could not, would not, let her destroy her boy!

Hannah didn't fall, rather crumpled in stages – to her knees, her hip, her hand, her elbow. Her head went down last.

The heavens opened. The wind was insane. It spat nails of rain into her face.

But Beatrice had her Pilates to thank for her excellent core control. She was far stronger than she looked. She was far better at standing up on a surfboard than Kit or Henry ever were.

She braced and pushed with her foot, and off the woman went, sprawling over the lip of the cliff. And it might have been all done and dusted then. But it wasn't. No such luck.

She had hoped to fling her into the sea, but when she looked, the body had somehow become lodged on a ridge below. Beatrice had to scramble down after her. So irritating!

She managed to reach her, careful not to lose her balance, and by pushing and shoving her along with her foot, clinging to the grasses in the crevices of the rocks at the side to keep her balance, she managed to roll the body off the ledge, rolling her around and down, like the Gloucester cheese at the Cooper's Hill Cheese Roll. Kit did it one year; sprained his wrist the silly boy. Over and over she went. Beatrice laughed. Nerves. Hannah caught her once more, another kick as her leg shot out, but that might not have been voluntary.

And by then they were almost at the blowhole.

Beatrice knelt over her. She was curled into herself like a

giant foetus, the side of her face ruined, bits missing, splattered with blood and mud. She seemed to focus on the face above her for a second and she cried out. It was such a horrible animal noise that Beatrice smashed the hammer into her teeth, a reflex action to shut her up. Then she hauled her up under her armpits, heavy as a sack of potatoes – not that Beatrice had ever lifted a sack of potatoes – dragged her across the wet rocks the last few inches, and flung her into the mouth of the blowhole.

Of course, just her luck, right at that moment, the sea spumed up so hard she feared the body would be hoisted aloft, the waterspout like that of a giant whale. But she'd gone in. Beatrice peered over the edge just to make sure, but there was no sign of her.

She sat there a good while to get her breath back. The waterspout caught her a couple of times before she galvanised herself to stand. She threw the screwdriver and the hammer and Kit's phone into the blowhole after her. Then she started to make her way back down.

Then she saw him – the man in the balaclava! God! Her heart lurched and she started running. She couldn't tell if he'd seen her and she had no way of knowing if he'd seen what had happened.

The rain hurtled against her as she ran, and she slipped a few times, but ploughed on and . . . she thought GOOD – it will wash all traces of that vile woman off her: her hands, her hair, her cheeks, her coat. A deluge! Almost biblical.

She was barely aware of how she managed to stagger all the way back to Falcon.

She was soaking, freezing by the time she got indoors. She leant against the wall, trembling spasmodically, and attempted to arrange her face in case Charlotte was home, but she wasn't, thank God.

She had a very large double vodka to steady her nerves. She assumes she had quite a few more.

In the morning Kit came.

She had no real idea how bad she looked.

He told her about the attack. Charlotte battered and whisked away to hospital. The man in the balaclava. Awful!

Useful.

The police interviewed Beatrice. Why wouldn't they believe the same man had attacked her too? Shock is convenient – details slip away. What other explanation could there be?

When her coat had dried, before Kit came in the morning, she has a vague recollection of ramming the pink waterproof into the very bottom of her supply box. And she forgot about it. She only thought of it once she'd arrived on the mainland. She should have thrown it into the sea. Too late then. No one would seek it out, surely. Her DNA would still be on it. But . . .

No one looks in those supply boxes. Always busy and a little chaotic, the changeover days, even more so in May. No one checks the personal belongings of the guests. There's only an issue if something goes missing. Like a barmaid.

She does recall her heart battering as she got on the helicopter to leave the island. She feared someone might shout, 'STOP! MURDERER!' But, of course, the barmaid hadn't been missing very long then.

Charlotte had left earlier than Beatrice, keen to be away. She went to recuperate with her mother in Bath, so Beatrice was on the helicopter by herself. She had waited until the actual day of her return ticket, so no one could suspect she'd rushed away.

Kit stayed behind to search. Foolish boy.

There followed one, two weeks back in London when Beatrice tried to blot it all out. Poor Primrose was left to her own devices.

Then she stopped. She gave herself a good talking-to. That woman wasn't worth risking her health for.

She now tells herself she had only done what any good mother would do – protect her child. Kit might hate her now, but he will come to understand it was done out of love . . .

And how dare some barmaid tell her to *keep your fucking nose out of my business.* He's her son! It is her business!

She would do anything for her boy. A parent's job is to protect their child. She would do it again.

82

Christie

It is a lovely peaceful night; Finn, a big boy now, into everything, a dead weight, fast asleep next to her on the sofa as she watches TV with the volume low, her feet up on the little beanbag Tommy likes to sit on. She helps herself to another Malteser and nuzzles into him. It's rare that she has a chance to put her feet up. The twins and Tommy are with their dad. Finn's full of a cold so she kept him home.

When Sam was living here she could never settle at night, waiting for him to come home, always on edge, listening out for him whether she was sitting down here on the sofa or up in bed. Now she knows he's not coming back, she can relax. She falls asleep easily.

Yeah, some nights she has to get up and come down for a few drinks until she feels able to go to sleep again. But not often.

Those are the nights she's back at the North End. Those nights she jerks awake.

If she'd got to the bloody barmaid that afternoon she would have gone for her, she knows that. But, in the end, she didn't have to. She stood in the gale and the driving rain, pressed herself into the lee of the rocks, her hip pushed hard against the unforgiving granite crag, and she watched Beatrice Wallace do the job for her.

Christie might have stopped her or tried to. Didn't.

If the police had come after her, if they'd found her pink coat, she would have told them what she saw. But they didn't push it, so she didn't need to.

Because if she told the police she'd seen Beatrice Wallace attack the barmaid, Beatrice could just as easily lie and say Christie had done it. And who would they believe – someone like her, or someone like Beatrice?

Best leave it be.

She has enough on her plate with the boys as it is.

83

Thor

He is thrumming with excitement, almost squirming in his seat. His first time on the helicopter. His first time meeting one of his online playmates in real life.

He's arranged to meet her at the Travelodge, book in, then go to a café overlooking the sand at Towans beach. She said she wanted to see the sea. Rhianna she calls herself, *RhiRhiSweetSixteen*.

That's not her real name.

It's not her real age either. She told him she was fifteen. Almost. Didn't matter much either way to him.

Fourteen-year-old Rhi-Rhi. What fun he'll have with her.

It is an effort not to bounce up and down in the seat of the taxi, but the driver is taciturn and doesn't seem to notice his eagerness. Hayle in November, hardly a riveting proposition.

He will put on his Marilyn Manson T-shirt and his eyeliner as soon as he gets there. The bitch had better turn up, otherwise all the screenshots he has of her will be off the Cloud and up online. He thinks of those images again. He can hardly wait. His online pal *BDE666* has given him plenty of ideas and *Van Damme* is always grateful for the images.

Standing at reception someone is waiting for Thor. The one who sent the last few messages, *RhiRhiSweetSixteen*. Not her name. Not her age. A much older woman, with short blonde hair. She spritzes it up into a quiff on a night out, but today it's combed flat for work. There is tension in her jaw, tiredness around eyes that have seen too many things she'd rather not see. All part of the job; a job that has left her loving her two rescue Staffies more than most people.

Rhi-Rhi – otherwise known as DCI Maggie (Margaret) Banks, part of a special team investigating internet grooming as part of the National Crime Agency's Child Exploitation and Online Protection unit. Not a mother herself – doesn't need to be to feel absolutely fucking furious at what goes on. And while in no way excited like Thor, she is antsy. She picks a rough bit of nail, gnaws at it.

A gift, the girl, the real Rhi-Rhi, breaking down and telling her parents and the parents immediately getting in touch. Rarely happens. Shame, the great inhibitor.

Maggie very much wants to meet *Thor*, aka twenty-five-year-old Alec O'Donnell. Some pathetic, socially inept incel. Bullying bastard. She can hardly wait.

Then they will trawl through his computer and find who else he's been chatting to. They've already got a location for another person of interest who calls himself *Van Damme* – from the island of Bryher. He's a consumer rather than producing the disgusting content. Still scum.

84

Kit

It is a blustery day. A bouncy castle boat ride over to St Mary's to catch the flight, which means they won't fly over Tresco on the way back to Penzance. When the helicopter takes off, Kit doesn't look back. He has the feeling that he'll not return to the island.

The wind makes the helicopter lurch as it lands at Penzance, making him feel queasy.

He nods to a couple who'd been staying at the Old Ship as they disembark, but he can't face the small talk.

He fusses over Primrose when she's released from her cage. She gazes up at him with trusting eyes the colour of chocolate drops. She seems to be in a trance. The dog remains quiet in the taxi to the station. She sits on his lap and doesn't seem entirely present. The new vet gave her some calming tablets before the flight and she didn't make a sound on the way over. Kit wouldn't mind some of those tablets himself.

He needs a coffee before he can brace himself to get on the train back to London. He needs a moment.

He walks slowly at the dog's pace, hauling his one wheelie case behind him. He'll have the rest of his things sent over later. They make their way inland, away from the harbour where a wind with the taste of winter is cutting across the water with malice. Primmy squats for a wee, then sits in the puddle, perplexed. He has to tie her up outside Boots and buy some baby wipes to clean her up. When he comes back out she is staring up at the sky, watching the gulls making lazy loops above despite the force of the wind.

He sits in a café which welcomes dogs. Messages a few friends. Charlotte's Insta is now labelled *Charlotte's Journey* and she's gained several thousand more followers, rebranding herself as a *Mental Health Advocate/Survivor*. Good for her.

Earlier this morning, Sergeant Jack Moore came over from St Mary's with a detective from the mainland to take his mother into custody. She went quietly, as they say.

The last thing she said to him was, 'It was an accident, darling,' her face a pantomime of grief.

She never told him what really happened. He guesses she never will.

He has no idea what will happen to her next, or where he'll go, what he'll do. At some point he'll need to try and unravel his emotions, but he is unable to do that right now – it is too raw. He has the responsibility of the dog, that's as far as he can think. He'll try and do what Hannah did, live in the moment, wring every last drop out of life while he can.

By the time they head to the train, Primrose is trotting once more, her head held high.

The Blowhole

She told them where. She didn't tell them why.

So well spoken. You could hardly believe what she'd done.

She admitted her injuries weren't from the man in the balaclava but from the barmaid. Swore it was self-defence, an accident.

She said they might find her in the blowhole – although it would be more accurate, what was left after so many months being battered by seawater.

A few tatters of material, bones, hair. Fragments. Hardly a person.

The team gather the equipment ready to descend at low tide. It is a beautiful day.

85

Hannah

Above, the birds cry their *if onlys*.

Below – she is nothing but pain.

The rain splinters her thoughts into fragments.

Memories like lightning.

He lay in her arms and sobbed. She stroked his hair, kissed his temple, soothed him. They spent the night together.

Christie didn't believe they'd never fucked. No one believed that. The gossips made up a story of an affair.

Sam loved her in a way. Trusted her. Hated her, ashamed that he'd allowed her to see the part he kept so well hidden – the tenderness he attempted to anaesthetise with alcohol when his wife lost her temper and pummelled him.

A kick. She curls away from the pain. A fleeting image of a baby.

The gossips made up a story of a pregnancy.

A flash of Kit sobbing against her breast. She kisses his eyelids and soothes him. He is grieving for his father.

Above her, a face, a gash of rage.

Below her, boiling water.

She fights. She fights until the breath is kicked out of her.

Then she falls.

Her light explodes into rocks and spume and the roar of the waves and the shrieks of dead gulls and she is all sound and sensation.

She flickers a moment . . . then goes under.

And she flies apart into a billion atoms. And she is the sea.

Acknowledgements

I love the Isles of Scilly and hope to go back one day if the people there forgive me for this book and don't *Wicker Man* me or *Midsommar* my Geoff. The real Tresco isn't anything like the one depicted here, nor are any characters based on any of my real friends I met there: Sue, Hobbsie, Robin, Anna, Joan, Jo, Jeremy, and everyone else. The Tresco in these pages is more like the Upside Down in *Stranger Things*, or perhaps a David Lynch version of *Doc Martin*.

There is no barmaid-encrusted blowhole, the Old Ship in these pages is not Tresco's New Inn, there is no *Book of Sea Stories and Songs*. I have taken liberties. I also took their barman.

Me and my Geoff have been married twenty years. Of all the bars in all the world, I walked into his while holidaying on Tresco. Ours was a long-distance relationship for a couple of years, me hurtling from London to Penzance on the sleeper train before getting the helicopter or the Scillonian across to the islands.

We had our wedding blessing on Tresco a couple of days after we'd run the Tresco marathon, with celebrities including Bill Bryson, Blake Morrison, Charlie Dimmock and Jenny Agutter, some doing a lap each, others the whole shebang. It is seven and a half times around the island to do 26.2 miles. Geoff had a pint of Betty Stoggs on his last lap. I only realised at twenty miles that the final half-lap would include the worst bloody hill. I recall falling across the finish line sobbing, 'I love you, Jenny Agutter.' It was one of the highlights of my life.

Such was the state of our legs due to this event, after we knelt to pray at our wedding blessing, we had to be hoisted to our feet by the husband-and-wife couple officiating. They styled themselves the BOGOF vicars, Buy One Get One Free. The BBC's *An Island Parish* chronicled the unusual way clergy operate on the islands.

I have spent Christmas, Easter, August and the manic month of May during the gig championships on Tresco. I've risked hypothermia swimming in the sea on New Year's Day; I've risked death by sea sickness getting there.

I've been privileged to see the island in all its glory, in all its seasons, and to watch how hard everyone there works. If you can visit, do! If you can't, the art of Richard Pearce (who Geoff calls Dad) and Kathy Todd can show you some of the magic.

Thanks also to the entire Viper team who bring my books to you – from the office cleaners to Momma Viper, Miranda Jewess. Thanks to all the bloggers and authors who raise me up on the socials. And huge thanks to you for reading.

Ten percent of the royalties of this book will go to the Cystic Fibrosis Trust. Geoff and I ran the Tresco marathon in aid of this charity because beautiful Jade Hingston from the island was born with CF.